FRIEND
OF ACFL

What people are saying about

let them eat fruitcake

"A winsome tale of friendship with a dash of holiday madness. Delightful!"

—Robin Jones Gunn, best-selling author of the Sisterchicks® novels and the Katie Weldon series

"This fun romp with the Bloomberg Place girls has it all—snappy dialogue, complex relationships, and a fantastically diverse cast of characters that kept me reading nonstop!"

—Camy Tang, author of *Only Uni* and *Single Sashimi*

let them eat fruitcake

let them eat fruitcake

Melody Carlson

86 Bloomberg Place

David C Cook®

transforming lives together

LET THEM EAT FRUITCAKE
Published by David C. Cook
4050 Lee Vance View
Colorado Springs, CO 80918 U.S.A.

David C. Cook Distribution Canada
55 Woodslee Avenue, Paris, Ontario, Canada N3L 3E5

David C. Cook U.K., Kingsway Communications
Eastbourne, East Sussex BN23 6NT, England

David C. Cook and the graphic circle C logo
are registered trademarks of Cook Communications Ministries.

This story is a work of fiction. All characters and events
are the product of the author's imagination. Any resemblance
to any person, living or dead, is coincidental.

LCCN 2008930398
ISBN 978-1-58919-106-8

© 2008 Melody Carlson
Published in association with the literary agency of Sara A. Fortenberry

The Team: Andrea Christian, Erin Michelle Healy, Jaci Schneider, and Susan Vannaman
Cover Design: The DesignWorks Group, Charles Brock
Interior Design: The DesignWorks Group
Cover Illustration: Rob Roth

Printed in the United States of America
First Edition 2008

1 2 3 4 5 6 7 8 9 10

061308

With love,
to my daughter-in-law and friend,
Lisz Carlson

One

Megan Abernathy

"I am just back from the worst Thanksgiving ever!" declared Kendall. She peeled off her coat, discarding it on the sectional next to Megan.

"Too bad," said Megan with a speck of feigned interest. The truth was she really didn't want to hear about Kendall's day. It wasn't as if Megan's had been particularly good. Before Kendall came in, she'd been absently watching the 49ers annihilate the Seattle Seahawks. The Seahawks had been Megan's dad's favorite team, and she knew that if he were still alive, they'd be watching the fiasco together, commiserating. And this was the first Thanksgiving that she'd spent alone—at least until now.

To be fair, it was her choice. Several weeks ago, she'd encouraged her mom to join a friend on a Mexican cruise during Thanksgiving week. And then Megan had declined Marcus's invitation to spend the holiday at the beach with his family. She wasn't ready for that.

"I am utterly exhausted." Kendall flopped down in the club chair, leaned her head back, and sighed as if she'd just completed the Portland Marathon.

"And why is that?" asked Megan. She was trying not to be selfish, but it was hard to muster even a twinge of empathy for Kendall right now, perhaps because she'd been having her own little pity party. For a party of one.

"I don't know why I let Amelia talk me into coming to their place. It was bad enough that she was cooking dinner, since she barely knows how to make toast, but she didn't bother to warn me that her sister and brother-in-law were bringing both their newborn baby *and* a teething toddler along."

"Did you think her sister would leave her children home?" ventured Megan. She muted the Doritos commercial, although so far the ads had been more entertaining than the actual football game.

"No, of course not. But she might've considered hiring a babysitter to watch the little monsters in the other room so that the grown-ups could properly enjoy themselves. Or at least try. Not that we wouldn't have still heard the screaming brats. Who knew two small children could spoil things so badly?"

Megan nodded with sympathy that was about as genuine as Kendall's faux fur coat laying limply next to her like a slain polar bear. "So, it was a bit of a circus then?"

"It was like being held hostage at a screaming, pooping, puking, baby fest." Kendall rolled her eyes dramatically. "Note to self: Never have children."

"And never attend holiday dinners where other people's children are present?"

Kendall nodded. "Absolutely."

Megan was about to make some sort of excuse to exit but heard the front door opening. To her relief, Lelani came in.

"Hey, Lelani." Hopefully Lelani would join them, and Kendall could continue to pour out her troubles while Megan slipped off to her room.

"Hey, what's up?" Lelani took her time to remove and hang her navy wool coat on the hall tree, carefully unwinding her knitted scarf and hanging it neatly as well.

"Come tell us how your Thanksgiving went," urged Megan. "Poor Kendall's was a disaster."

Lelani sat down next to Megan. "It was okay," she said without much enthusiasm.

"So everything is smoothed out with your aunt and uncle now?" asked Megan.

"As smoothed out as it can be." Despite her weak smile, Lelani seemed discouraged.

Earlier in the fall, her aunt had accused Lelani of flirting with her overweight, middle-aged, and balding uncle, which seemed preposterous. Lelani was a beauty who could catch the eyes of most guys without even trying. Consequently, Lelani had avoided her relatives for more than a month. Finally, the aunt had come forward and apologized to Lelani. Apparently one of her aunt's friends had gently hinted that the problem lay with her husband and not her niece.

"Before I could get out of there, my aunt actually cornered me, begging me to move back in with them." Lelani sounded weary. "She wants me to help with the children in exchange for free rent."

"So you had to spend your day with children too?" asked Kendall with what seemed sincere compassion. "I am *so* sorry."

"Actually, the children were great."

Kendall blinked. "Really?"

"Yes. It was the adults who drove me nuts. Honestly, I couldn't get away from there fast enough."

"Did you tell your aunt you were tied into a yearlong lease?" asked Megan.

"I reminded her of that fact, but she seemed to think it was no big deal."

"No big deal to her," said Kendall with a sly grin. "But I plan to hold you to that lease."

Lelani sort of laughed. "That's sure not how you felt last month."

"Well, things change," said Kendall. "And I'm glad that you're both home. Now if we just had something good to eat." She glanced around. "Where's Anna, anyway?"

"Probably still with her family," said Lelani. "Come to think of it, I could probably still show up over there."

"Did Gil invite you?" asked Kendall.

Lelani nodded, then picked at the cuff of her silk blouse. "But I wasn't sure how his parents would react."

"They still don't know that you're dating?" asked Megan.

"We're not really dating," said Lelani quickly.

Kendall laughed. "If you're not dating, what do you call it?"

"Well, we can't call it dating," explained Lelani. "Not until I meet his parents."

"You have met his parents," pointed out Megan.

"I've only met them as Anna's friend and roommate," continued Lelani. "Not as their son's girlfriend—not that we're calling it that."

Kendall shook her head. "Methinks you protest too much."

"Out of respect for Mr. and Mrs. Mendez," said Lelani firmly, "we need to proceed slowly and carefully."

"But I've heard Anna say that her parents treat Gil differently from her. She said that Latinos aren't nearly as protective of sons as they are of daughters."

"Maybe so, but our age difference could be a concern."

Kendall laughed so loudly that she snorted. "You are like, what, a year older than him? That is so ridiculous, Lelani. They need to get over it."

"Maybe."

"What they should be thinking about," said Megan, "is what perfectly gorgeous children you and Gil would have."

Lelani frowned. "That's getting the carriage *way* ahead of the horse."

"Ugh, children!" Kendall groaned, then stood. "Please, do not even use that horrid word in my presence today." She headed toward the dining room, then paused. "Hey, is anyone else hungry?"

"Is that a hint or what?" asked Megan quietly.

"Duh." Lelani stood now. "She obviously wants us to come fix something."

"And you're going to?"

Lelani shrugged. "I'm actually pretty hungry too. My aunt's turkey was a little on the underdone side, and eating pink turkey concerned me."

Megan stood as well. "Come to think of it, I'm kind of hungry too. I had a microwave meal that was a little on the overdone side. Think *wooden* turkey."

Soon the three of them were foraging together in the kitchen. Kendall opened a bottle of red wine and filled three glasses, her contribution to their meal. And Megan managed to put together a fairly decent-looking green salad, topping it with Gorgonzola and pine nuts. Lelani fixed a nice plate of crackers and cheese. Still, without a trip to the grocery store, this meal, skimpy as it seemed, was probably as good as it was going to get today.

"Hey, everyone," called Anna. She emerged through the garage door carrying two plastic bags, as if bearing gifts.

"Is that food?" asked Kendall hopefully.

"Yep. My mom insisted on sending home the leftovers. I didn't think anyone would complain."

"God bless your mom," said Megan eagerly.

They all chattered as they helped Anna unload the leftovers, heaping sliced turkey and candied yams, and even some pumpkin empanadas onto plates, then carrying them into the dining room, which Lelani had already set for three.

"We need another place setting," said Megan, quickly running to get it from the kitchen and thinking that this really wasn't halfbad for a Thanksgiving meal. And far better than moping around by herself.

Soon they were all seated around the table, their little makeshift family of four. And after Megan said a Thanksgiving prayer, Kendall held up her glass to make a toast. "Here's to holidays without children."

Anna frowned in a confused sort of way.

"Kendall had a bad day with Amelia's sister's kids," explained Megan.

Anna nodded. "Oh, right."

"And I want to propose a second toast," said Lelani. "Here's to good friends and happy times throughout the rest of the holiday season."

The response to this toast was much more enthusiastic.

"Speaking of holidays," said Megan. "Do you plan to go home to Hawaii to celebrate with your family, Lelani?"

"Yeah," said Kendall eagerly. "Maybe you'd like me to join you?"

"Why just you?" protested Anna. "I'd like to come too."

"Don't leave me out," said Megan quickly. "I'm the one who asked about it in the first place."

"Christmas in Hawaii," said Kendall dreamily. "I'll have to get in to the tanning salon and—"

"Don't book your flight yet," said Lelani calmly. "That is, unless you're going without me."

"Meaning you're not going home for Christmas?" Kendall frowned.

Lelani firmly shook her head. "No. I am definitely not. In fact, I'm sure I'll be working right through Christmas Eve and then again on returns day, since half the people at Nordstrom have already begged for time off."

"I would think you could talk Mr. Green into—"

"I already promised him that I'd be around," said Lelani.

Megan suspected that Lelani was still trying to make up for their misguided accusations against Lelani's supervisor when Kendall had gone missing and he somehow seemed implicated. Even now, the whole incident seemed more like something that Megan had imagined. Anyway, it was definitely an event that all four girls wanted to forget.

"Okay, so Hawaiian holidays are out," said Kendall with disappointment. "Anyone else have an exciting idea?"

"You could join me and my family," said Anna in a less than enthusiastic way. "Although I'd love to do something besides watch nieces and nephews breaking piñatas and fighting over candy."

"Count me out," said Kendall.

"That's right," said Anna. "You've decided you hate kids."

"*Hate*'s a bit strong." Kendall narrowed her eyes. "As the late W. C. Fields used to say, I love children … if they're cooked properly."

"Ugh," said Lelani. "That is disgusting."

"It's a joke," said Kendall.

"Since when did you become an expert on W. C. Fields?" asked Lelani.

"Since I did a paper on him in college."

"A paper on W. C. Fields?" queried Megan with skepticism. "What kind of class was it?"

"Filmography." Kendall grinned. "Here's another W. C. quote: 'I cook with wine, sometimes I even add it to the food.'"

"He said that?" asked Anna. "My mom has that on her fridge."

"Yep. That was old W. C. Want to know another interesting fact?"

"Sure," said Lelani.

Anna nodded, although she looked as wary as Megan felt.

"You're going to like this one, Megan."

"Huh?"

Kendall nodded and continued. "Did you know that W. C. Fields was an agnostic his entire life?"

Megan shrugged. "Why should that surprise anyone?"

"And he was found reading a Bible on his deathbed."

"Seriously?" Megan peered curiously at Kendall now. Was she pulling their legs?

"Yep. He reportedly said that he was looking for a loophole."

"A loophole?" Lelani frowned like she didn't get it.

"You know," said Kendall. "So that he could get into heaven despite the kind of wild and crazy life he'd lived."

They all laughed, but even as she did, Megan wondered if Kendall was looking for a loophole too.

"Okay, as interesting as W. C. Fields is," said Lelani, "let's get back to Christmas. I just got a really great idea."

"What's that?" asked Anna.

"Well, since no one seems to have any really firm plans, how about if we have a big Christmas party right here?"

"What kind of Christmas party?" asked Anna.

"An old-fashioned one," said Lelani. "You know, on Christmas Eve."

"This would be a cool house for a party," said Megan. "Craftsman-style homes are great to decorate."

"And even better since you guys fixed it all up," added Kendall.

"And we could get a tree and bake goodies and put up lights and all sorts of fun things," said Lelani eagerly. "I've never had a real mainland Christmas before."

"That's right," said Anna. "That must've been weird, celebrating Christmas in eighty-degree weather."

"Oh …" Kendall sighed dreamily. "A sunny beach and a cabana boy bringing me a mai tai sounds like a perfectly lovely Christmas to me." She gazed hopefully at Lelani. "Are you absolutely, positively sure you don't want to rethink going home for the holidays and taking me with you? I could buy your ticket."

"First of all, cabana boys are in Mexico, not Hawaii," said Lelani. "Second of all, no, I am not going home."

"Besides that," said Megan. "You can't afford even one ticket to Hawaii, Kendall. Remember, you're broke."

Kendall made a pouty face. "Thanks for reminding me." She pointed at Lelani. "Well, you did promise to go out with me some-time—are you backing out on that too?"

Lelani frowned. "All you want to do is go clubbing, Kendall. And I'm not into that. Thanks anyway."

"Count me out too," added Megan.

"Me too," said Anna.

Kendall leaned back in her chair. "What a bunch of party poopers."

"Hey, I'm the one trying to get a party off the ground," persisted Lelani. "How about it? Doesn't anyone want to host a Christmas party here?"

Anna and Megan both agreed it would be fun.

"Fine," said Kendall. "If Hawaii is out, and no one will go club-bing, I guess I'll agree to having a Christmas party here. And I might even help decorate, since that sounds sort of fun, but do not expect me to be involved in the baking. As you know, I'm fairly hopeless in the kitchen."

"Of course." Anna winked at Lelani and Megan.

"Well, that is, unless you make fruitcake." Kendall got a sly grin now. "I do know a thing or two about that."

"Meaning?" Megan waited for Kendall's predictable response.

"Meaning you guys make the fruitcake and I'll add the rum … or brandy … or whatever it is they soak that stuff in. Yum!"

"You mean you actually *eat* fruitcake?" said Megan.

"Eat it, drink it … sure, whatever." Kendall laughed.

"You must be the only person I know who likes it."

"And you'd actually serve it at our Christmas party?" Lelani almost looked as if she was rethinking her idea.

"That's right." Kendall's eyes glinted with mischief. "And here's what I have to say to anyone who comes to our party—*let them eat fruitcake!*"

The other girls chuckled at this, but Megan got it. Somehow, she knew exactly what sort of party Kendall had in mind. Although Lelani was probably imagining a sweet, old-fashioned Christmas Eve celebration with good food and gifts and singing, Megan suspected that Kendall was envisioning a rock-out, drink-till-you-drop, party-hardy kind of Christmas Eve.

"Does it snow here for Christmas?" asked Lelani with wide eyes.

Kendall laughed. "Don't get your hopes up."

Megan wasn't about to say anything just now, but she knew that she wouldn't be getting her hopes up either.

Two

Anna Mendez

"Honestly, Edmond," said Anna for the second time. "I cannot go out with you tomorrow night."

Edmond adjusted his glasses, then smiled hopefully as he leaned over her desk holding out a pair of tickets. "But I got these just for you."

"Tickets for what?" She knew Edmond was a Blazers fan. Hopefully he hadn't assumed she was into sports, since nothing could be further from the truth. But maybe it was too early for basketball. How would she know?

"For the ballet. They were supposedly sold out, and the seats are in the orchestra section."

Anna frowned and turned off her computer screen. Never mind that she was supposed to be editing a children's book that was due last week. But the Thanksgiving weekend had gotten in the way and now, a week later, she was really in a crunch. Even so, this was Edmond's family's publishing company. If he didn't care, why should she? "Why didn't you ask me first?"

"I wanted to surprise you. You said you loved the ballet, Anna."

She blinked. "I told you that I used to dream of being a ballerina, Edmond. But then I took ballet lessons and quickly discovered that I have absolutely no grace. Plus I'm too short."

His smile faded. "So, you really won't go with me?"

"I *can't* go."

"And you're not even going to tell me why?"

Anna pressed her lips tightly together. No way was she going to tell Edmond that she was being forced to be one of twelve bridesmaids in her cousin Maria's over-the-top traditional Latino wedding. She knew he'd expect her to invite him to accompany her. Knowing Edmond, he'd probably even talk her into it. But that was just not going to happen. For one thing, it was going to be thoroughly humiliating to wear that silly hot-pink satin dress—with ruffles, no less! She did not need Edmond there to witness her embarrassing discomfort. Besides that, and perhaps even more importantly, she didn't want to go through the painful process of introducing Edmond to everyone in her large extended family. Although she'd gone out with him several times now, she just wasn't ready to bring him on board as the new *boyfriend*. Her parents hadn't even met him yet. And her mom would throw a fit if, say, Tia Elisa were to meet him first.

"I'll tell you this much," she said with a weak smile. "It's a family gathering—and I am not looking forward to it at all."

"Then don't go."

She laughed. "If only life were that simple."

"Come on, Anna," he pleaded. "Now you've got my curiosity going. What could possibly be that bad?"

"These lips are sealed."

He grinned now. "Hmm … is your family part of some weird cult? Do you wear black robes and remove chicken parts from people's bellies?"

"Oh, Edmond!" Despite herself, she laughed. "If it was something like that, I might actually invite you to come."

"So what is—"

"Just give it a rest." She shook her finger at him.

"Fine." He tried to look offended but was unconvincing. "If that's the way you want to be."

"Okay, here's the deal, Edmond. If you promise to quit bugging me about this, I'll take you to my family's restaurant for dinner next week."

"Seriously?" He brightened now.

"Sure, my mom's dying to meet you."

"What day?" he asked eagerly.

She considered this. "They're closed on Mondays. So how about Tuesday?"

He shook her hand. "It's a date." He held up the tickets. "And maybe I can exchange these for next weekend."

Anna wasn't sure how to respond. It wasn't like she knew much about the ballet, but on the other hand, it might be interesting. "Sure," she said with a smile. "And now if you could leave me alone for a bit, I might be able to get some work done before your uncle observes me slacking on the job."

Edmond laughed. "Right, Anna, that's something that they're always saying around here. 'You know that Anna Mendez, she's a real slacker.'"

Anna waved him off and returned her attention to her computer screen, but she could tell that Edmond was still hovering.

"How's the Ramsay Rowan book coming?" he asked quietly.

"Well, I thought we might actually make some progress now that Ramsay's out of rehab, but she's even harder to track down now."

"I don't know why my uncle contracted a kids' book from someone like Ramsay." Edmond shook his head.

"You mean besides the potential to sell a boatload of books?"

"That's only if Ramsay stays clean and doesn't embarrass us."

"I know." Anna sighed. "She hasn't been out of rehab for a week yet, and I'm worried she's going to fall off the wagon again."

"I haven't seen anything in the tabloids."

She peered curiously at him. "You read the tabloids?"

"Felicia says it's part of my job—publicity, you know."

"I'm glad I don't work in marketing." She gave him a warning glance. "Uh, speaking of work, Edmond, are you going to get any done today?"

"Hey, talking about the Rowan book *is* work. By the way, some samples of the illustrations are supposed to come in this afternoon."

Anna stood up. "Well, why didn't you say so? I saw the FedEx guy leaving just a little while ago."

"What are we waiting for?" said Edmond as he took off toward the marketing department with Anna on his heels. He quickly shuffled through the FedEx packages until he found the right folder. Then they went to his office, which was even smaller than Anna's. As she waited for him to open it, she had to remind herself that Edmond Dubois, sans the surname, was actually an Erlinger. He'd kept this secret from her for quite a while, acting like he was Felicia's lackey, when he was really a member of this old publishing family. But he was happy to pay his dues, and Anna appreciated that attitude.

"Here we go," said Edmond as he peeled back the attached layer of parchment paper to reveal the painting beneath.

"Oh!" Anna didn't know whether to be happy or sad. "That's really good, Edmond."

"You sound disappointed."

"Just for the illustrator. I mean, what if the book doesn't happen and she's put so much work into this? It doesn't seem fair."

"The illustrator still gets paid for what she's produced. Plus, she gets to keep her work."

"Oh … well, okay."

Anna was about to leave when Edmond asked her if she wanted to do dinner and a movie.

Anna frowned. "Tonight? I can't."

Now Edmond looked exasperated.

"Sorry, but really I can't."

"Another family thing?"

She nodded. "Believe me, if I could get out of it, I would."

His eyes lit up now. "It's a wedding, isn't it?"

She narrowed her eyes. "Hey, we made a deal, Edmond, I promised to take you to La Casa Del Sol if you quit talking about—"

He pressed his forefinger over his lips now. "Mum's the word."

"I need to get to work."

But he followed her down the hallway, and she could tell he wanted to say something.

"What?" she turned and stared at him.

"Well … I can't believe you don't want an escort, Anna. I mean, it's a wedding, right? And you'll be by yourself and—"

"Edmond Dubois!" She gave him her best threatening look.

"Nothing," he said quickly. "I was saying nothing."

"Good!" She turned on her heel and walked off. Of course, she knew it didn't take a genius to figure out that she was going to a wedding, but sometimes Edmond's persistence reminded her of a pit bull. And she didn't need him pressuring her to take him along.

Fortunately, that was the last she saw of him for the remainder of the afternoon. And to make sure she didn't see him again, she went out the back exit, which wasn't so odd since she'd driven her car today. But even so, she felt sneaky as she hurried to start the engine in her little

Mini Cooper. The only reason she'd driven today was because she knew she'd be in a hurry. She wanted to go home and change without risking being late to the rehearsal.

⚬

"Hey, Anna," said Lelani as they both entered the house simultaneously. "What's the hurry?"

"I have to be at a wedding rehearsal at six," she said as she set down her bag. "And it's in the city."

"Oh, yeah, Maria's wedding."

Anna blinked. "How do you—" Then she nodded. "I'll bet my brother invited you to come."

"He did."

"And did he warn you?"

"He said it would be cultural experience."

"That's one way of putting it. Are you going to go?"

"Sure." Lelani smiled. "I think it'll be interesting."

Anna rolled her eyes. "I wish I felt the same. Anyway, excuse me, but I need to get ready."

Anna would've been just as happy not to change her outfit, but because it was casual Friday at the publishing company, she had worn jeans to work. And she knew that would not be acceptable attire for Maria's rehearsal and celebration dinner. The other thing Anna knew, from years of experience, is that it never paid to rock the family's boat. Not unless one's personal stakes were extremely high. In the case of Maria's wedding, they were not.

"Have fun," called Lelani as Anna emerged wearing a charcoal-colored business suit. Okay, it wasn't exactly festive party wear, but it was the best she could do quickly. And it was better than jeans.

Of course, as soon as Anna entered the church, she knew she'd made a mistake. As usual, everyone seemed to be wearing flamboyant colors, and the crowded center aisle of the sanctuary resembled a Latino rainbow. The whole place smelled of too much perfume.

"Oh, Anna, who died?" teased Anna's younger cousin Eva as she handed Anna a mock bouquet of plastic flowers.

"No one," said Anna as she stretched to kiss Tia Elisa's cheek.

"You didn't have time to change into party clothes after work?" Tia Elisa gave Anna a sympathetic frown.

Anna just nodded. Some things were better left unsaid.

"We need all members of the wedding party to go to the back of the church," called out another one of Anna's aunts. Tia Marguerite was the self-appointed wedding coordinator. Whether invited or not, she usually forced her way into a power position at all family weddings. Anna dreaded to think what would happen if she ever decided to get married. Perhaps she'd simply elope.

Anna went back to join the other bridesmaids, all of whom seemed to be in the appropriate party mode. Anna tried to fit in, with a forced smile and appropriate laughter. She knew the rules. She also knew this was going to be a long evening. And tomorrow would probably be even longer.

"Hey, Anna, did you hear that Maria had a meltdown today?" whispered Caroline. Caroline was Maria's older sister and one of Anna's favorite cousins. She could usually trust what came from Caroline's lips.

"A meltdown?"

Caroline nodded. "The stress was getting to her."

"I don't know why people go to so much trouble over weddings," said Anna, keeping her voice low. A statement like that could be considered treason in this crowd.

Caroline shrugged. "It almost makes you want to go to Vegas, doesn't it?"

Anna laughed. "I was just thinking the same thing."

"Not that you two have anything to worry about in that regard," said Eva from behind them.

"What?" Caroline and Anna said in unison as they both turned around to peer at their eavesdropping younger cousin.

"I mean it's not like you two are getting married any time soon." Eva looked at them innocently. She wasn't even nineteen yet—but she had already acquired that I-know-everything sort of attitude that so many twenty-somethings seemed to take on.

"And why should we want to?" asked Caroline. "I'm not even thirty and Anna is—what?"

"Twenty-five," Anna supplied.

"That's like old maids," said Eva smugly.

Caroline took in a sharp breath, then looked at Anna.

"No," said Anna carefully. "It's like young women who want to have a life before they get tied down with a husband and children."

Fortunately Tia Marguerite started clapping her hands and trying to get everyone's attention. And Anna hoped that her comment, which was obviously heard by most of the wedding party, would not get her into trouble.

As usual, it took quite a while for their oversized group to go through the paces a few times. But finally, Tia Marguerite was marginally satisfied, and they were all excused to the restaurant where the festivities would continue. If the dinner weren't being held at Anna's family's restaurant, which had been closed for the occasion, Anna would have considered making a quick appearance and then leaving. But she knew she wouldn't get off that easily. Nor would she be allowed to help in the kitchen, which would be preferable to being questioned as to when her "big day" might be coming. Or worse, to being the target of sympathetic glances. She was, after all, the girl whose heart had been broken not so very long ago—at least in their eyes. To Anna, it had been another lifetime.

The truth was, Anna had been thinking about Jake a lot less since moving into the house on Bloomberg Place. And it had helped enormously to spend time with Edmond these past few weeks. Sure, he was nothing like smooth, good-looking Jake. Anna had even considered Edmond to be somewhat nerdish at first, but he had grown on her. To be perfectly honest, he had grown even more appealing when she discovered he was part of the Erlinger family. Not that she was proud of her reaction.

Anna had participated in two family weddings since breaking up with Jake and, she told herself, this one should be different. Really, her aunts should've forgotten all about Anna's broken heart by now.

But before the night was over, she knew that was not the case. She almost reconsidered asking Edmond to be her escort to the wedding. Ugly hot-pink dress or not, it might be worthwhile having a guy on her arm.

But when she called Edmond's number and got his voicemail, she could not bring herself to swallow her pride and ask him. Really, she would sound so desperate and sad and pathetic. Anna hung up without even leaving a message. She knew he had caller ID, and if he wanted to, he would return her call. If he begged to come with her, well, that would be different. She would give in. And all would be well.

Three

Lelani Porter

It had been a long day at the Nordstrom cosmetics counter and, even though it was Friday, all Lelani wanted to do was to put her sweats on, put her feet up, and put in a DVD. She knew there was no chance of Gil popping over, since he was helping with the wedding rehearsal dinner at the restaurant tonight. And that was fine with her, because she was looking forward to a quiet evening at home.

She'd just heated a bowl of soup and was about to turn on the TV when she heard Kendall calling her name from the stairs. Tempted to jump up and hightail it to her bedroom, she knew it was too late when Kendall came bursting into the living room looking, as usual, like a million bucks. Well, a million bucks in that blond, slightly plastic, Barbie sort of way, which really wasn't Lelani's cup of tea.

"There you are, Lelani." Kendall smiled triumphantly. "Didn't you hear me calling you?"

Lelani set the remote down. "Sorry, I was just turning on the TV."

Kendall frowned. "You look like you're ready for bed."

"Not really, but I was ready to relax. I was just about to have some soup and watch this—"

"No, you're not," said Kendall sharply. And before Lelani could protest, Kendall snatched the bowl from her.

"I thought it was okay to eat in—"

"That's not the problem." Kendall chuckled as she set the bowl on a side table. Then she reached down and grabbed Lelani's hand, pulling her from the sectional. "No canned soup for you tonight. I'm treating you to dinner."

"But I—"

"No buts," said Kendall as she pushed Lelani toward the hallway leading to her room. "You go and put on something fun. You and I have big plans."

"But I'm—"

"I said no buts, Lelani, and I mean it. Besides, if you'll remember, you promised me that you'd go out with me sometime."

Lelani did remember. It was an evening not too long ago when Kendall had been depressed about her life and how it wasn't going anywhere. She'd said that was one of the main reasons she shopped and drank too much. She also said that she wanted to change. Feeling sorry for her, Lelani had offered to go out with Kendall just to prove there were ways of having fun that did not involve clubbing and drinking and hooking up with guys.

"I draw the line at clubs," Lelani repeated, just in case Kendall dared revisit the topic.

"We're not going to a club. Come on, come on," urged Kendall as she stood in the doorway to Lelani's bedroom.

Lelani just stood in front of her closet, blankly staring at the contents. Really, the last thing she wanted to do tonight was to go out with Kendall.

"Let me help." Kendall was going through Lelani's closet now. She pulled a brightly colored dress out and thrust it at Lelani. "Here. Wear this."

"It's a sundress," said Lelani. "And it's freezing out."

"Wear a jacket over it."

Instead, Lelani put a long-sleeved shirt on beneath it. Then she pulled on some black jeans, some warm socks, and a pair of black Stuart Weitzman boots that she'd gotten on sale at Nordstrom last week. "Will this work?" she asked Kendall.

"I suppose. But you need a little sparkle." Kendall dug out some hoop earrings, a beaded necklace, and several bangle bracelets. "That should do it."

Lelani made an exasperated face, then reached for her heavy wool coat, her scarf, hat, and gloves.

"You look like you're going to the North Pole," complained Kendall as Lelani turned off her bedroom light.

"When you've lived in Hawaii your whole life, places like Oregon happen to feel like the North Pole."

"Whatever." Kendall grinned as she opened what looked like a new D&G bag, then fished out her keys. "Okay, let's go."

"Where?" Lelani frowned. "And if I remember correctly, my promise was to take *you* out, Kendall. We were going to do something that you wouldn't regret the next day. And no hangovers either."

"I won't regret this," said Kendall as she tugged Lelani into the garage. "Neither will you."

"Where are we going?" demanded Lelani.

"Trust me." Kendall opened a car door. "This is going to be totally cool."

"And you promised me dinner," Lelani reminded her as she got into the passenger's seat.

"Of course, no problem. I'm sure that food is involved."

Lelani shook her head as Kendall backed out. "What have I gotten myself into?"

"Just take a deep breath and chill," said Kendall as she drove down Bloomberg Place. "Later on, you'll thank me for this."

"And you swear we're not going clubbing, right?"

Kendall turned on the CD player and cranked it up loud enough to end the conversation. It was also clear that Kendall was heading for downtown Portland. Finally, Lelani decided she didn't care. Worst-case scenario, she'd grab a cab and go home. And later she would tell Kendall that she'd kept her part of the promise even if Kendall hadn't.

As it turned out, Kendall passed right by the club district and stopped in front of a large hotel. "Come on, girlfriend," said Kendall. "The fun's about to begin." She handed the keys to a parking valet, then linked arms with Lelani and led her into the lobby. Lelani hadn't been paying attention to which hotel it was, but it was clearly a nice one, with marble floors and oriental carpets, huge vases of fresh flowers, and crystal chandeliers. There was also a restaurant and lounge.

"Are we eating here?" asked Lelani as she glanced toward the restaurant.

"This way," Kendall directed her toward the elevators.

"Are we getting a room?" asked Lelani.

"We're going to a party," said Kendall as she pushed the number for the top floor.

"A party?" Lelani frowned.

"See, I knew you'd act like that," said Kendall. "That's exactly why I didn't tell you."

"What kind of a party?" Lelani was imagining a bunch of drunken guys who'd come to the city for some kind of convention. Plumbers, maybe.

"A wrap party."

"A wrap party?" Now Lelani was imagining wrap sandwiches,

which actually didn't sound too bad. Unless it was a party with lots of rappers and loud music—that was not appealing.

"You know, it's for the end of a production—for the cast and crew to celebrate."

"You mean for a movie?"

"Duh."

"What kind of movie?" This time Lelani was imagining some kind of slimy porn producers trying to lure unsuspecting girls to a room and get them drunk, then take skanky photos.

"A very good movie." Kendall smiled proudly. "I met a guy on the camera crew and he invited me to come tonight and said to bring a friend."

"A friend?"

"An attractive friend."

Okay, this was making Lelani concerned, and they were almost at the top floor. "Seriously, Kendall, what do you know about this movie or these people?" But before Kendall could answer, the elevator doors opened, dumping them into a small foyer with several other people who seemed to be waiting for something.

Lelani felt slightly relieved to see that these people looked fairly normal. But still, she reminded herself, she was with Kendall, and who knew what kind of trouble that girl could get into? Lelani noticed a brass sign on the wall. "Presidential Suite?" she whispered to Kendall.

"Yeah." Kendall nodded. "Pretty swanky, huh?"

"Can I help you?" asked a guy who acted more like a security guard than a host, although he wasn't wearing a uniform.

Kendall's brow creased as if she was trying to remember something. "Oh, yeah," she cupped her hand around her mouth and lowered her voice. "*Yosemite Sam* sent me."

The man nodded. "Right this way, ladies." Then he opened the double doors, placing himself like a barricade to the others in the hallway, as if he wasn't going to let them inside. Lelani caught an envious glance from a pretty girl about their age.

"Seriously," she whispered to Kendall. "What *is* this?"

"I told you. It's a wrap party." Kendall led the way into a large but crowded room. The music was loud, but at least it felt warm in there.

"For a movie?" continued Lelani skeptically. "But we're not in Los Angeles."

A middle-aged blond guy who wore his pale blue shirt untucked asked, "Do you think LA is the only place to make films?"

"Excuse me?" asked Lelani.

"Haven't you heard that many excellent films are being made here in the Northwest?" he continued. "Right here in downtown Portland, for that matter."

Lelani stood a bit straighter now. "I'm sorry, I don't think we've met."

He smiled and held out his hand. "I'm Aaron Stone."

Lelani blinked. *"The* Aaron Stone?"

He laughed. "The only one that I know of."

Kendall gave her a sharp elbow then stepped forward. "Mr. Stone," she said smoothly. "I'm Kendall Weis and this is my friend Lelani Porter. One of your crew invited us to the wrap party, I hope that's okay."

He nodded at Kendall but seemed to be keeping his eyes on Lelani. "It's always a pleasure to have some new faces around. Perhaps you hadn't heard, Lelani, but we just finished shooting *Never Mind.*"

"Never Mind?" said Lelani with interest. "I loved that book."

"Hopefully you'll love the movie, too."

"And that was filmed right here in Portland?"

"For the most part."

She shook her head as she unbuttoned her heavy coat. "I had no idea that people made films up here."

"She's from Hawaii," said Kendall apologetically. "We're still trying to bring her up to speed."

Lelani gave Kendall a look.

"What part of Hawaii?" he asked with raised brows.

"Maui." She went on to explain which part of the island, and he said that he knew just where it was. He and his wife visited Maui on a regular basis and were even considering buying property there.

"That's why she's so bundled up." Kendall was still trying to insert herself into the conversation. "She says Oregon feels like the North Pole."

He laughed. "I'm with you there, Lelani. I'm an LA boy, and this cold, wet weather makes me happy to wrap. Anyway, once you get acclimated, feel free to toss your coats in there." He nodded toward a door. "And you girls make yourselves at home. There are food and drinks over there and—"

"Hey, Aaron buddy." A guy was waving from the other side of the crowded suite. "You gotta hear this."

"Enjoy," said Aaron.

"Wow," said Lelani as they went into the adjacent room and dropped their coats on the bed. "I am glad I came."

"What did I tell you?" said Kendall proudly.

Lelani nodded. "Very cool."

But it wasn't long before the "cool" factor wore thin. While it had been interesting to have a brief conversation with a famous director, the rest of Lelani's encounters felt more like pickups. Besides that, Kendall was drinking too much. Plus, the food was not all that great.

"So you're really not an actress?" a guy named Barney asked her for what had to have been the fourth time.

"No, I'm not." Lelani glanced across the suite to see if she could spot Kendall. But the room was packed now and, to Lelani's surprise, it was getting hot.

"And you're not looking to become an actress?" asked Barney.

"No."

He grinned, and she knew that Barney, like Kendall, had over-imbibed. "That's too bad, because I'm pretty sure the cameras would love you." He squared his fingers into a box and squinted at her. Judging by his goofy expression, she wouldn't be surprised if he was seeing two of her.

"Excuse me," she said as she spotted Kendall. Then she pushed her way through the crowd and grabbed Kendall by the elbow. "Let's go," she said.

"No way," said Kendall.

"Way," insisted Lelani. "And you've had too much to drink. I'm driving."

"You can drive if you want, but I'm not going." Kendall smiled at the attractive man standing next to her. "Do you know who this is?" she asked Lelani.

Lelani peered at the dark-haired man, then shook her head.

Kendall linked arms with the guy and grinned like she had just been awarded a grand prize, or maybe an Oscar. "This, my friend, is Matthew Harmon."

The name sounded vaguely familiar, and Lelani knew he had something to do with Hollywood, but she couldn't really place him. "Hi, Matthew," she said politely. "I'm Lelani Porter."

He nodded. "Have I seen you in anything?"

"She's not an actor, silly." Kendall playfully punched Matthew in the shoulder.

"Too bad," said Matthew.

"Thanks," said Lelani. "And nice to meet you, but I really need to go."

Now Kendall put her hands on her hips and frowned. "Go ahead and leave, Lelani. Take my car if you want. I'll catch a ride later."

"Fine," said Lelani. She pasted a smile on her face but walked away from Kendall with clenched fists. Why had she ever trusted that girl in the first place?

"Leaving so soon?" asked a sound technician Lelani had spoken to earlier. He had actually seemed like a nice guy, and he told her how he missed his wife and even showed her photos of his preschool-aged kids. Still, most of the guys she'd talked to here made her feel she was on shaky ground—like they figured she was crashing their party for one thing only: to hook up with a celebrity. And nothing was further from the truth. Sure, it had been nice meeting some famous people, but now she just wanted to go home.

She made her way to the bedroom, located Kendall's D&G bag, and dug out her car keys as well as the valet parking stub. If nothing else, Lelani figured she was preventing Kendall from driving under the influence tonight. And Lelani had fulfilled her promise as well. If she thought there was any way to get Kendall away from this party without creating a huge scene, which would only make Kendall dig her heels in more deeply, Lelani would have tried. As it was, she knew it would be a losing battle. A battle she didn't have the strength to fight.

Lelani picked up her coat and bag and heard her cell phone ringing. As usual, she checked the caller ID. Her biggest fear was always that it would be from home in Maui, that her mother would be calling with some kind of bad news. She didn't know why she always thought like this, but she did. Fortunately it was Gil.

"Hey, Gil," she said eagerly. "What's up?"

"I finally got out of the kitchen," he told her.

"They had you working in the kitchen?"

"Actually, I offered." He chuckled. "So what've you been up to tonight?"

"You're not going to believe this," she began. Then, sitting there in the bedroom, she quickly replayed parts of her evening, including speaking with Aaron Stone.

"That sounds interesting." But even as he said this, she could sense a question in his tone.

"Interesting, yeah, but I'm leaving now."

"Oh?"

"Naturally, Kendall doesn't want to go home. But I'm taking her car. She's in no shape to be driving anyway."

"And you're just leaving her there?"

"She said she can get a ride."

"I suppose."

"What else can I do?" she asked with uncertainty.

"I don't know."

"Seriously, Gil. Do you think I should stick around? I mean people are really partying hardy now, and it's starting to feel a little like a meat market, if you know what I mean."

"No, of course I'm not saying you should stay there," he said. "But I guess I'm wondering why you went with Kendall in the first place."

For no explainable reason, his insinuation really irked Lelani. But she didn't say anything. Still, what did he think of her?

"Sorry," he said quickly. "That came out all wrong."

"No …" Someone else was coming into the bedroom. She stood and picked up her scarf and things. "But I better go."

"Where are you, anyway?"

"To be honest, I don't know," she admitted as she left the suite. "Some swanky downtown hotel."

"Hey, I'm still downtown too. Want to meet for coffee?"

"Sure. Let me go down to the lobby and figure out where I am, and I'll call you back, okay?"

"Great!"

She shut her phone and rode down the elevator with a couple who never even looked at her because they were busy locking lips. She was tempted to tell them to get a room but knew that sounded juvenile. Still.

She fixed her focus on her phone as she slowly punched in Gil's number, getting ready to call him back when she figured out where she was. She had mixed feelings regarding his statement about why she'd gone out with Kendall tonight. On one hand, she couldn't agree more. She'd known it was risky. But on the other hand, it was unsettling to realize that Gil seemed to be getting more and more attached to her— and protective. And yet she really liked him, and she liked spending time with him.

What worried her most was that his feelings for her might be stronger than hers toward him. Like things were moving too fast. And yet she didn't want to lose him either. But at the same time she didn't want to lead him on or, even worse, use him. Gil was too nice of a guy for that—and he was the brother of one of her roommates. Lelani knew she needed to be careful.

Four

Kendall Weis

"Where did your friend go?" asked Aaron Stone.

Kendall ran a perfectly manicured fingernail over the edge of her martini glass as she thought about this. "Oh, you mean Lelani?"

"Yes, the lovely Lelani from Maui." Aaron smiled as if he thought this was clever. "Has she ever done any acting?"

Kendall frowned. "No."

"I asked her the same thing," said Matthew Harmon with a bit too much interest.

"That girl has the most classic features," said Aaron. "You know who she looks like?"

Matthew nodded eagerly. "Rita Hayworth."

Aaron considered this. "Maybe a little, but I was thinking of the great Hedy Lamarr."

"Didn't she do some nude scenes?" asked Kendall, trying to keep a toehold in the conversation. After all, she had taken some filmography classes during her short stint at college, and she'd been trying to put it to use tonight.

"In Europe," said Aaron, "before her career was launched over here."

"Oh, yeah," said Kendall, nodding as if she knew all about this.

"Do you think she has any interest?" persisted Aaron.

"Who?" Kendall opened her eyes wide as if she'd forgotten who they were speaking of.

"Your friend from Maui," said Matthew.

"The lovely Lelani," said Aaron.

"Oh, I don't think so." Kendall shook her head dramatically, tilting her chin at what she felt was a photogenic angle and wishing that these two would notice her and forget about silly Lelani.

"Why not?" asked Matthew. "I thought all girls dreamed of opportunities like this."

"Not Lelani," said Kendall quickly. "She's not like that at all."

"What does she do?" asked Aaron.

Kendall considered this. To admit that Lelani worked at the Nordstrom cosmetic counter might somehow suggest that she would be interested. Like makeup and actresses—didn't that just go together? "Well, she was in med school," said Kendall. "And although she's taking a break, I think she's very serious about going back to it."

"So she's not just beautiful, she's smart." Aaron smiled with way too much interest. And Kendall wished they'd change the subject.

"Yes. But she isn't into things like acting or popular culture. I mean, she thinks I'm shallow," said Kendall. "Lelani is a very serious girl. She wants to be a doctor and that's it."

"Too bad." Aaron shook his head, then wandered off.

Kendall nodded to Matthew. "It really is too bad," she said to him. "I think Lelani would be beautiful on the big screen. Her features are flawless."

Matthew smiled at Kendall. "Yours aren't too bad either."

She brightened. "Why, thank you very much."

"Can I freshen that drink for you?" he offered.

"That would be very nice." Kendall watched as Matthew meandered across the crowded room and over to the bar area. With those broad shoulders, slim hips, and a walk that said he knew who he was, he was a seriously stunning guy. Not only that, but he thought she was pretty too—or something to that effect. Okay, it had totally miffed her that he and that stupid Aaron Stone were acting all gaga over Lelani in her pathetic little outfit of a sundress over a shirt and jeans.

To think that Kendall had dressed to the nines for this party. Her shiny blond hair was perfection and her teeth were straight and whitened. Why couldn't they imagine her face on the big screen? Lots of people compared her looks to Paris Hilton's. And, while Kendall thought she was actually prettier than Paris, she didn't like being compared to Lelani. In the past, she'd tried to get Lelani to go clubbing with her. Who could resist two gorgeous girls out on the town? Maybe it was time to rethink that plan. As Matthew made his way back through the crowd toward her, Kendall was extremely glad that Lelani decided to leave early. She smiled at Matthew and decided it was time to turn the charm factor up a notch or two. This guy was worth getting her hooks into.

"Here you go, Kendall." Matthew handed her a fresh martini.

"Thank you." She looked over the edge of the glass, giving him her best sultry expression and then frowned.

"Is something wrong?" he asked with concern.

She smiled now, tipping her head slightly to the right. "No, I was just thinking about Lelani … how it's a shame she's not into acting." Kendall shook her head sadly. "It's just not fair that some girls have all the looks and absolutely no interest in using them." She sighed. "And then there are some who would do anything to make it in Hollywood."

His brow lifted slightly. "Anything?"

She laughed as if she was embarrassed, then waved her hand in a dismissive way. "Oh, you know what I mean."

They continued to chat and he continued to "refresh" her drink, and before long it seemed that Matthew was the only guy in the room. She was captivated by him and, unless she was mistaken, he felt the same about her. It was almost magical ... and definitely chemical. Every time his hand brushed against her skin, she felt like she was melting. She also felt like things were getting a little blurry and fuzzy, but even so, Kendall was having a good time. At least she thought she was. Then she realized that Matthew was speaking to her and she hadn't even responded.

"What?" she peered up at him, then blinked when it seemed he had two heads weaving back and forth.

He nodded to the nearly empty hotel suite. "I think the party's pretty much over and I was just asking if you have a way to get home?"

"Home?" She tilted her head as if considering this concept.

"I mean Lelani took your car, right?"

"Lelani ..." Kendall sort of nodded. "Oh, yeah."

"So ... I could give you a ride ... or I suppose you could crash in my room if you like."

"Your room?" She smiled slowly.

"Okay, then." He took her hand and they got on an elevator and went up or down, she wasn't sure, but the next thing Kendall knew she was in another hotel suite—one that was neat and clean and quiet. And standing in front of her was this great-looking guy. Okay, maybe he did have two heads, but he was pouring her another drink and then they were kissing ... and kissing ... and kissing ...

>◦<

Kissing was the last thing Kendall remembered when she woke up the following morning, and even that memory was foggy. She had a nasty headache and a rumbling stomach, and she was lying by herself in a strange bed—totally naked, it seemed. She lifted the sheet to make sure, then frowned. Yep, she was naked as a jaybird. And she didn't even remember how she'd gotten this way. Oh, to be sure, it wasn't the first time, but it *was* something that she'd been trying to put a stop to ... something her roommates had warned her was not only stupid and dangerous, but just plain slutty.

But this was different. She had spent the night with the famous actor Matthew Harmon. And he was really into her, and she was definitely into him. This was definitely different. In fact, she felt certain that this relationship would go the distance. This was the real thing— the guy she'd been waiting for. Okay, not waiting, exactly, but she'd been looking for, hoping for ... and now he was here! Then she looked to the other side of the bed to see that, while slept in, it was vacant. So he wasn't actually here-here, but he was in-her-life here.

She sat up to look around the room, but this only made her head feel worse. The hotel suite was strewn with clothes, but no sign of Matthew Harmon. She sighed and smiled, hugging herself. She, Kendall Weis, had just spent a romantic night with a famous actor. This was a whole new beginning!

Just then her stomach turned upside down. She rushed to where she hoped the bathroom was and soon found herself sprawled on the marble tile and hugging the toilet. Not a pretty sight, she knew, but before long it was over. And fortunately Matthew hadn't popped in to find her worshipping the porcelain throne. That was something.

She took a quick shower, then located a thick white terry robe and finally went to search for her purse. She'd caught sight of her face in the mirror only to see it was a disaster. No way did she want Matthew to see her like this. This wouldn't be the face of the woman he wanted to spend the rest of his life with—which she knew he would. He had to be as into her as she was into him. Where was he, anyway?

She snatched up her D&G bag, then returned to the bathroom, locking the door behind her while she attempted to put what was wrong right—or at least try. After a hard night of partying, it could be a challenge to transform blotchy skin, puffy eyes, and dark shadows into smooth, sleek perfection. But she'd had plenty of practice.

As she worked to do damage control she pondered two regrets: 1) She couldn't remember a single thing, past that last drink and kissing session, about being with Matthew last night, and 2) she didn't have a fresh outfit to put on this morning.

"Coffee, anyone?" called a male voice from the other room.

Kendall took one final look at her face. Not perfect, but not bad. "Coming," she called, trying to make her voice sound light although her head was still throbbing.

"How you feeling?" he asked as she emerged from the bathroom.

She smiled. "Pretty good ... considering."

"Considering how wasted we got last night. I woke up with a severe headache. I took a walk and got some Starbucks."

"You're an angel," she said as she eagerly took a cup.

"I wasn't sure what you like," he said. "I guessed mocha."

"Perfect." She sat down in one of the club chairs by the window and pretended to enjoy a sip. The truth was she was feeling nauseated again, but hopefully she'd get past it before too long. She wasn't about to let that or anything else spoil her day. She smiled as Matthew sat down in the club chair across from her.

"You're certainly easy to please."

Kendall laughed. "Really? Some of my friends accuse me of being high maintenance."

"I suppose it's all a matter of perspective."

"It's been so great getting to know you," she said happily.

"That was quite a party."

"It makes me wish I lived in LA," she said dreamily.

"Seriously?"

"Oh, yeah."

"Why?"

"I think I'd fit in down there better than I do up here."

"You don't like Portland?"

She shrugged. "It's okay, but I grew up here, so I suppose it seems kind of ordinary to me ... a little boring."

"It's a beautiful city, Kendall."

She brightened. Maybe Matthew would consider living here some of the time, and in LA some of the time when his career really took off the way she knew it would. And, of course, that would allow her to enjoy both places too, since she was feeling more and more certain that they had a future together.

"Did you know that Portland was picked as the number-one city to live in for twenty-somethings?" she asked.

"Really? Number one in the country?"

"That's what I heard."

"Wow, that's pretty cool."

"Even so, LA sounds really good to me."

"Well, it is warmer down there." He pretended to shiver. "Like just now I was outside and it was rainy and windy and—*brrrrr*—it made me want to go home."

She nodded. "I totally get you."

"Which reminds me ... I should get busy." He set down his coffee and slowly stood.

"Busy?"

"Packing. It's already past ten and I haven't even showered yet."

She frowned. "Packing? Does that mean you're leaving?"

He gave her a halfhearted smile. "Remember, Kendall, I told you last night that I was leaving today. The filming here is wrapped up. And my flight's at one thirty this afternoon."

She tried to remember him mentioning this but came up blank.

"I thought I'd have time to take you home in the rental car, but we slept in … and now I'm thinking that's not going to work. I hope you don't mind catching a cab." He was stuffing things into a gigantic wheeled duffel bag as he talked, acting like this sudden departure was no big deal, like he spent the night with strange girls in strange towns, then took off the next morning all the time. And maybe he did. But somehow Kendall had convinced herself that this was more than that. At least she had hoped so.

"You're a great girl, Kendall," he continued chattering. "And we had a fun time. You'll have to give me your number for the next time I'm up here."

"When will that be?" she asked, knowing she sounded too eager. Or maybe it was too desperate. Whatever it was, she knew it sounded all wrong.

He stood up straight and studied her with a blank expression, a pair of boxers dangling in his hand. "I, uh, I don't really know …"

"I mean, do you have another movie you'll be doing up here?"

"Not that I know of."

"Oh."

"My next movie is going to be shot down there—on the lots to save a few bucks, you know."

"Uh-huh." She almost could feel tears in her eyes now. How could he be leaving her so soon? She had sincerely believed this had been something more than a one-night stand. She'd imagined them spending the day together … and then the night … and then who knew? How could he just leave?

He smiled at her. And it was that gorgeous Hollywood smile that she'd admired on the big screen, those sweet wrinkles at the creases of his blue eyes, and his straight white teeth. "You're not feeling bad, are you?"

She took in a quick breath, then forced a smile. "No, no. Of course not."

He looked relieved. "Oh, good. I thought you understood."

Then he went into the bathroom and before long she heard the shower running. While he was in there, she got dressed, taking her time and hoping that she didn't look as rumpled on the outside as she felt on the inside. Rumpled and dirty and used up.

When he emerged from the bathroom, he looked clean and fresh in the other thick white bathrobe. He grinned as he toweled his hair dry. "Ah," he said happily. "Much better." Then he tossed the towel to the floor and stretched out his arms. "Come here, babe."

Feeling hopeful, like maybe he'd had a revelation in the shower, she ran straight into his arms and held on tight. He felt good, smelled good. Maybe he'd decided he couldn't live without her after all. Maybe he wanted to take her home with him. Maybe he had an engagement ring for her in the pocket of his bathrobe, a little something he'd picked up at the jewelry shop downstairs, something he'd eventually replace with more karats once they got settled down in the land of sunshine. It could happen. Dreams really could come true!

"It was a pleasure getting to know you, Kendall," he said with a sense of finality. "You're really a great girl." Then he gave her a long kiss and released her. "Sorry I can't stick around longer."

"You could come back up here to visit," she said hopefully. "Or I could come down there to see you."

He frowned. "It wouldn't work for you to come down there, Kendall. Not for me, anyway. Remember?"

"Remember?" She frowned and for the second time wished she hadn't drank so much.

"I told you last night."

She blinked. "What was that?"

"You know ... that I'm married."

"Married? *You told me you were married?*"

"Yes. You said it was okay."

"I said that?"

He laughed. "Oh, yeah, that and a lot of other things."

"Oh ..."

"And I told you that I'm mostly faithful to my wife." He looked slightly sheepish now, like he was embarrassed or uncomfortable, or his conscience was bothering him. Not that this made her feel any better. It did not. Not even a little.

"I mean, it's no secret that my marriage has had its share of problems," he continued. "It's hard when both partners have a career. Sometimes we pull in different directions. But we're trying to work things out."

She was picking up her purse now, shoving some things inside and moving toward the door like a robot.

"I'm sorry," he said. "I didn't mean to hurt you, Kendall. I thought you understood."

"Oh, I understand," she said slowly, woodenly. "I understand completely."

Five

Megan

"Do you think you could've picked a colder, wetter, windier day to put these lights up?" Megan yelled down at Lelani. She strained to loop the string of lights around one of the hooks that they'd put in along the top of the porch. Rain was running down the back of her neck and the ladder was wobbling slightly.

"I'm sorry," Lelani called up from where she was supposedly holding the ladder, although Megan wasn't so sure. "I thought we'd finish up before the weather changed on us. The Channel Two forecast said it wasn't going to rain until later today."

"It wouldn't be the first time they were wrong," yelled Megan.

"We're almost done," said Lelani.

Megan finished hanging the strand, then hurried down the ladder. "I'm freezing," she said as she stomped her wet feet on the porch steps.

"Me too," said Lelani. "Let's get in—"

"Who's that?" asked Megan, glancing out to where a cab was pulling up.

"It must be Kendall," said Lelani.

"Why's she in a cab?"

"Because I drove her car home last night," explained Lelani. "But I didn't realize she hadn't come home yet."

Kendall ran through the rain up the walk and paused on the

51

porch to study her soaked housemates. "What on earth are you guys doing?"

"Putting up Christmas lights," said Lelani.

"In this weather?" Kendall shook her head as she opened the front door. "You're flipping crazy."

They all went inside, and Megan and Lelani began to peel off their soggy outer clothes while Kendall watched with a deep frown. "I can't believe you guys," she said. "You couldn't pay me to hang Christmas lights in the rain."

"It's my fault," admitted Lelani. "I wanted to get the lights up this weekend, and it wasn't raining when we started."

"When did you start?"

"Around eight this morning," complained Megan as she peeled off her wet socks.

"I'll make you some hot cocoa, Megan," offered Lelani.

"I'm taking a hot shower first," said Megan.

Megan took a quick shower, then put on sweats and fuzzy slippers. When she came back out, Lelani had dried off too and was just pouring cocoa into mugs. Kendall, it seemed, was capitalizing on Lelani's peace offering too.

"Do you forgive me?" Lelani smiled as she handed Megan a steaming mug.

"I don't," said Kendall from behind her.

"I wasn't talking to you," said Lelani.

"Well, I don't forgive you anyway," said Kendall hotly.

"Why don't you forgive her?" asked Megan as she took a mug of cocoa. "What did Lelani do to you, anyway?"

"Just abandoned me at the party last night," said Kendall.

"Did you really abandon her?" Megan asked Lelani.

"Kendall told me to take her car," said Lelani. "Besides, she was too drunk to drive."

"Kendall!" Megan frowned at her. "I thought you said you weren't going to do that anymore."

"I just had a few drinks."

"She was plastered," said Lelani.

Kendall scowled. "Who even says *plastered* anymore?"

"Wasted, snookered, inebriated, smashed, drunk …" Megan shook her finger at Kendall. "It doesn't matter what you call it, it all equals the same thing—major stupidity."

"That's right," agreed Lelani. "And to let you drive like that would be even more stupid."

"Thanks a lot." Kendall sniffed like she was about to start crying.

"Sometimes the truth hurts," said Megan in a gentler tone.

"Seriously, Kendall," said Lelani. "What about getting drunk is fun?"

Kendall shrugged. "I don't know."

"Are you still going to counseling?" asked Megan.

Kendall glared at her. "None of your business."

"Sorry," said Megan. "It's just that you told us that you wanted our help, remember? You said you wanted to change."

"So, where did you stay last night?" asked Megan.

"That is none of your business either," said Kendall.

"I'll bet I can guess." Lelani grinned slyly.

"If you must know," said Kendall, "I spent the night with Matthew Harmon."

"Matthew Harmon the actor?" asked Megan.

Kendall nodded smugly. "That's right."

"I heard he'd been making a movie in town."

"It was a wrap party," explained Lelani. "I actually had a nice conversation with Aaron Stone."

"*The* Aaron Stone?" Megan blinked.

"Yep." Lelani laughed. "I said the same thing. But he's actually pretty normal and nice."

"Of course he's normal," said Kendall defensively. "They're all normal. What did you think they'd be?"

"I don't know." Lelani shrugged. "Snobs, maybe?"

"And you actually slept with Matthew Harmon?" Megan asked Kendall.

"Why not?" Kendall had a hard-to-read expression. Megan wasn't sure if it was pride or embarrassment.

"Why not?" repeated Megan. "Well, for starters he's married."

Kendall didn't say anything.

"How did you know that?" Lelani asked her. "I didn't notice him wearing a wedding ring."

"Maybe he took it off to shoot the movie," said Megan. "But I do know he's married."

"How?" demanded Kendall.

"I saw him being interviewed on the local news a couple of weeks ago. They showed some footage of his other films and they had a shot of him with his wife. She's an actor too, but not as well known as him. I think her name is Heidi something."

"Heidi Hardwick?" asked Kendall suddenly.

"Yes, that's right," said Megan.

Kendall looked somewhat disturbed by this.

"Who's Heidi Hardwick?" asked Lelani. "I mean what's she been in? Would I know her?"

"She's in a TV series that just premiered," said Megan. "I can't remember what it's called. It's on Fox. But she's really pretty—dark hair, dark eyes." Even as Megan said this, she thought she saw Kendall flinch. But maybe it was for the best. The sooner Kendall realized that it was wrong to get wasted, wrong to sleep around, and especially wrong to sleep with married men, the better it would be for her and everyone.

"Anyway, Heidi Hardwick seems to be hot, and I'm guessing her career is about to take off."

"Matthew said their marriage has had some problems," said Kendall.

"I'm not surprised," said Lelani sharply.

"No, I mean before this," said Kendall. "He said it's hard having two careers going in totally different directions."

"And I'm sure that last night's little fling won't help much," added Megan.

"Maybe their marriage is ending," said Kendall with what sounded like too much hope.

"You mean you'd *like* them to split up?" asked Megan.

"If they're unhappy …"

"Meaning you'd do what you could to help them split up?" asked Lelani.

"Meaning … what will be will be." But the gleam in Kendall's eyes seemed to suggest more.

"I can't believe you, Kendall," said Megan.

"Look," Kendall narrowed her eyes. "I did not know that Matthew was married. At least I don't remember him telling me that—last night—although he said he did."

"Being drunk does that to a person," said Megan.

"Well, whatever. But I didn't knowingly sleep with a married man."

"Fine," said Megan. "But now that you know he's married, would you do it again?"

Kendall considered this. "It depends ..."

"It *depends*?" Megan knew her voice was too loud, but she couldn't help herself.

"If I thought that Matthew and I had a future together, and if I thought his marriage was over, sure, I'd probably sleep with him again."

"Oh, Kendall!" Lelani just shook her head. "You're pathetic."

"No, I'm honest. If you can't take the truth, don't ask."

"But he used you," protested Lelani. "He used you for a one-night stand, Kendall, doesn't that hurt a little?"

"Look, you guys." Kendall grew serious. "It was more than just a one-night stand. I know you won't get it. I don't expect you to. You're both such Goody Two-shoes and I know you'd never do anything like this. But then you might not ever meet your true love, either."

"Matthew Harmon is your true love?" Megan knew her tone was sarcastic, but how could she help it? Was Kendall totally insane?

"Maybe." Kendall held her chin up.

Lelani just shook her head.

Kendall looked from Lelani to Megan, then back to Lelani again. "I don't know why I'm even telling you guys this, but I think I'm in love with Matthew."

"In love with Matthew the guy," asked Lelani, "or Matthew the celebrity?"

"With Matthew the guy." Kendall sighed. And it actually looked like she had stars in her rather bloodshot eyes. "Seriously, I've never felt quite like this before."

"After spending one night with him?" demanded Lelani. "One night when you were pretty much wasted?"

"Why would I expect you to get this?" Kendall set her mug down on the table with a clunk, then stood up, walked off, and loudly stomped up the stairs.

"I guess I wasn't too tactful," said Lelani.

"You and me both," agreed Megan. "But I just couldn't help myself. I cannot believe her sometimes."

"Just sometimes?" Lelani frowned.

"Well, I guess I'd hoped that she was changing. I mean, I know she's Kendall and, well, kind of a loose cannon. But I thought the counseling was helping some. And she'd asked us to be sort of like her support group."

"Maybe we let her down," said Lelani.

"We can't control her."

"Well, I never should've agreed to go to the wrap party with her last night."

"I don't know …"

"I mean it was actually kind of fun. But even Gil questioned me."

"Why?"

Lelani shrugged. "I think he was kind of jealous. And the truth was, even though it started out to be fun, I started to feel like I was there for the wrong reasons. Or that the guys there assumed I was there for the wrong reasons."

"Like you wanted to sleep with Mr. Hollywood too?"

"Exactly. Although nothing was further from the truth."

"Well, that seems to be why Kendall went."

"Yes, and I figured that out once we were there. I saw her eyes light up when she spotted Matthew, like she had this whole thing all worked out in advance. I honestly think she'd set her sights on him long before she talked me into going with her. Like she had this great big plan to get him in the sack with her." Lelani frowned. "I know that sounds mean, but in hindsight, I think it was a setup, and I actually feel a little sorry for Matthew."

"What about his wife?"

"Yeah, it must be some marriage."

"Still, it's so weird. I mean, I can't imagine wanting to sleep with a guy simply because he was a celebrity." Megan drank the last of her cocoa.

"And now Kendall thinks she's in love?" Lelani sadly shook her head.

"I think she's *in crush*. And I'm sure it won't last long."

"Especially since they're done filming in Portland now."

"I wonder if he's still around."

"It sounded like most of the cast and crew were going home today. My guess is he's gone, or Kendall wouldn't have come home."

"As irritating as Kendall can be, I still feel a little sorry for her," admitted Megan.

"She does tend to be her own worst enemy."

"Well, maybe she'll learn something from this." Megan picked up the mugs and took them into the kitchen.

"And me, too."

"Huh?" Megan peered at Lelani.

"Well, to just say no."

"No?"

"To Kendall."

Megan laughed. "Just say no to Kendall. I'll have to remember that line."

"You're lucky you weren't here last night. She probably would've roped you into going too. Where were you, anyway?"

"Marcus picked me up after work and took me to dinner."

"So … is it getting serious?" Lelani's eyes lit up like this would be a good thing.

"No, not really." Megan sighed. "I mean, he's a sweet guy. But we are so different. I'm not sure if it will ever get serious."

"I'm not sure that's what Marcus thinks."

"Well, I've made it clear to him that I'm a Christian," declared Megan, "and that I don't plan to get serious with a guy who isn't."

"And yet you go out with him?"

Megan shrugged. "Maybe that's a mistake. But when he popped in and told me he had made a reservation at Tullah's … well, I was hungry."

"You ate at Tullah's?"

Megan actually smacked her lips. "It was great."

"So it's okay to compromise your values if it entails really good food?"

Now Megan frowned. "I guess that does sound a little flaky."

"I'm not trying to be critical," said Lelani quickly. "I'm just curious."

"The truth is I'm trying to figure things out myself," she admitted. "Sometimes life doesn't seem totally black and white. I think I used to believe that. But the older I get, the more I question this."

"Meaning you really do like Marcus?"

Megan nodded. "But at the same time I'm not totally comfortable with that feeling."

"Because of your religious beliefs."

"Yeah, basically. You see, my dad was a really strong Christian. Well, my mom, too. But my dad used to talk to me about waiting for the right guy. Not that I've quit waiting. I mean, I'm still a virgin."

Lelani glanced away.

"Okay, too much information," said Megan quickly. "I know, I know. But my point is that my dad had these high expectations for me.

He told me that he'd been praying for my future husband since I was a little girl. And he really believed there was this one, special, perfect guy for me. You know how dads are."

Lelani's brow creased. "I guess."

"Anyway, I suppose I didn't think about it too much during college. I mean I was involved with a guy who I thought was The One. But then he wasn't. And then life was busy, and Dad got sick. And now that he's gone … well, more than ever, I want to do this thing right. But at the same time, I'm not even sure I know how." Megan frowned. "Does that make any sense?"

"I don't know." Lelani patted her on the back. "But if anyone can figure it out, Megan, my money's on you."

Megan nodded, but she wasn't convinced. And she wondered why everyone else seemed to assume that she had things under control. Did she really exude some false sense of confidence? Or did she simply take her faith seriously, whereas they didn't? Or maybe, and she hoped this was it, maybe they could see God shining through her.

Still, when it came to her relationship with Marcus, she felt generally mixed up. She'd been praying for God to guide her, but so far he wasn't being too clear. She didn't feel like it was wrong to spend time with Marcus. He was a genuinely good guy, and he'd been a good friend to her. He was helpful and trustworthy and straightforward. And she was being honest with him. She never said anything to get his hopes up as far as a long-term relationship. Mostly, she told herself, they had a nice friendship. And, really, what was wrong with that? It wasn't like he was complaining. Maybe, if she were to be completely honest with herself, she would have to admit that perhaps she was the one who wanted more. And that was the part that seemed wrong.

Six

Anna

"Oh, you poor thing," said Kendall when Anna stepped out of her bedroom wearing the detestable bridesmaid dress.

"It really is awful, isn't it?" Anna held out her arms and turned around to show off the horrible bow in back.

"It belongs in the hall of fame for ugly bridesmaid dresses."

"I just don't get why brides insist upon torturing their bridesmaids like this." Anna grimaced to think how far back this stupid outfit had set her pocketbook. "Really, what's the point?"

Kendall laughed. "Isn't it obvious? The bride wants to make sure she's the prettiest one at the wedding. Naturally, she has to make her bridesmaids look like a bunch of dogs to accomplish this."

"Seriously? That seems absurd. Would you do that to your bridesmaids?"

Kendall gave her a sly grin. "Now what do you think, Anna?"

Of course, Anna suspected Kendall would probably pull a stunt like that. Hopefully Anna wouldn't be around to participate by then. "Well, I wouldn't do it," declared Anna. "I'd want everything about my wedding to be pretty—even the bridesmaids. And I wouldn't have more than three at the most."

"So are you planning a wedding?"

"Me?" Anna firmly shook her head. "No, of course not."

"You and your little publishing friend aren't serious then?"

"Not that serious, that's for sure. By the way, his name is *Edmond.*"

"Yes, Edmond. Well, you could do worse than marry the son of the publisher."

"He's not the son. He's a great-grandson."

"Whatever. Is he picking you up?"

"No. I'm going by myself." Anna was still surprised that Edmond hadn't returned her call last night. Okay, even though she hadn't left a message, he should've checked his caller ID. And he should've called by now anyway. Perhaps it was just as well.

"You're joking." Kendall stared at Anna with horror.

"My parents haven't met him yet." Anna reached for her coat.

"So?"

"So … you don't know my parents." Anna slipped her cream-colored trench coat over the poofy dress and attempted to button it over the layers.

"You look like the Michelin Man," observed Kendall.

"Thanks a lot. I needed to hear that." Anna tried to fasten the belt around her midsection, but thanks to the bunches of fabric beneath, it was impossible.

"Well, you're obviously not concerned about looks if you're willing to go to a wedding looking like that and *without* an escort."

"Obviously." Anna made a face at Kendall before she headed down the stairs. "And if I fall down, I expect I'll just roll along like the Michelin Man."

Kendall chuckled. "Now, that'd be something to see."

Anna just hoped Kendall wouldn't push her.

"Are you sure you don't want to ride with Gil and me?" offered Lelani.

"Thanks anyway," Anna told her. "But bridesmaids are expected to be there early. Don't ask me why—all we ever do is stand around."

"I'm surprised you don't take the dress and change there," said Lelani.

"Yeah," added Megan. "Aren't you worried about wrinkling?"

Anna rolled her eyes. "I'm actually hoping that this will flatten it out."

"See you there," called Lelani.

Anna waved, then went outside. At least it had quit raining now. Maybe her hair wouldn't frizz after all. Not that anyone would be looking at her hair in this dress.

The only comforting thing about wearing a horrid bridesmaid dress is that you're not alone. And once Anna was with the others, lost in a sea of hot-pink satin, she didn't feel quite so conspicuous.

"I've decided to boycott all weddings when I turn thirty next year," said Caroline. "I'm done."

"Even mine?" asked Anna. Of all the cousins, Caroline was one of the only ones that Anna would've actually wanted in her wedding.

"Okay, maybe yours. But only if you promise to have moderately dignified dresses."

"Definitely dignified."

"So, do you have a groom in mind?" asked Caroline.

"Not really." Although she went on to talk a bit about Edmond. "But it's not really serious," she said finally.

"Sounds interesting." Caroline winked. "Will he be here?"

Anna explained that he hadn't met her parents yet and, unlike everyone else, Caroline got it. "It's not easy be part of a humongous Latino family."

"Yes, when I tried to explain it to Edmond, I asked him if he'd seen *My Big Fat Greek Wedding*."

Caroline laughed. "Yes. That's just about perfect."

"Except he hadn't seen it."

Finally it was time to line up. The music was beginning to play, and following the four flower girls, Anna was the first bridesmaid to be escorted down the aisle. She tried not to notice the looks she got, reminding herself that other ugly dresses would be right behind her. Her escort was a kid with a bad complexion who appeared to be about fifteen. Probably related to the groom. As usual, the procession and ceremony seemed to take forever. And by the time Anna was finally escorted back up the aisle—the first to enter and last to exit, since she was obviously Maria's least favorite cousin—her feet were killing her and she wished she'd thought to bring a spare pair of shoes for the reception.

"At least I have a good excuse not to dance," she said to Caroline as they sat in their assigned seats at the "reject table," as Caroline had dubbed it. Maria and Daniel's least favorite members of the wedding party sat here. "I have blisters the size of quarters on both heels."

"These pumps are the worst," complained Caroline. "But at least they were fairly cheap."

"I wonder where old bridesmaid shoes go to die."

"How about old bridesmaids?" said Caroline. "Seriously, if one more well-meaning aunt inquires as to my marital status, I think I'll scream."

"I think I may throw—" Anna saw something—rather, someone— that made her want to duck under the table.

"What's wrong?" demanded Caroline. "You look like you just saw a ghost."

Anna swallowed hard. "I did."

"What?"

"The ghost of boyfriend past."

"Jake?"

"Yes." Anna glanced over her shoulder, trying to spot the nearest exit. "I'm going to make a fast break, okay?"

"Sure." Caroline nodded. "I totally understand."

So, with her loathsome hot-pink shoes in hand, Anna stood, and without looking back, headed straight for an exit sign, only to discover that it was an emergency exit. As tempting as it was, she knew an alarm would sound if she pushed it open. And even if Maria wasn't her favorite cousin, Anna didn't want to spoil her reception.

So, staying on the perimeter of the room, she made her way to the front exit. When she got there, Jake seemed to be waiting for her. Short of running straight past him, which would probably appear melodramatic, it seemed her only recourse was to simply force a smile and say, "Hey, Jake."

"Anna, I've been looking all over for you." Then he actually reached out and took her hand, the one not holding the shoes. "It's so great to see you."

"Really?" Anna frowned.

"Yeah. I've been thinking about you lately."

"Oh?"

"Yes. And then I come to Daniel's wedding and the first girl I see walking down the aisle is you! I couldn't believe my eyes." He squeezed her hand.

"Really?" Anna felt slightly dizzy. She vaguely wondered if she'd actually blasted through that emergency exit, tumbled over the rail of a second-story fire escape, landed smack on her head, and was now semi-conscious and delusional. She blinked and stared at her old boyfriend.

"I know it sounds crazy, Anna. But it seems like fate."

"Fate?" She pulled her hand away from his and stepped back.

"Were you leaving?"

"Well, I …"

"Don't go yet, Anna. We need to talk."

She narrowed her eyes. The last time he'd told her they needed to talk, he confessed to falling in love with someone else.

"Kayla …" Without meaning to, she said the name. But at least it was out there in the open now. "What about Kayla?"

"We broke up, Anna. She wasn't really who I thought she was."

"Oh."

"Are you okay?" He bent down to peer at her face. "Do you need to sit down or anything?"

She nodded, and he led her through the hotel lobby, past an enormous Christmas tree and over to a quiet couch in a corner. But even after she sat down, it seemed her head was spinning. And she'd had only one glass of champagne. "This is very weird, Jake."

"I know. But really, Anna, it seems like fate to me. I mean I was thinking of you and wondering how to get ahold of you, and then you walk down the aisle in that hideous dress."

She laughed. "It *is* hideous, isn't it?"

"It's pretty bad."

She held up the shoes. "And these shoes are going straight into the trash when I get home."

"Do you still live at home?"

So she explained her new housing arrangements and, to distract herself from how bizarre this felt, she told him a little about her housemates and their various quirks. "But, all in all, we're starting to feel more like a family. In fact, we're even going to have a Christmas party, which should be interesting."

"Good for you, Anna. I mean for moving out. I never wanted to say anything, but your parents made it easy for me to break up with you."

"Oh, and so Kayla didn't really have much to do with it, then?"

"Yeah, yeah. Kayla turned my head. I can admit it now." He gave her a charming smile, the same one she used to love. "I'm sorry, Anna. I know I was a jerk. Can you forgive me?"

She frowned. "I don't know."

"Seriously, Anna. I really was just thinking about you. It's so cool to see you here tonight. Just like old times."

"How long ago did you break up with Kayla?"

He considered this. "I guess a couple weeks, but it seems like longer. It was right after Halloween."

"Oh." She wondered why he thought it seemed like longer. Was it because he was missing Kayla? Or just because he'd moved on? Still, she didn't want to ask. She didn't want to appear overly interested.

"It was a little uncomfortable coming to the wedding without a date," he said.

"I don't see why. A lone guy at a wedding is a hot commodity. I'm surprised the single girls weren't lined up to dance with you."

"How about you, Anna? Do you have a date here?"

She pressed her lips together, then shook her head. Why was he so darned good-looking anyway? And why was he doing this to her?

"So, you're not dating anyone, then?"

"Well, there's a guy ..."

He nodded with a slightly grim expression. "A guy ... well, of course, why should that surprise me? Is it serious?"

"Oh, I don't know ..."

"Meaning it's *not* serious?"

"Meaning *I don't know.*"

"But he's not here with you."

"Yes, well, I didn't want him to come."

Jake's dark brows arched hopefully. "So, maybe it's *not* serious."

"I just didn't want to subject him to everything yet. I mean, other than Gil, he hasn't even met my family."

"Speaking of Gil," said Jake, "who's that girl with him?"

"Lelani. She's one of my housemates."

"Wow, she's hot." Jake got a sheepish smile. "Sorry, but I'd have to be blind not to notice."

"I know, she's gorgeous. She's also really nice."

"Well, Gil looks smitten."

"Yes, he's been like that since the first time he met her."

"Are they serious?"

Anna frowned at that word again. "Serious? I'm not even sure how you define serious, Jake. They're not engaged, if that's what you mean. They go out sometimes. But Lelani is kind of mysterious. It's like she has some deep, dark secret. Or maybe she's just not sure what she wants to do with her life. She quit premed and seems a little confused. Anyway, I think she keeps Gil at arm's length. Although I know she really likes him too." It was a relief to talk about someone besides herself. Consequently, she probably told Jake more than he needed to know. But it did seem to move the conversation into a different direction.

As they continued to talk, Jake filled her in on his current job. He'd just been hired by a new software company and seemed to like it. Then Anna told him about her work at the publishing house and even the Ramsay Rowan project. And to her amazement, she started to relax a little. It almost felt like old times. But it also felt weird. Kind of like an unsettling déjà vu. Like history might repeat itself. And like maybe she should be careful.

"Want to dance?" he asked finally.

"Sure, why not?"

So they returned to the wedding reception and joined the others on the dance floor. And after a couple of songs, Anna realized that she was actually having fun.

"Okay, tell me about this guy," said Lelani. The two couples were taking a break together. The girls found a table while Gil and Jake went to fetch drinks.

"Oh …" Anna shrugged. "Jake's just an old friend."

"What about Edmond?" Lelani's gaze pierced Anna, like she knew what was up.

"I know this is crazy," Anna admitted. "I mean, Jake is the same exboyfriend who totally broke my heart. That was almost two years ago. And I was so over him."

"No way. This is that guy?"

Anna nodded. "He said he'd been thinking about me lately. Apparently, he broke up with the … the other girl, and he'd been wanting to call me. And then we meet at this wedding totally by accident. I had no idea he was a friend of the groom."

"Wow."

"Jake keeps saying that it's fate."

"What do you think?" Lelani peered carefully at Anna now.

"I don't know."

"But you're still into him?"

"Sort of."

"Poor Edmond."

Anna frowned. "What am I going to do?"

Lelani just shook her head. "I have no idea."

"Edmond is so sweet."

"Yeah."

"But Jake, well, he was my first love, Lelani. Isn't that supposed to mean something?"

"I'm not sure."

"But Edmond has been so good for me."

Lelani tipped her head to clue Anna that the guys were returning.

"Listen to your heart, Anna," Lelani said quietly.

That sounded good, but at the moment, Anna's heart was saying all kinds of unrelated things. On one hand, she was remembering how deeply hurt she'd been when Jake dumped her for someone else. On the other hand, she remembered what it felt like to be in his arms. She hadn't forgotten his kisses. And she remembered how she had pined for him, how at one point she would've done anything to get him back.

Then she remembered how good it felt to realize she was over him—or so she thought. And how it had been great getting to know Edmond. He made her feel special, and he respected her. Edmond had been so good to her. He knew how to make her laugh, and she felt so comfortable and happy when she was with him.

With Jake, well, she was on pins and needles. And yet that felt strangely good too. How was she supposed to listen to her heart when her heart felt so fragmented? So confused.

Instead she decided to listen to the music, to get lost in the dancing, and to be swept away by the moment. She'd figure out her heart later!

Seven

Lelani

"What's going on with Anna?" asked Gil as he and Lelani danced a slow dance together. Lelani could tell that the wedding was winding down, and yet she didn't want it to end. Despite all of Anna's complaints about Latino weddings, Lelani felt slightly enchanted and surprisingly at home. And she felt wonderful being in Gil's arms.

"You mean with Jake?" she asked quietly.

"Yes. What is she doing with him?"

"Dancing?" She smiled with her eyes.

Gil chuckled. "Do you know who he is?"

"You mean her ex?"

"Her ex who broke her heart."

"She told me."

"I just hope she knows what she's doing."

"She's a big girl, Gil." Lelani chuckled. "Okay, she's a petite girl, but she has a big spirit, and she's very smart."

"She's smart on some levels," said Gil. "But I'm not so sure about matters of the heart."

"She'll figure it out."

Gil nodded, then pulled Lelani closer to him. Wanting to cling to this moment, she nestled her head onto his shoulder and sighed. If only life could be this sweet and simple all the time.

But then the song ended and the lights came on and all too soon it was time for the bride and groom to make their getaway. Maria threw her bouquet and one of the bridesmaids, not Anna, caught it. But when Daniel threw Maria's garter he wadded it into a ball and pelted it like a football. It sailed beyond the groomsmen and straight at Gil, who caught it before it put his eye out.

"Uh-oh …" Gil tossed Lelani an uncomfortable smile.

"Don't worry," she said. "I don't take these things seriously."

Gil pocketed the garter and asked her if she was ready to go. Lelani didn't know whether to be relieved or disappointed when she realized the magic of the evening was gone now. But as Gil got her coat, she told herself it was for the best.

"Oh, there you are," said Gil's mother as she hurried to Lelani. "I hoped you were still here."

Lelani smiled. "Yes. Gil's getting our things." She barely knew Mrs. Mendez and wasn't quite sure what to make of this woman yet. She was friendly and sweet on the surface, but beneath lay something else. Something fiercely maternal and protective—not only of Anna, but Gil as well. It sort of frightened Lelani.

"So, what did you think of the wedding?" Gil's mother's dark eyes were studying Lelani closely, peering at her as if she expected to spy something sinister.

"It was lovely."

Mrs. Mendez looked surprised but simply nodded. "Oh?"

"Yes. It was perfectly delightful. I've had such fun and met such interesting people."

"Here you go," said Gil as he joined them. He draped Lelani's coat over her shoulders and smiled at his mother. "We're heading out now, Mom."

"But I was talking with Lelani."

"Oh?" Gil nodded. "What are you talking about?"

"The wedding." Mrs. Mendez's brow creased.

"And?" Gil waited.

"I was telling your mother that I had a great time," said Lelani. "I totally enjoyed myself."

"And it's getting late," said Gil, glancing at his watch.

"Too late to talk to your mother?" asked Mrs. Mendez.

Gil chuckled. "No, of course, not. What do you want to talk about, Mom?"

"Anna," she hissed, glancing over her shoulder as if worried that someone might be listening. Although that seemed unlikely. Most of the guests, including Anna and Jake, had left by now.

"What about Anna?" Gil's voice was getting impatient.

"What was she doing with that—that man?"

"Jake?"

"Yes! What was she doing with him?"

"Dancing?" Gil's eyes met Lelani's, and she was afraid he was going to laugh.

"Yes, dancing. But why?"

"If it's any comfort," said Lelani, "they didn't come together. And Anna was pretty shocked to see him."

Mrs. Mendez nodded. "Yes, that's a relief."

"But it's possible they could get back together," said Gil.

"No!" Mrs. Mendez firmly shook her head. "That boy—he is not good for our Anna."

"Anna is an adult, Mom."

"She is still my daughter."

Gil laughed now. "Yes, and she will always be your daughter." Then he hugged his mother. "And I will always be your son. But we will live our own lives, Mom. And now I need to get Lelani home."

Fortunately, that seemed to quiet his mother. And she actually smiled. "Drive safely."

"Where's Dad?" asked Gil.

"Getting the car."

"Shouldn't you go out to meet him?"

She shrugged. "There's no hurry." Then she grabbed Gil's arm. "Don't forget what I said about Christmas Eve, Gil."

"I won't." Gil kissed her on the cheek. "Now, you take care, Mom."

Lelani smiled and said her good-bye, then they made a quick getaway.

"Sorry about my mom," said Gil they waited for the parking valet to bring his pickup.

"Why?"

"Oh, she can be a little pushy."

Lelani laughed. "It's just because she loves you."

"I guess." Gil waved toward a white Cadillac idling across the driveway. "There's Dad, waiting, as usual, for my mom."

"Your dad's sweet."

"He's a good guy."

After they got into the pickup, Lelani asked Gil what his mom meant about not forgetting Christmas Eve.

"Oh ..." He shook his head. "Apparently Anna told Mom that you girls were throwing a Christmas party, and my mom's nose got out of joint."

"But your parents could come," said Lelani quickly. "And you're invited too, of course."

"That's not going to happen. I mean with my parents. There's no way my mom will go to someone else's party."

"Oh." Lelani frowned. "And it was my idea to have it. Am I ruining your family's Christmas?"

Gil laughed. "Not at all. My mother needs to learn that she can't expect Anna and me to come running every time she calls. Sooner or later, she's going to need to let us go and lead our own lives."

"But it *is* Christmas, Gil. And families should be together. I hadn't even considered that when I got the idea for the Christmas party."

"It's okay, Lelani."

"But your mother is going to hate me."

He chuckled. "My mother always takes a passionate dislike to anyone that Anna or I show interest in. But once she gets to know them, it gets better."

Lelani wasn't so sure. In fact, she felt fairly certain that Mrs. Mendez would like her even less the more she got to know Lelani and her history. "I just don't want to be the spoiler for your family's Christmas, Gil. Maybe I should cancel the Christmas party."

"That's ridiculous. Go ahead with it. I know Anna is excited about it. And I'd like to come too."

Now Lelani was imagining Mr. and Mrs. Mendez home by themselves. "But your parents, Gil. Won't they be lonely?"

He laughed. "No way. They'll have a houseful of relatives. It's the same thing every year."

"Except you and Anna won't be there."

"You won't be home with your parents either, Lelani."

"That's true. But Maui is a bit of a commute."

Gil didn't respond, and Lelani suspected he wanted to ask her more but was simply being polite.

"Besides, I don't think they want me around."

"Why?"

"It'll be their first Christmas with the baby ... with Emma."

"But what about you? Don't you want to be there too? I mean, she is your baby."

Lelani considered this. "To be honest, I've been thinking about her lately. Like I'll see a baby that's about her age—about six or seven months—and they are so adorable. And I think I am missing out on that."

"Can't you change your mind?"

"I don't know. I mean, of course, I'm sure I can change my mind. But my parents. They'd be upset. And we made a deal—they don't want me coming back so soon. So far, they're the ones holding everything together. They're the ones who paid for my college and supported me ... and I let them down."

"Life happens."

"I know."

"You need to forgive yourself, Lelani."

She didn't say anything. Maybe he was right on some level, but at the same time it seemed impossible ... unimaginable.

"I know you don't like talking about this," he continued. "But burying your feelings isn't good for you either."

"I know."

"Eventually you'll have to face it."

"Eventually, but not this Christmas."

"As long as you're not torturing yourself."

Lelani didn't respond to that either. And, fortunately, Gil changed the subject back to Anna and Jake. "It's going to be interesting to see what happens," he continued. "I was actually getting attached to old Edmond."

"Me too."

"And it's obvious that Edmond really cares about Anna."

"And she cares about him, too."

"But she might not be in love with him." Gil sighed. "Not like she was with Jake, anyway."

"But Jake hurt her," Lelani pointed out. "Do you think it's possible to fall back in love with someone who hurt you like that?"

"Could *you?*"

Lelani knew that he was referring to Ben now. Emma's father. And the truth was Lelani wasn't sure. Ben had hurt her more than anyone. He'd deceived her about being single, and then when she found out she was pregnant he abandoned her. Even so, she still remembered how it felt to be totally in love with him. In the past, she had imagined Ben searching for her, telling her he was wrong, that he wanted her back, that he wanted to take care of her and Emma, that they would be a family.

"I guess it's complicated," she finally admitted. "I mean matters of the heart. On one hand, you can feel like you totally despise someone who has hurt you. Like Anna probably felt toward Jake. But then that person appears to change, he apologizes, he says the right things, he pulls you in, and then everything is turned upside down."

"I know," said Gil firmly.

"You know *what?*"

"I know that Anna will be sorry if she goes back with Jake."

"Really?" Lelani frowned at him now. "You're starting to sound like your mother."

"Maybe so, but I think history can be the best predictor of the future."

"Meaning?"

"Meaning it's simple and straightforward, like math or science. You put two and two together and you know they equal four. You put Anna and Jake together and you know it equals trouble."

Lelani wasn't sure that he was only talking about Anna and Jake anymore. She suspected that somehow she and Ben had slipped into his metaphorical equation as well.

"It's too bad some people think with their hearts instead of their heads," stated Gil.

"Which do you think with?" she asked him.

He paused as if weighing his answer. "Maybe both."

"I'd like to think that I do too. But I have to admit that it hasn't always been the case."

He pulled up in front of the house on Bloomberg Place and let out a loud sigh. "I'm sorry, Lelani. I'm sure it must've sounded like I was lecturing you. Anna tells me that I can get all high and mighty sometimes. I probably sounded like that now."

She smiled at him. "No. I like talking with you."

"It's just that I really do care about you." He turned and looked at her. "And sometimes I sense that you're tormented."

"Tormented …" She nodded. "Yes. That sounds about right."

"And, being a guy, well, I guess I just want to fix it."

"But you can't."

"Right. But I want to help if I can."

"You do help, Gil. I mean, you're right … I *don't* like to talk about it. I *do* want to shove it away and pretend it's not there. But it's always there, you know, bubbling beneath the surface. And it helps me to know that you know about everything and that I can talk to you if I need to."

"Any time."

"Thanks."

Then he got out, helped her out of the pickup, and walked her to the door. "I know we've been saying that we're just friends, Lelani, but

I need to be honest with you. I feel like you're more than that. Or maybe I just wish you were more than that."

She didn't know what to say.

"But I don't want to push things either," he told her.

She looked up at him. "I really did have a lovely time tonight."

He smiled. "I did too."

This time she reached out and took his hand. "And I'm sorry I'm such a basket case sometimes."

"You're not a basket case."

"Well, I probably hide it, but I know that you know what I'm like underneath."

"You've got a lot to deal with."

"And I appreciate your patience with me, Gil. Really, I do."

He nodded and squeezed her hand. "And you're getting cold, Maui girl. You better get inside and get warm."

Then, to her surprise, she kissed him on the cheek. Then, feeling self-conscious, she turned and hurried inside the house. She closed the door and leaned against it and wondered why she had done that. Here she'd been managing to keep things under control and she goes and kisses him. But on the cheek, she reminded herself as she locked the door. Hadn't he kissed his mother on the cheek earlier tonight? Really, he shouldn't assume that it meant anything.

And yet as she went to her room, she had a distinct feeling that it did mean something. Or that she wanted it to mean something. And that worried her.

Eight

Kendall

"You expect me to believe that you actually slept with Matthew Harmon?" Amelia looked skeptical as she blew the steam off her latte. "Come on, girl. In your dreams."

"I *did*," protested Kendall. "Just ask Lelani if you don't believe me. She went to the wrap party too."

"Right. Like I'm going to call someone I barely know and ask her if my best friend is lying to me."

"Fine, then don't believe me." Kendall held her head high, glancing across the crowded coffee shop. She was curious as to whether anyone had overheard her confession about Matthew. Not that she cared, since she was rather proud of the fact that she was involved with Matthew Harmon. But everyone seemed to be engaged in their own conversations or reading the Sunday paper.

"Furthermore," said Amelia indignantly, "why did you ask Lelani to the wrap party and not me?"

"Because you're married."

Amelia rolled her eyes. "So?"

"So, I wanted to take a single friend."

"You wanted to take a single friend, but then you end up going to bed with a married guy?"

"I didn't know he was married."

"Everyone knows he's married, Kendall. Have you not heard of Heidi Hardwick? Get real."

"Okay, I sort of knew who she was, but I honestly didn't know they were married. Or maybe it was some kind of Freudian trick, like I knew on some level of consciousness, but I simply forgot."

Amelia laughed. "Yes, obviously it was some kind of Freudian trick."

"Anyway, he's not happily married."

"How do you know that?"

"He told me."

"Before or after you slept with him? That is *if* you actually slept with him."

"After." Kendall frowned now. "Well, to be honest, it might've been before, too. The night we met is still kind of blurry."

"You were drinking, obviously."

"It was a party."

"Just how drunk were you?"

Kendall gave her a sheepish smile. "Pretty wasted."

"So how can you be sure you actually slept with him then? Maybe you hallucinated or imagined the whole thing."

"Because I was in his room the next day. With him."

Amelia seemed to be coming on board now. And when she asked for specifics, Kendall was glad to give them to her. Sure, it was possible that Kendall was fabricating some of the details, since she really couldn't remember that much about the actual event, but she knew how to make it sound good.

Amelia shook her head. "Well, you are a piece of work, Kendall."

"A good piece of work?"

Amelia laughed. "Let's just say an interesting piece."

"But there's a problem now," said Kendall sadly.

"What?"

"I think I'm in love."

"In love or infatuated?"

"In love."

"How can you be so sure? I mean you admit it was a one-night thing, right?"

"Yes. But he's such a cool guy. And he liked me. And I'm sure if he wasn't married, well, I might have a real chance."

"What makes you so sure?"

"It's hard to describe. But something about the way he held me, the way he spoke to me, I could tell he really cared about me."

"Maybe he was just appreciative of the free sex."

"Amelia!" Kendall frowned.

"Get serious, Kendall. A guy like Matthew Harmon can have practically any girl he wants—or at least any girl who's giving it away. I mean he's obviously not faithful to his wife. You were simply at the right place at the right time. You were drunk. And you're easy."

"Thanks a lot." Kendall felt like walking out on Amelia right now. What kind of friend was she anyway?

"Come on, Kendall, you know that guys are like that. Easy come, easy go. Use her then lose her."

"Not all guys."

"No," said Amelia with cutting sarcasm. "Guys like Matthew Harmon, the ones who cheat on their wives, they're definitely different."

"He *was* different."

"Fine. Whatever." Amelia was checking her cell phone now, always a sign that she was bored with the conversation. For that matter, Kendall was fed up with her "friend's" criticism. When Amelia got married she turned into some kind of moral snob, like she'd never partied or slept around before. It was getting pretty aggravating, too. And here Kendall thought Amelia would be so impressed, and that she'd be fascinated to hear about Kendall's amazing encounter with a real film star.

"Are you jealous?" asked Kendall suddenly.

"Jealous?" Amelia laughed in an unconvincing way.

"You know, because I'm still single. And because I took Lelani, not you, to this really great wrap party, and we hung out with famous people, and I slept with a great-looking celebrity?"

"Why on earth would I be jealous of that?"

"Because you're a boring old married lady," teased Kendall. "And your days of fun are over and gone."

"And you're insane."

"And you're jealous."

"Puh-leeze." Amelia snapped her phone closed. "Arden and I are fabulously happy and I am not jealous." She stood now. "But here's a word of advice for you, Kendall."

"What?" Kendall stood too, hooking the strap of her Hermès bag over her arm.

"Do not get involved with a married guy."

Kendall frowned.

"I'm serious, Kendall. It never works."

"What makes you such an expert?" asked Kendall as they exited the coffee shop together.

"A mutual friend."

"Who?"

"Laura."

"Laura Stein?"

"Yes."

"She's involved with a married guy?"

"Yes. And she'd kill me if she knew I told you."

"Then why did you?"

"Because I'm making a point. Laura is miserable."

"She never looks miserable to me." Kendall paused by her car now.

"She's good at hiding it, but trust me, she's miserable."

"Why?"

"Because the guy keeps promising to leave his wife."

"And?"

"And he never does."

"Maybe he's going to."

"No. He's not. They never do."

"Never?"

"I saw it on *Oprah*."

"Yeah, right." Kendall shook her head and unlocked her car.

"I'm just warning you. A married guy who's cheating on his wife will say anything to get what he wants and, believe me, he wants it both ways. It's a lose-lose situation, Kendall. And you'll be the big loser."

"Thanks a lot." Kendall made a face. "But just so you don't stay up nights worrying about me, I am not going to be having an affair with Matthew."

"Good."

Kendall told Amelia good-bye and got into her car, slamming the door a little too loudly. "Amelia is such an idiot." Of course, she smiled as she said this, giving a dainty little finger wave to Amelia as they drove in opposite directions down the street.

Kendall continued talking to herself as she turned down Bloomberg Place. "Like I'm really going to have an affair with Matthew Harmon. Like that's even possible."

But as she drove down the street, she wondered, *what if it was possible?* Seriously, maybe she had given up on this guy too easily. What if she gave this her best shot? What if she went down to LA and surprised sweet Matthew with a little visit? Naturally, she'd make sure that she looked absolutely stunning. She'd get the hottest outfits together, and her hair and nails and everything would be total perfection. She'd book a room in a great hotel and then she'd just "happen to run into him." And who knew what might happen after that? Anything was possible.

As she pulled into her driveway, she felt extremely hopeful. Seriously, why couldn't she win Matthew away from that stupid Heidi Hardwick, a selfish woman who cared more about her career than she did for her husband?

Kendall hurried straight to her room and got online, and before long she was convinced that Matthew's marriage was doomed.

She spent the next couple of hours reading everything she could find about both Matthew and Heidi. It was an established fact that they'd had marriage troubles the past several years, although, according to one source, the couple had been trying to fix them lately. Allegedly, anyway. Who knew what was really true and what wasn't? Still, if Heidi's career was taking off like everyone seemed to be predicting, she might become a bigger star than poor Matthew before long. And in that case, Matthew might need someone in his corner to encourage him. He might need someone like Kendall to come home to.

Kendall closed her laptop and smiled. This might not be as impossible as she'd assumed. Even if it was difficult, it could be well worth the trouble. Besides, Kendall liked a challenge.

It was time to go shopping. The only problem was that Kendall was broke. She'd taken Megan's advice and used December's rent money, recently collected from her housemates, to pay the minimum balance on her credit cards. She'd known it was a bad idea, but Megan had been insistent. "You need to get your finances under control," she'd urged. Megan had also encouraged her to cut up all of her charge cards, but that's where Kendall had drawn the line. Instead, she had promised to seal them in an envelope and stick them in a drawer and forget about them.

It was time to get those plastic cards out. And, she told herself, this was different from just careless spending or being a "shopaholic" as her housemates liked to say. This was a serious mission and an investment in her future. Winning Matthew Harmon could change things for Kendall, permanently and wonderfully.

Kendall drove straight to the mall and hit her favorite stores, but she soon realized that this mission would be a bigger challenge than she'd expected. It was December and she wanted to find cool clothes that would work in sunny Southern California. Finally, she went to a boutique that specialized in cruise and vacation clothes.

"Kendall," said a female voice from behind her.

Kendall had been standing in front of a three-way mirror, checking herself out in a turquoise blue Gucci bikini. Surprised, she turned to see that it was none other than Laura Stein trying on a coral-colored sundress.

"Laura," said Kendall happily. "How *are* you?"

"Great," said Laura. "What do you think of this dress?"

"Nice." Kendall nodded. "And it looks like you've been tanning, too."

"Yes, I'm going on a Caribbean cruise next week."

"Ooh, that sounds wonderful."

"How about you?" asked Laura.

"I'm going down to LA." Kendall frowned. "But, obviously, I

haven't been tanning. The salesgirl said this color might make me look tanner, but I'm not seeing it."

"You can get a spray-on tan," suggested Laura.

"Really? Does that work? Or do you end up looking all drippy and orange?"

"No, it works. I've done it before. You know, when something comes up short notice and you want to look good."

"I'll check it out." Kendall did another turn to examine her back-side. "Do you think this cut makes my thighs look fat?" she asked Laura.

Laura laughed. "Yeah, what are you, like a size two?"

"Actually, this bikini is a size four." Kendall frowned.

"No, you look awesome." Laura ducked back into the dressing room cubicle.

"Thanks." Kendall returned to her cubicle and took off the bikini and decided it really did look good. But as she tugged on her jeans, she got an idea.

"I wouldn't dare wear a bikini like that," Laura called over the divider. "I stick with one-piece suits these days. Much more slimming for my kind of figure."

"I thought you were looking really good," called Kendall.

"Thanks, you're sweet."

With her bikini in hand, Kendall waited for Laura to emerge from the dressing rooms. "Do you feel like grabbing some lunch?" Kendall asked. "I just realized that I haven't eaten a thing today and I'm starving."

"Sounds great."

So they both finished up their purchases, and before long Kendall was sitting across from Laura Stein and confessing the whole thing about Matthew Harmon.

"Wow," said Laura. "That's wild."

"Do you think I'm crazy?" Kendall set her spoon back in her bowl of half-eaten soup.

"I, uh, I don't know."

"Because there's more to my story," said Kendall.

"What?"

"Well, the reason I'm going down to LA is to visit Matthew."

"Really?" Laura's brows lifted.

"I feel certain that his marriage is just about history. And I'm afraid if I wait too long someone else will jump in ahead of me."

"What makes you think his marriage is in trouble?"

So Kendall filled Laura in on all she'd read and heard. "Really," she said finally, "I think it's just a matter of time."

"And timing …"

"Exactly." Kendall leaned forward expectantly. She hoped that Laura would give her some little jewels of advice.

"I assume that you know about me." Laura looked evenly at Kendall.

Kendall kind of shrugged, then nodded.

"I figured that's why you told me about you and, uh, Matthew."

"I thought you'd understand." Kendall smiled. "And it just seemed meant to be. I mean, who would've thought I'd run into you today? And here we're both kind of involved in the same thing. Cool, huh?"

Laura pressed her lips together as if she wasn't sure whether to speak or not.

"Go ahead," Kendall urged her. "You can tell me anything."

"Well, I'll tell you this, Kendall. It's not easy being involved with a married man."

Kendall frowned. "Then why do you do it?"

Laura sort of laughed. "I suppose it's because I'm in love."

"So am I."

"And I think … in time … my situation will work out. But it's not for everyone."

"Are you saying I can't handle it?" Kendall felt defensive.

"I'm saying you have to be patient."

"I can be patient."

"I mean really, really patient. Most guys in this situation do not want to be rushed or pushed, you know what I mean?"

Kendall nodded. "I get that."

"And the very worst thing you can do …"

"What?" demanded Kendall.

"The way to ruin everything … is to tell the wife."

"Tell the wife? Why would anyone do that?"

"I'm just warning you. It's like a death sentence. A friend of mine was in a similar situation and time went by and she got fed up, you know, impatient. And she told the wife."

"Why?"

"She thought it would end the marriage and she'd get her man."

"What happened?"

"Well, the guy got really ticked. He broke off the affair and he and his wife got marriage counseling and they're doing fine now."

"And your friend?"

"She's *not* doing fine."

"Oh."

"So, be forewarned, Kendall."

Kendall held up a thumb. "Gotcha."

"And here's another bit of advice."

"Okay?"

"It's best to not even think about the wife, and don't ever talk about her to, uh, your lover. Just pretend like she doesn't exist."

Kendall nodded. "Well, I guess that makes sense. I don't think I'd want to talk about her anyway."

"You think that now, but things change. Most of all you just need to remember to be patient."

"And that's working for you?" asked Kendall eagerly.

Laura gave her what seemed a halfhearted smile. "Mostly."

"But you're going on this great cruise with him, right?"

Now Laura brightened. "Right."

"Cool."

"Well, I hope it goes well for you, Kendall. Let's stay in touch, okay?"

"For sure." Then Kendall thanked her and hugged her. "Bon voyage," she called out cheerfully as she and Laura parted ways.

Nine

Megan

"I need you to do an install over at Mrs. Fowler's today." Vera Craig shoved a design notebook toward Megan on Monday morning with an exasperated expression.

"By myself?" Megan set aside the notebook to hang up her coat. So far neither of her bosses at the design firm had expected Megan to do a complete installation by herself. She had helped them numerous times, and she'd been their gofer dozens of times, but to do a complete installation on her own ... "Are you sure?" she asked Vera.

"Is that a problem?" demanded Vera.

"No. I mean I don't think so. But I've never done an install by myself. Usually we go—"

"Look, Megan, it's time to be a big girl, okay?" Vera was obviously in one of her moods. "Sometimes we do installations together, sometimes we don't. If it's a problem for you, we can always look for another line of—"

"No," said Megan quickly. "It's fine. I just wasn't sure I understood."

"Good." Vera tapped a blood-red nail on the thick design folder. "Here's the plan. It's all in there. Most of the accessories are in the van, but there's a box by the back door that just came yesterday. You're only doing one room, a parlor of sorts, and the larger pieces of furniture should be arriving at the house around two, I believe. The movers will help you get them into place."

Megan nodded. She really wanted to ask why Vera wasn't coming along, but she also knew that questions would probably get her lambasted. So she kept her mouth shut.

"I'll have my cell phone if you need to reach me." Vera grabbed her coat and bag, then hurried out of the design shop.

Ellen chuckled from where she was sitting at the receptionist desk. Megan hadn't even noticed her come in, but she suspected that Ellen had been lying low and listening to Vera's spiel. "Good luck," she said.

"Good luck?" Megan went over to Ellen's desk.

"Yeah. Mrs. Fowler is, uh, well, different."

"What kind of different?"

"She's old for one thing."

Megan shrugged. "So?"

"And I guess you'd call her eccentric."

"Is that why Vera isn't doing this herself?" asked Megan.

Ellen pressed her lips together, and when the phone rang, she eagerly reached for it. Megan suspected that was all the information she was going to get from the receptionist. She wished that Cynthia were in so she could ask for some advice.

Well, maybe this would be an adventure. She loaded the large box into the already full van. Even if Mrs. Fowler was old and eccentric, why should that be a problem? If anything, it would probably be interesting.

✂

Mrs. Fowler's house, a Queen Anne–style Victorian, was in the historic section of town. When Megan drove through the narrow alley, hoping to park in the back, she discovered that the only available spot was filled with a large black Lincoln. So she went back around and parked in the front. The steps up to the front door were narrow and steep, and Megan knew this would pose a problem for all the things she needed to carry into the house. She rang the doorbell and waited. And waited and waited.

So she knocked loudly on the door. After a few more minutes went by, she rang the doorbell again, several times.

"Good grief!" screeched a tiny, wrinkled woman as she jerked open the heavy front door. She wore a blue bathrobe, and her white hair was sticking out in every direction in a slightly frightening way. Glaring at Megan, she asked, "What do you think you're doing, making enough racket to raise the dead like that?"

"I'm sorry, but I—"

"Who in the world are you, and why are you waking me up at this hour of the morning?"

"I'm terribly sorry to wake you up, Mrs. Fowler. I'm Megan Abernathy and I'm from—"

"I don't know any Abernathys." She was starting to close the door now.

"Wait," said Megan, actually putting her foot in the door. "I'm from Sawyer & Craig."

"I don't know any Sawyer Craig and I want you to leave at—"

"The interior-design firm," insisted Megan. "Vera Craig is—"

"Vera, you say?" The woman opened the door just a bit more, looking at Megan curiously.

"Yes. Vera Craig sent me. I'm an assistant at the design firm and Vera asked me to come here and put your—"

"Where is Vera?"

"I, uh, she couldn't be here and she asked—"

"But Vera is supposed to finish my parlor for me," said the old woman with uncertainty. "All the old furnishings are gone now."

"Yes," agreed Megan. "I have all the things that Vera ordered for you, and more furniture will be coming this afternoon. I'm here to put your parlor back together."

Mrs. Fowler frowned. "But how will you know what to do?"

Megan smiled, hoping to exude confidence. "Because I have the design plan. Vera wrote it all out, and by the end of the day, I should have everything in place for you."

"You're sure?"

Megan nodded. "Yes. But it would be helpful if I could park my van in back of the house so that—"

"That's impossible."

"But why?"

"My car is back there."

"I could move your car for you."

"No." She firmly shook her head. "No one is allowed to drive that car except me. And I do not drive."

"But how am I—"

"Don't be bothering me with your foolish nonsense, young lady, you are most certainly not going to drive my car. Of all things!"

Megan sighed. "Okay. Then I'll need to bring everything through the front door. Can you leave it unlocked for me?"

"Unlocked?"

"Yes. So that I can bring in the boxes and things."

Mrs. Fowler's hand was on her chest as if she was truly shocked. "I cannot leave my front door unlocked. Someone from the street might walk in and murder me."

"But—"

"Most certainly not."

"Then do you want me to knock every time I bring a load of things up? Or shall I simply ring the doorbell?" Megan knew impatience was creeping into her voice, but she didn't really care. No wonder Vera had passed this cantankerous client off onto her!

"I most certainly do not want you banging on my door or ringing my doorbell."

"Then I guess your parlor will have to remain like it is," said Megan.

"Do you have any identification?"

"Identification?"

"Yes. To prove that you are really who you say you are."

Megan held up the folder with Mrs. Fowler's name on it. "Look, this is Vera's plan for your parlor, would you like to see it?"

Mrs. Fowler squinted as Megan flipped through the pages of drawings and photocopies of various furnishings. "I suppose that looks right," she finally said. "Come inside and I will give you a key."

"A key?"

"So you can let yourself in and out. But you must give it back to me."

"Of course."

Mrs. Fowler opened the door wider now. "Come in. Wipe your feet first."

Megan wiped her feet, which were not dirty, then followed the little woman inside. The house seemed to have all its original woodwork and floors intact. In fact, Megan suspected that little had changed in this house over the years. The worn oriental carpets looked old. The heavy, carved wooden furnishings looked old. In fact, Megan was curious why Mrs. Fowler wanted to change anything.

"Here is the key," said Mrs. Fowler. "Don't lose it."

"No, of course not."

"The parlor is in there," said Mrs. Fowler, pointing to a set of French doors off to the right.

"Thank you."

"Do not break anything," warned Mrs. Fowler as she paused to look in a large, smoky mirror that hung above a marble-topped table.

"I'll be very careful."

Mrs. Fowler frowned at her reflection, attempting to smooth down her wild hair. "Now, if you will excuse me, I will return to my morning routine. And I do not wish to be disturbed."

"I'll be as quiet as possible," promised Megan. The truth was, she hoped Mrs. Fowler would not disturb her. The sooner she could finish this installment, the happier they both would be. Still, Megan wanted to throttle Vera!

After several trips from the van to the house, Megan wished she'd worn more comfortable shoes. High heels and steep steps were a painful combination, to say the least. She had decided to use the hallway outside the parlor as the staging area. But as she was opening a carton, she heard Mrs. Fowler cry out. "What is all this?"

Megan went out to the hallway to see Mrs. Fowler neatly dressed in a pale pink pantsuit, and her hair was somewhat in place, but her hands covered her mouth as if she'd just walked in on a crime in progress.

"I need to stage—"

"Get this garbage out of my hall at once!"

"It'll all be gone by the end of the day."

"At once!"

"But I need to—"

"If it is not removed, I will be forced to call the police," cried Mrs. Fowler.

Megan walked over to stand by her. "You don't understand. I can't put all these boxes in the parlor and have enough room to work in there."

"I understand that you have created a big mess."

Megan wanted to scream. Instead, she remembered last year, when she did her student teaching in a first-grade classroom. Perhaps some of those skills would come in handy now. "Do you ever cook, Mrs. Fowler?"

"Cook?"

"Yes. Do you bake cakes or pies or—"

"I'm an excellent baker."

"Okay." Megan took in a deep breath. "When you're getting ready to bake a cake, you have to get out all the ingredients, like the flour and sugar and butter and eggs and—"

"Yes, yes, of course."

"Well, it sort of makes a mess, doesn't it?"

"I suppose."

"And that's like what I'm doing now. I need to make a little bit of a mess, but when I'm finished, it'll all be cleaned up and gone."

"You're certain of this?"

"Yes, of course."

She sighed loudly. "Well, then ..."

"Perhaps if you stayed in another part of the house," suggested Megan.

"Perhaps." But something about the old woman's expression hinted that this was not going to be the case.

"If you'll excuse me," said Megan, "I need to get back to work." Megan went back into the parlor, where she'd been trying to get everything arranged for hanging the green velvet drapes. Fortunately, Vera had opted to use the original hardware, so that all Megan had to do was get them hung and then steamed. Of course, this was easier said than done. Fortunately the van, as usual, was equipped with a stepladder and steamer, as well as other tools of the trade. Still, Megan wished she could've had the help of Henry, the handyman often hired for larger jobs. Not that this was a large job. But doing it alone was a challenge.

It was nearly noon by the time Megan had the heavy drapes in place and steamed, and her arms were aching. She stepped back to admire her work. Not bad.

"What on earth!"

Megan turned to see Mrs. Fowler standing in the doorway and frowning up at the drapes.

"Aren't they beautiful?" asked Megan, although she could tell by the old woman's expression that this was not her sentiment.

"They are green!"

Megan nodded. "Yes, of course."

"They are not supposed to be green."

"What?"

"They are supposed to be red."

"Red?"

"Yes!"

Megan went to look in the file, searching until she found the color sketch, which clearly depicted the drapes as green. "See?" she showed it to Mrs. Fowler.

"See what?"

"Vera's sketch. The drapes are green."

"I do not care about this silly drawing. The parlor drapes are meant to be red."

Megan didn't know what to say. And so she decided it was high time to call Vera. Let her come over and sort this out. But, naturally, Vera was not answering her phone. Megan tried Cynthia's cell phone, and to her relief, Cynthia answered.

"Sorry to bother you," said Megan quickly. Then she explained, with Mrs. Fowler listening, about the problem.

"Oh, dear," said Cynthia.

"What?"

"Oh, I can't believe that Vera sent you there by yourself."

"You're telling me."

"And I really can't help you. I'm at Serenity Spa, not getting a treatment, but I'm about to make a big presentation for redecorating the whole place."

"What should I do?"

"Please, Megan, do what you can to handle it."

"Right." Megan closed her phone and looked at Mrs. Fowler and forced a smile. "I can see that you're frustrated," she said. "So, you don't like the color green?"

Mrs. Fowler seemed to consider this. "No, I like green."

"But you don't like green drapes?"

She frowned slightly. "No, I do like green drapes."

Okay, Megan became even more confused. "Do you mind if I ask you something, Mrs. Fowler?"

"What?"

"Well, I've noticed that your home is lovely. Really, really beautiful."

"Thank you."

"And everything in it almost looks original to the house. It's like a wonderful piece of history."

Mrs. Fowler smiled proudly. "It is, isn't it?"

"Yes. It's amazing. All your beautiful antique pieces and amazing rugs and lamps—it's really incredible."

"The house has been in my family since it was built in 1894. My parents gave it to my husband and me for a wedding present back in 1938."

"So I'm curious as to why you decided to redecorate your parlor. It must've been very nice before."

Mrs. Fowler frowned now. "Yes, it was lovely."

"But you wanted to change it?"

"My husband died in this room."

Megan nodded. "Oh, I'm sorry."

"Yes. I am too. Harold was a dear man. He died in here about a year ago, shortly before Christmas. And I couldn't come in here after that."

"I understand."

"But this is where our family always celebrated Christmas." She pointed to one of the big bay windows. "The tree always went right there."

"I see. And what color were the drapes before?"

"Red."

Megan considered this. "But if you want the room to be different, why would you want the drapes to be red again?"

Mrs. Fowler began to cry. Megan stepped closer to her and put an arm around her frail shoulders. "I want it to be the same," she sobbed, "the same as before …"

"You mean when your husband was alive?"

"Yes."

Megan didn't know what to say. And so she just stood with Mrs. Fowler as she cried. And finally, Mrs. Fowler stepped back, removed a lace-trimmed handkerchief from her pocket and dabbed her nose and eyes, then looked back at the drapes. "I suppose green will be fine."

The rest of the day wasn't without its complications, but Megan and Mrs. Fowler seemed to have made it past a crossroads of sorts. And each time Mrs. Fowler came into the parlor suggesting a lamp be changed to a different spot or the rug repositioned, Megan did not argue. After all, it was the old woman's house. Finally, just past five, all the furnishings were in place, all the boxes had been hauled away by the movers, and it seemed Mrs. Fowler was happy. Or as happy as she was going to be.

"And do you have plans for Christmas?" asked Megan as she handed Mrs. Fowler the house key. "I mean now that your parlor is back together?"

Mrs. Fowler shook her head. "No, my children live too far away. Most of my friends are in nursing homes or dead. I will probably be alone this year."

"My roommates and I are having a Christmas party," said Megan. Okay, it was a crazy idea. "Would you like me to send you an invitation?"

Mrs. Fowler looked surprised, but then she smiled. "Why, yes, dear. That would be very nice."

"Great," said Megan. "And I already have your address."

"Thank you for helping with my parlor," said Mrs. Fowler as she slowly walked Megan to the front door. "I know I'm not a very pleasant person anymore, but I wasn't always this way. It's not easy being old and alone."

Megan reached out and took one of Mrs. Fowler's small, wrinkled hands. "You know, it's not easy being young and alone either." She told Mrs. Fowler about how her father died last summer, and how she was still getting over it.

"You are a dear child," said Mrs. Fowler as Megan was finally saying good-bye. "I hope you will come visit me again."

"I will," promised Megan.

"Maybe I'll redecorate my bedroom."

Megan nodded and waved, but she really hoped that Mrs. Fowler wasn't serious about any more decorating projects.

Ten

Anna

"Have you been avoiding me?" Edmond was hovering over Anna's desk, looking down at her with a worried expression.

"Me?" She gave him her best innocent look.

"I left you a couple of messages on Sunday, but you didn't call back."

"Sorry. I was so exhausted after all that wedding stuff. I kind of crashed yesterday." Okay, that was partially true. But the rest of the story was that Jake had stopped by the house and invited her to a late lunch. And, after that, she didn't really want to talk Edmond. Not that her feelings for him had changed, but she didn't want to have to admit that she'd been with Jake. Mostly she felt confused.

"And then all morning, I get the feeling you're hiding from me. Are you?" He adjusted his glasses and sighed.

"No."

"But something's wrong, isn't it?"

"Look," she said. "I've really got to finish with this edit. It's due to the proofer and UPS pickup is at four. Can we talk later?"

He frowned. "I guess so. But if something's wrong, I just wish you'd tell me."

"Nothing is wrong," she assured him.

He brightened slightly. "So, are we still on for tomorrow then?"

"Tomorrow?"

Now he looked totally crushed. "Our dinner date?"

"Oh, yeah." She nodded as if she hadn't forgotten all about her promise to take him to her family's restaurant on Tuesday. "Sorry, Edmond, I'm just distracted with this project. I really need to finish it ASAP."

"Okay, I'll quit bugging you."

"Thanks." She gave him her best smile, then turned back to her computer screen. Still, she had a hard time focusing. Really, what was she going to do?

Four o'clock came and went, and Anna realized she'd missed the UPS pickup. She finished printing out the book at a quarter to five, and she knew she could make it to the UPS store if she made a run for it. So she turned off her computer, grabbed her coat and her package and took off. "I've got to get this to UPS," she told the receptionist on her way out. Of course, she realized that this also provided a perfect escape from having to discuss things with Edmond, but it wasn't as if she had planned it.

After the package was safely on its way, Anna decided to do something a little out of character. She went to her mom and dad's home. But first, she turned off her phone. She told herself she was doing this for her parents' sakes. They always got miffed if she or Gil got calls on their cell phones while they were visiting. They thought it was rude, although Anna had noticed that both her parents seemed to be using their own cell phones more these days. Maybe things were changing.

"*Mi'ja*," said her mother when she came in the door without even knocking. "What are you doing here?"

"You don't want me to stop in and visit?" asked Anna as she peeled off her coat. "Or do I need to phone ahead and make an appointment first?"

"Of course you're always welcome. Anytime." Her mother frowned now. "But, tell me, is something wrong?"

"No, of course not."

"*Mija?*" Her mother put both hands on Anna's cheeks and looked directly into her eyes now. "What is going on with you?"

"Nothing."

But her mother wouldn't let her off the hook or let go of her cheeks either. "Okay, what is going on with you and that—that—*Jake Romero*. I can hardly stand to speak that snake's name."

Anna pulled away now. "Jake is not a snake."

Her mother's brows shot up. "That's not what you used to say, Anna. You used to call him Jake Snake too."

"Fine. He hurt me, okay?"

"He broke your heart." Her mother's voice was dramatic now. "How can you let him back into your life, *mija?*"

"We're just friends, Mom."

She waved her hand at Anna. "Friends today. What will you be tomorrow?"

"Actually, I was planning on bringing Edmond to the restaurant tomorrow," said Anna as she followed her mother into the kitchen.

Her mother actually smiled now. "Edmond? The man who owns the publishing company?"

"His family owns it, Mom."

"Yes, but he sounds like a good man." She checked a pot of meat on the stove and went back to chopping an onion.

"You don't even know him." Anna picked up a carrot and took a bite. "You've never even seen him."

"But I heard your voice when you told me about him, Anna. It sounded like he made you happy. And it doesn't hurt if his family is wealthy."

"You'd want me to marry someone just because his family is well off?"

"If he's a good man."

"But not a Mexican?"

Her mother frowned now. "I don't know …"

"Jake is only half Latino, Mom. You used to complain about that. Now you want me to be involved with a rich gringo?" Anna tried not to laugh.

"I just want you to be happy, Anna. That's all any mother wants."

"Really?" Anna wasn't so sure. This didn't sound like her mother.

"Now tell me more about Lelani," her mother said eagerly.

"Well, she's obviously not Latino either."

"She is beautiful, though."

Anna nodded and took another bite of carrot.

"I think your brother is in love with her."

Anna laughed. "Duh? Ya think?"

"For an editor, your speech isn't very proper."

"Since when did you become an English expert?"

"I try." Her mother shook her head.

"Sorry." Anna picked up an avocado. "Want me to peel this for you?"

"Thank you."

"Am I invited to dinner?"

"Of course." Her mother turned to Anna with tears running down her cheeks.

"Are you crying?"

"It's the onions."

But Anna wasn't so sure. "Is something wrong, Mama?"

Her mom shook her head as she rinsed the knife. "No, *mi'ja*. It's just the onions. Although I suppose I am sad to think that my children have grown up so quickly … how they have left me behind to go their own ways."

"But that's what we're supposed to do, right?"

"I suppose. Yesterday your brother gave me a long speech about how I need to let go of my children. But it's not easy. My children are my life. How do I let you go?"

"It's not like you're losing us," said Anna, "and you know that we love you, Mama. We always will."

"Yes, I know." She smiled and nodded. "Okay, now tell me more about this beautiful Hawaiian woman that my niño has fallen for. Is she a good person?"

"Lelani is very nice," said Anna. "She's a hard worker. And she was going to med school to become a doctor, but she dropped out."

"Why did she drop out?"

"I don't know for sure. But I think it was some kind of personal tragedy. She doesn't talk about it. She moved to Oregon last summer. And, really, she seems kind of lost sometimes. I mean, I don't think she really likes her job, but she doesn't complain about it. And I don't know if she really likes living here—"

"Do you think she'll move back to Hawaii?"

"I don't know." Anna considered this. "To be honest, I guess I don't know that much about her."

"But you share a home with her, Anna."

"Yes. But we all have our own lives."

"I know, I know. Gil keeps telling me the same thing."

"If you really want to get to know her, why don't you invite her over for dinner or something?"

"That's a good idea, Anna. And maybe you and Edmond too?"

"I don't know."

"What do you mean, you don't know?"

"It's complicated, Mom."

"Aha!" Her mother pointed a meat fork at her. "I knew that Jake Snake was coming back into things."

"That's not it. Not exactly."

"What is it, then?"

"I don't know. I think I'm confused. I mean, you're right, Jake was a jerk. And I thought I was over him. But then, at Maria's wedding, well, I could tell he was different. He's changed, Mom."

"Changed? A snake can't change his stripes, Anna."

"Why not?" Anna set down her knife and stared at her mom. "Why can't a person change?"

Her mother made a face. "I have a bad feeling about that boy, Anna. That's all I know. I don't trust him."

"You don't trust who?" asked Gil as he came in through the garage door.

"Jake." Mom nodded to Gil. "And I thought you felt the same."

Gil looked uncomfortable now. "I guess we all feel protective of Anna." He smiled at his sister. "What are you doing here?"

"Having dinner."

He studied her as if he questioned this but didn't say anything.

"We'll be a family again tonight," their mother said happily.

"Sorry, I've got a date."

"With Lelani?" asked Anna.

"Yes, as a matter of fact."

"What are you and Lelani doing?" asked their mom.

"If you must know, I'm taking her to do some Christmas shopping for her family back in Maui. She wants to get the packages all wrapped and in the mail before it's too late."

"Smart girl." Mom tossed the chopped onion into the pan with the meat. "And she must be a thoughtful girl to be thinking of her family, sending them gifts."

"She is," said Gil quickly, making his getaway. Anna could tell he didn't want to have this conversation with their mother.

Fortunately, Mom was talking about Maria's wedding now. Saying what she liked and didn't like about it. It seemed that mostly, she didn't like it. Or perhaps she simply felt that she could've done it better. "One thing is for certain," her mom said as they were setting the table together. "Your Tia Elisa will not be coordinating your wedding, Anna."

Anna laughed. "I think I'll get married in Las Vegas if the opportunity ever arises."

"Las Vegas?" said her dad as he sat down in his chair. "No daughter of mine is getting married in Sin City."

"I'm kidding, Dad."

"She may be kidding about Las Vegas," said Mom, "but not about her opportunities. Our Anna has two boys after her now."

Dad frowned. "Is one of them Jake Romero?"

Anna waved her hand. "Don't worry about him, Dad. And you're going to meet my friend Edmond tomorrow." She explained her plan to bring Edmond to the restaurant, and then her mother told him about how "wealthy" Edmond was. Well, fine, let them think what they liked.

After dinner, Anna told her mother to take a break while she cleaned up the kitchen. Naturally, her mother was shocked, but she didn't refuse. Then Anna took her time, keeping an eye on the stove's clock as she worked. Her plan was to hang out here until eight. Then she would drive home, take a nice long shower, and go to bed. And she would "forget" to turn on her phone. She knew she was avoiding Edmond, but she didn't know what else to do.

☙❧

"There she is," said Megan when Anna came into the house. "The woman of the hour."

"What?"

"Your boyfriends have been calling here," said Kendall. "On the landline, no less. Apparently you've lost your cell phone."

"Oh?" Anna reached into her purse. "I guess it's turned off. I was at my parents' for dinner, and they're kind of old-fashioned."

"Whatever." Kendall rolled her eyes. "Anyway, I told them both that you'd call them when you got home."

"So, who is the other guy?" asked Megan quietly. Kendall was on her way upstairs, and Anna was standing with her phone in her hand, trying to decide what to do.

"The other guy?" she asked absently.

"You know," said Megan, "the one who's *not* Edmond."

"Oh, right. The other guy is my old boyfriend, ex-boyfriend, Jake."

"And you're dating both of them?"

Anna sank down in the club chair across from Megan. She still had her coat on and her cell phone in hand. "Not exactly. But sort of."

"That sounds tricky," said Megan.

Anna nodded. "Yes. And I don't think I'm really cut out for it. That's why I hid out at my parents' tonight."

"To escape the guys?"

"Yes. I don't know what to do, Megan." Anna felt close to tears now. "I'm so confused."

"For starters, why don't you take off your coat?" suggested Megan.

"Then tell me what's going on."

Megan hung up Anna's coat while she quickly replayed the whole thing. "The weird part is that everyone in my family seems to be opposed to Jake."

"Because he hurt you?"

"Yes. And then, of course, Gil likes Edmond."

"Edmond is a great guy, Anna."

"I know, I know."

"But you still have feelings for Jake."

"I guess I never stopped."

Megan's brow creased like she was trying to figure something out. "So how do you feel when you're *with* Jake?"

"How do I feel?" Anna thought hard about it. "Well, sort of nervous, you know, because we're not technically back together."

"But is it a good nervous?"

"I'm not sure. I mean I kind of get butterflies in my stomach. But I also feel kind of edgy and uncertain. And I suppose I've got my guard up."

"That seems normal."

"To be honest, I still feel hurt for the way he dumped me."

"But he's apologized?"

"Yes. Several times."

"Do you worry that something like that could happen again? That he might leave you for someone else?"

Anna pressed her lips together and thought hard about this. "Yes, I think so."

"Well, I suppose that's normal too."

"I suppose."

"And how do you feel when you're with Edmond?"

Anna considered this. "Well, up until Jake popped back into my life, I thought I felt pretty good."

"Like how do you mean?"

"Edmond makes me happy. He makes me feel safe. And I know I can trust him."

"But no butterflies?"

Anna giggled. "Actually, I do get butterflies with Edmond too. But it's not the same as with Jake. Maybe it's because Jake was my first love."

"Or maybe it's because Jake's more risky," suggested Megan.

"Risky?"

"You know, like a bad boy."

"I don't know."

"Sorry," said Megan. "I probably sound like I'm trying to psycho-analyze you."

"Actually, it's helpful. It makes me think about things differently."

Megan smiled. "Well, some girls would love to have your problem."

"What?"

"Like Kendall, for instance." Megan chuckled. "She acts all aggra-vated about the phone calls, but I think she's just jealous."

"Kendall, jealous of me?"

"I think she wishes she had two guys calling for her, too."

Anna shook her head. "Not me. It's too stressful."

"So are you going to call them back?"

"Not tonight. I need some time to think about everything."

"Well, I'm sure you'll figure it out."

"I hope so." But as Anna went to her room, she didn't feel very hopeful. There was a tight knot in her stomach, and it wasn't from her mom's cooking, either. If only for her own sake, Anna needed to resolve this thing as soon as possible. She was just not the kind of girl who could casually juggle boyfriends and not get an ulcer from it.

Lelani

"Oh, Gil, that is absolutely perfect!" Lelani clapped her hands as he held up a pink fuzzy one-piece bunting with satin-lined bunny ears. "Perfect for here, that is." She frowned. "But way too hot for Maui."

"Oh, yeah." He hung it back on the rack. "Sorry, I forgot about the climate thing."

"Me too."

It felt odd to be shopping for baby things. And even stranger to be doing it with Gil. But at the same time it was fun. Gil brought a whole new perspective to everything, including her life. Being with Gil made Lelani feel hopeful, although feeling hopeful also made her a little nervous.

"Hey, Gil." A pretty blond woman in the crib section waved to them.

"Camille!" Gil waved back. "Come here, Lelani," he said, tugging on her arm. "I want you to meet someone."

"Hey, Gil," said a guy who joined them. He had dark curly hair and appeared to be Latino. And as Lelani got closer to this couple, she realized the woman was very pregnant.

"Lelani, this is my cousin Brad and his wife, Camille." Gil smiled nervously. "And this is my, uh, my friend Lelani."

Lelani put the pink dress she was holding into her left hand, then shook hands with the couple. "Pleasure to meet you." She smiled at Camille. "When are you due?"

"Last week," said Camille with a weary sigh.

"We came to the mall to walk around, just hoping she'd go into real labor," said Brad.

"Not that it's working." Camille put both hands on her back and shook her head.

"Have you been having false labor?" asked Lelani.

Camille's eyes got large. "How did you know?"

"Lelani was going to med school," said Gil.

Relieved at his quickness, Lelani nodded. "Yes. Obstetrics was one of my strong interests. That and pediatrics."

"But you're baby shopping too?" asked Brad.

"Trying to find something for a friend's baby," said Gil with a relaxed smile. "For Christmas."

"That's a sweet dress," said Camille. "We're having a boy."

"Well, congratulations," said Gil. "I missed you guys at Maria's wedding."

"We were all ready to go," said Brad.

"Then I thought I was in labor."

"So I grabbed the baby bags and we shot off to the hospital."

"And three hours later, the doctor sent me home."

"Was that false labor too?" asked Lelani.

"Yeah. Now I'm worried I won't be able to tell when it's the real thing," said Camille. "I mean I keep having those little squeezes and I think they're contractions. But the doctor called them braxton something or other."

"Braxton-hicks," supplied Lelani. "And that could be true, or you might really be in early labor. Unfortunately some labors can go on for quite a while."

"How long?" asked Camille with fearful eyes.

"It just depends, but I'll bet you're very close," Lelani assured her. "Try not to think about it unless they start coming closer together, then you can time them. Unless, of course, your water breaks, then you'll know you're in labor. The good news is that all those contractions are getting your muscles in shape to give birth—you'll probably have a great delivery."

Camille brightened now. "Gee, this was even better than going to the obstetrician. He's always in such a hurry, and then I get flustered and I forget what I want to ask him."

"Well, good luck," said Lelani. "I'm sure you'll do great."

"Thanks," said Brad.

"Let me know how it goes," added Gil.

"Oh, yeah," said Brad. "I already got a nice box of *It's a Boy* cigars."

She and Gil watched as the couple slowly walked away. "Wow, you were good just now," he told Lelani.

"Hey, I was thinking the same about you. Fast thinking about your *friend's baby*."

"Well, that was the truth."

She considered this. "Yeah, I guess so."

"But your medical advice was great, Lelani. You sounded like a real professional."

She kind of laughed. "Well, the truth is I had a lot of premature labor too. But I didn't want to say that."

"Anyway, I think you made Camille feel better."

"It's a scary time," she admitted. "I mean right before your baby's born. You're nervous about your unborn child, and no matter how much you read, you don't really know what to expect when you go into labor. But at least Camille has Brad by her side. He seems like a good guy."

"He is." Gil studied her for a moment. "So, did you have someone with you when Emma was born?"

"My mother offered, but when the time came … well, I just went in by myself. I didn't call my parents until it was over."

"Wow, you're a brave woman."

"Or just dumb."

"No, you're not dumb." He firmly shook his head. "Definitely not."

Lelani wanted to point out that she'd been dumb to get pregnant. Dumb to trust a guy who turned out to be a liar and a jerk. Dumb to let her parents push her around. Dumb to drop out of med school. Dumb to not even attempt being a mother. Dumb, dumb, dumb. She wondered why Gil didn't see it.

But, as usual, she pushed these thoughts away, focusing instead on finding Christmas presents for Emma and her parents.

"Let's look at toys," suggested Gil after Lelani purchased the little dress and a dainty pair of white Mary Jane shoes.

"Toys?" Lelani frowned. "But she's a baby."

"I thought you said she was almost seven months old."

"Yes, but that's still a baby."

"There are baby toys."

"How do you know so much about this?"

He laughed. "I pay attention."

As it turned out, he was right. There were baby toys. All kinds of things. But Lelani was very careful in her selections. She didn't want to send anything that wasn't safe. "You're sure a baby couldn't choke on this?" she asked the salesgirl.

"See on the box," pointed out the girl. "Safe for zero to twelve months."

"Yes, but …"

"They test these toys," the girl said.

"What about lead?" asked Gil.

"Those have all been recalled," said the girl impatiently. "Ages ago."

Even so, Gil read the back of the box to see where the toy had been manufactured. Finally satisfied, he handed it back to Lelani. "Seems safe enough."

She grinned at him. "You would make a great dad." But even as she said this, she wanted to take it back. It had come out all wrong. It sounded like a hint. Lelani took her things to the counter and focused on paying the clerk, chatting absently about Christmas and asking when it had last snowed in Portland.

"We did have snow last year," the girl said as she handed Lelani the bag. "But it was in February."

"That's right," said Gil. "And it was followed by freezing rain, which turned the city into a huge mess."

The girl nodded. "Yeah, it was bad. Wrecks all over the place."

"I guess I'm glad I don't drive," admitted Lelani as she and Gil left the toy store.

"If you really want to see snow, there are other ways."

"You mean the ski resorts?"

"Yeah. Timberline and Mount Hood Meadows are both open. I could take you up there sometime."

"But I don't know how to ski."

"I don't either, but we could just go up for the fun of it."

"That'd be great, Gil. I just really want to see snow before I go home."

Gil was quiet as they walked through the parking lot. Then after they were in the truck, he spoke up. "So, Lelani, do you think you'll go back to Maui to live? I mean eventually, like after your year's lease is up?"

"That was the plan. My parents made me promise to take a year off to figure out my life." She shook her head. "Although I think a year was more than I needed."

"Oh."

Now Lelani felt bad. Still, she didn't know what to say. She was simply being honest. If Gil couldn't handle that, well, there wasn't much she could do about it.

"Anyway," he said as he drove across town. "Let me know when you'd like to go see snow. Saturdays are probably the best for me."

"It'd be fun to go before Christmas," she said. "I mean if it's not too much trouble."

"No trouble at all. Let's see, there are only two Saturdays before Christmas. Which do you want to shoot for?"

"Maybe next," she suggested. "I think the weekend before Christmas might be busy, getting things ready for our Christmas party."

"Speaking of that, I tried to give my mother a little heads-up warning that Anna and I might have other plans."

"Was she okay with it?"

"I'm not sure. She's been acting differently the past couple of days. I'd like to think it's because I told her that she needs to let her children grow up. Maybe she's just pouting and will be back to her old bossy self before long."

"You like her to be bossy?"

He chuckled. "Well, I guess I'm used to it. We all are. Not that we do what she wants."

"At least your mother is out in the open with it," said Lelani. "Not like my parents."

"Yes, you usually know where you stand with my mom."

"My mom likes to play games."

"Such as?"

"Oh, you know. This thing with Emma. My mother acted like she was doing me this great favor, like I was so needy and she was rescuing me from a fate worse than death. But sometimes I think she was simply glad to get rid of me. I think she was secretly thrilled that I had a baby, and that her plan is to push me away forever and raise Emma as her own daughter." Lelani felt tears now. "I know that sounds horrible, Gil. But sometimes that's how I feel."

"But you could go back and get your daughter, couldn't you?" he asked with genuine concern. "It's not as if you gave her up for adoption, did you?"

"No. I did sign legal guardianship over to my parents, for medical things and insurance." Lelani fished a tissue from her purse. "But I'm sure there would be a battle if I tried to take her from them." She blew her nose. "And even if I did get Emma, what would I do? I can't support myself and a baby working at Nordstrom. And I can't go back to med school and support a baby—not without help from my parents." She shook her head, but the tears kept coming. "My parents are right, Gil. I'm a mess. And it's a good thing they can care for Emma while I figure things out. I should be grateful to them."

Gil didn't say anything, and for that Lelani was relieved. When they got to the house, she quickly gathered up her packages and hurried up the walk with Gil trailing behind her. "Hey, Lelani, I could've helped with those," he called.

"It's okay," she said quickly. "But you can get the door for me."

He opened the door for her and smiled hopefully.

"Thanks for everything, Gil," she said. "I know it's late and we both have work tomorrow."

He just nodded, but she could see a trace of hurt in his eyes as she

told him good night and went into the house, closing the door with
her foot.

"Here comes Santa Claus," Kendall called out as Lelani walked
through the living room.

"And here she goes," Lelani called back as she headed directly to her
room.

"Aren't you the friendly one," said Kendall with sharp disappointment in her voice.

Lelani closed the door to her room, dumped the packages on her
bed, peeled off her coat, and then sat down and really cried. It seemed
that all she did was hurt people. No matter how hard she tried, it
seemed that she brought pain to anyone she cared about. Oh, she wasn't
that concerned about Kendall. She didn't really want to hurt her housemate, but she knew that Kendall would get over it. That might not be
the case with others.

Despite her harsh words about her parents, she knew that she'd
brought pain and humiliation to them. They had put their hopes in her.
They had believed that she was working hard in school, and she was,
but then she got sidetracked. She'd made a mistake. One that couldn't
be undone. And their disappointment had been enormous. She had
wounded them deeply. She knew this.

And then there was Emma. How was she going to feel when she
was older and found out that her mother abandoned her as an infant?
And then there was Gil. Dear, sweet Gil. But what did Lelani have to
offer him, really? Sure, she could be his friend, but it seemed a very one-
sided relationship. He was the one doing all the giving, all the helping,
all the understanding. And for what? What could he possibly gain from
this? And how would he feel when she finally went back home? How
would his family feel when they realized that she had hurt him? Would

they think she had used him? Was she using him? How could she even be sure?

But maybe she wouldn't go back home. Maybe she didn't have a home. Really, where did she fit in? Not here. Not there. She wasn't going to be a doctor. She couldn't imagine working at Nordstrom forever. And even her interest in cosmetology school felt silly and wrong and phony. Who was she, really? And where was she going? More importantly, when would she stop hurting people?

Lelani was pacing now, trying to make sense of her life, but she felt more lost than ever. All she had were questions. Questions. Questions. Where did one go to find answers? Or were there answers? Or just this continuous struggle. And, if so, what was the point? She knew if she continued with this line of thinking, she might wind up in a full-fledged panic attack. She'd had enough to recognize the initial signs. Already her heart was racing and her jaw was tight and her fists were clenched. Just breathe, she told herself, relax and breathe. But she felt trapped, like it was too late. Her head was starting to buzz and all she could imagine was doom and gloom and disaster. Her life was a mess that could only get worse and—

Someone knocked on her door. She took another deep breath and steadied herself. It was probably just Kendall. She was probably hoping that Lelani would share a glass of wine and stay up late and listen to Kendall go on and on about her silly problems. Like Lelani didn't have enough of her own to deal with. She jerked the door open and was ready to tell Kendall to take a leap when she realized it was Megan.

"Oh." Lelani stared blankly at Megan, who stood barefoot in the hallway wearing her *I Love Lucy* pajamas and an uncomfortable expression.

"Sorry," Megan said quickly. "I know it's late, but I heard you walking around, so I figured you were still—"

"Sorry, am I keeping you up?" Lelani used the back of her hand to wipe a wet cheek, then quickly looked away.

"No, that's not it. I just wondered if you're okay."

"I'm having kind of a bad night. Sorry to disturb you."

"Do you want to talk?" offered Megan.

Lelani took in a deep breath, then slowly exhaled. She was afraid to talk, afraid if she opened her mouth, she'd spill out her whole story. She wasn't ready for her housemates to know everything about her. It was hard enough that Gil knew, but at least he seemed to understand.

"I don't know what you're going through," said Megan quietly. "But I do know what it's like to go through hard times."

Lelani nodded, swallowing hard against the lump in her throat. She didn't want to start crying again, and she knew any sympathy might undo her.

"And I don't want to sound like I'm preaching at you," continued Megan, "but I know that the only thing that gets me through hard times is God."

Lelani studied Megan closely now. "But how? I mean, *how* does God do that?"

Megan seemed stumped, or maybe just surprised.

"Because I do believe in God … the Creator," said Lelani slowly. "At least I used to. But how does he really get involved in your life? I just don't get that. Is it even possible? *I mean, how does God do that?*"

"It's hard to explain," said Megan. "But it's like you pray to him. You give your worries and concerns and fears to God, and then you trust him. And he gives you this peace."

"Peace?" Lelani knew her voice sounded strained.

"Yes. A sense of deep inner peace, despite circumstances. Like I said, it's hard to explain, but I know it's real. I know I've experienced it myself. It's a peace that sort of carries you along."

"I don't even know what peace feels like anymore."

"I know I'm probably not making much sense," continued Megan. "I'm not that good at talking about God. But I do know he's the only thing that gets me through stuff."

"I feel like I'm drowning," admitted Lelani.

"God is a lifeline," said Megan. "He wants you to grab hold of him."

Lelani considered this. "Just like that?"

Megan nodded. "It's actually really simple. You believe in him. You ask him to live inside your heart. You start a relationship with him. You pray and you trust and he leads you. And things get better. Well, not overnight. And it's not like you don't still have problems. But he makes you stronger ... so you can withstand them."

"I'd like to believe that."

"Ask God to help you, Lelani. That's all it takes. Just start talking to him. He's there. He's ready." Megan looked slightly uncomfortable now. "I could pray with you if you want."

"Oh, I don't know."

"I mean I don't want to push you."

Lelani reached out and took Megan's hand. "Look, I'm going to really think about what you said. And if I can do this, I will ask God to help me. Okay?"

Megan blinked. "Okay."

"But I'm kind of a private person, and maybe I just need to figure this out."

"I understand."

"Thank you." Lelani let go of Megan's hand.

"And if it's any comfort"—Megan kind of smiled—"I've been

praying for you. And I'll keep praying. I really do think God is up to something in your life."

Lelani sighed and shook her head. "I so hope you're right, Megan."

Then she closed the door and tried to remember exactly what Megan had just told her. Believe in God. Trust God. Pray to him. Really, it did sound simple. Okay, almost too simple. Yet, Lelani couldn't deny that she desperately needed help. She did feel like she was drowning, like she needed a lifeline to hold on to.

As Lelani got ready for bed, she remembered a time when she was fifteen and had been out surfing. She took a hard fall and had been pulled down by a sharp undertow and held down. She'd reached out to God then. And, like a lifeline, something or someone had pulled her to the surface and to air. That's what she wanted now.

Twelve

Kendall

"You're up early this morning," said Megan as Kendall trudged into the kitchen.

"Yeah, I noticed." Kendall poured herself a cup of coffee and tried to remember just why she'd set her alarm so early.

"Are you going out job hunting?" asked Megan.

Kendall laughed. "Not exactly."

"You might be able to get a job in retail right now." Megan paused to pour a cup of coffee. "Stores could be getting desperate with Christmas just a little more than two weeks away."

"No one needs to remind me of that fact," said Lelani as she joined them. "Every day they change the big gold sign at the entrance. Today it will be fifteen shopping days until Christmas."

"I was just telling Kendall that she could probably get a job in retail if she wanted," Megan continued, sounding more and more like Kendall's mother or sister. Kendall seriously wanted her to put a cork in it, but instead she just closed her eyes and sipped the hot coffee. That was one good thing about having housemates. Someone, not Kendall, usually made coffee. And someone, not Kendall, bought coffee. And sometimes, if she managed to get up in time, which wasn't the norm, she got to drink some too.

"Nordstrom is looking for gift wrappers," said Lelani as she poured some cream in her coffee.

"Thanks, but no thanks," said Kendall. She could just imagine herself wrapping packages—in another universe perhaps.

"Well, how about sales?" asked Megan. "Surely they need salespeople somewhere this time of year."

"You'd be a natural, Kendall." Lelani pointed at her. "You're such a shopper and you know all the designers and everything."

"And that's how I intend to keep it. I'll stay on my side of the cash register and you stay on yours. Okay?"

"But when are you going to start earning a living?" persisted Megan. "You know your finances are a mess and you've got a bunch of bills—"

"Yes, but they're *my* finances." Kendall smirked at the two worker bees. "And they're *my* bills. And besides, I think I may be coming into some money soon."

"Seriously?" Lelani looked skeptical.

"Wait and see." Kendall tightened the belt on her bathrobe and nodded with confidence. Wouldn't they be singing a different tune when she was living the life down in LA, inviting them to come down for her wedding or maybe a movie premiere or just to hang around her beautiful house and sparkling pool? Kendall had bought a book yesterday. Yes, a book, a real hardback book. It was the first one she'd purchased since college. *The Seven Secrets of Sensational Success*, or something to that effect. And the first secret was to visualize what you wanted.

Consequently, Kendall had been imagining all sorts of lovely things, starting with Matthew Harmon by her side, an enormous diamond on her finger … and then the house, the pool … and Matthew's successful film career, of course! And even a little Chihuahua named

Pinkie—complete with a rhinestone collar! Or perhaps Pinkie's collar had real diamonds. It was hard to tell, since it was a daydream.

"I'll bet she's been buying lottery tickets," said Megan.

"It's getting pretty high," said Lelani. "I was feeling tempted myself the other day."

"You know what they say the odds of winning the lottery are," said Megan, the spoiler.

Lelani frowned. "I think I heard you had a better chance of getting hit by lightning."

"Twice," added Megan.

"You two are so cheerful this morning," said Kendall wryly. "I wonder why I don't always get up and have coffee with you."

"It must be because we're getting into work mode," said Megan. "I don't know about you, Lelani, but I had quite a day yesterday." Then Megan began to drone on about redoing some old lady's parlor, and Kendall couldn't get out of the kitchen fast enough.

Seriously, she wondered why anyone would put up with jobs like those two had. Lelani was on her feet all day trying to make wrinkled old rich women look younger, and Megan worked for the Wicked Witch of the West doing old lady houses. Kendall chuckled to herself as she took her coffee upstairs. And to think these girls gave her a bad time for not working. Who did they think they were fooling?

Kendall sat down and began making a list. She still had some shopping to do, plus she needed to book her flight and hotel. She knew some people did that online, but she thought she should seek the advice of a travel agent. And she would buy some lottery tickets. You never knew.

But before she would do any of this, she would call her mother. And before she called her mother, she would make sure to rehearse the conversation. There was no point in making this call if she didn't handle it right. Hopefully her mom's cell phone would be on. If not, Kendall had concocted a compelling message and was all ready to leave it—a message that would entice her mother to call back right away. But to her surprise, her mother actually answered.

"Hi, Mommy," Kendall said cheerfully. "How are you and Daddy doing?"

"We're doing well, Kendall. How are you?"

Kendall could hear the cautious tone of her mother's voice. But that wasn't unexpected. Her parents usually figured that when Kendall called, it was to hit them up for money. And, okay, that was usually the case. But today Kendall wasn't about to tip her hand.

"I'm doing great. I've been going to my counseling. And my housemates and I are planning a Christmas party and everything is cool."

"Well, that's good to hear." Her mom's voice relaxed. "And how's the job situation?"

"Well, December didn't seem like the best time of year to get a job. Besides that, I've been thinking about going back to school."

"Oh, that's wonderful, Kendall. Your father will be so happy to hear it."

"And I've had another exciting development, Mommy."

"What's that?"

"I met this guy. He's just the greatest. And he's actually an actor." Now Kendall felt pretty certain that her mother, a woman who knew less about TV and movies than anyone on the planet, wouldn't know a thing about Matthew or his sorry little wife.

"An actor?" Once again the caution crept back into her voice.

"A very successful actor named Matthew Harmon. He was filming up here in Portland. In fact, I got to know his director, too. Aaron

Stone. Have you heard of him?"

"That name does sound vaguely familiar."

"Yes. He's one of the top directors. Anyway, Matthew and I totally hit it off, Mommy. And he's such a great guy. He kind of reminds me of Daddy. He's a little bit older, and he's thoughtful and smart and responsible, and he really cares about me."

"Really?"

"So anyway, I just wanted you to know about this. I mean I don't usually tell you much about the guys I see. Well, because usually there's not much to tell."

"Well, thank you, Kendall. I appreciate that."

"But, here's the thing. Don't tell the other kids, okay? I mean not until it's really set in stone, you know. I can just imagine Kate or Kim getting all gaga over the fact that I'm dating a famous actor. I don't want that. Not until we've set the date."

"Set the date?" Now her mother sounded very interested. "Kendall, are you and this Matthew person thinking of marriage?"

Kendall giggled. "Yes! Isn't it exciting? And, of course, I'll want you and Daddy to meet him. Where are you guys now anyway?"

"We're at a lovely lake about an hour from Charlotte, North Carolina."

Kendall tried to imagine her parents and their big fancy motor home parked next to a lake, but it just seemed so far away. "It sounds nice."

"Very."

"So, you're not anywhere near Southern California then?" Kendall sighed. "If you were, maybe you could meet Matthew."

"Oh, we'd love to meet him. Let me see. We'll be heading west after the New Year. Maybe we could plan something later in January."

"Like your daughter's wedding?"

"Oh, sweetheart, that would be so wonderful!"

"I'm going down to visit him this weekend," continued Kendall.

"Give him our best."

"And, depending on how it goes, well, I might just stay on."

"So this relationship is really moving quickly then?"

"Absolutely."

"Well, I'm very happy for you."

"Thanks." Now Kendall waited. She was actually crossing her fingers.

"Is there anything we can do for you, dear?"

"Oh, I don't know. I mean Matthew is really rich and he'll probably insist on paying for everything for my trip. I mean since my budget is a little tight right now. You see, I've been paying off my bills and trying to get everything in order. One of my roommates has been helping me to manage my finances. But it would be nice to go down there and not feel like I was a total charity case."

"Of course. And your father and I were going to send you a little something for Christmas, Kendall. I don't know why we couldn't send it early."

"Oh, could you, Mommy? That would be fantastic. The last thing I'd want is for Matthew to think I'm after him for his money."

"No, you definitely don't want to look like a gold digger."

Soon it was all arranged. Kendall's dad would do an online transfer directly into Kendall's account. In a few hours, she would be celebrating Christmas early.

"Thanks, Mommy!" she cried. "I'll let you know how it goes, and we'll be sure to pick a date that works for everyone."

"I'm so happy for you!"

Then Kendall hung up. "Mission accomplished," she said. "Well, part of the mission." Then she picked up her new book and reread chapter one about visualizing success. Not only could she see success coming her way, she could smell it too!

Thirteen

Megan

"What sort of spell did you cast on Mrs. Fowler yesterday?"

"What?" Megan looked up from her desk to see Vera frowning down at her.

"Mrs. Fowler. Remember? The old lady in the Victorian house?" Vera carefully removed her pigskin gloves, still glowering at Megan.

"Yes, I know who Mrs. Fowler is," said Megan slowly. "But what are you talking about?"

"She left a message saying that she needed to talk to someone at the firm today."

"Oh?" Megan considered this. "Is something wrong?"

"I wouldn't know. When I called Mrs. Fowler, she insisted she needed to see the girl with red hair. I assume she must be speaking of you."

"I think she has memory issues," said Megan.

"So I explained to her that I was her decorator, but she insisted that wasn't so. She said the girl with the red hair was both her decorator and the only person she wanted to speak with."

"Well, she's just confused." Megan tried to mask the irritation she felt.

Vera leaned down and, placing both palms down on the edge of Megan's desk, peered at her with narrowed eyes. "Confused, or are you trying to steal one of my clients?"

Megan actually laughed now. "Vera, if *your* memory is still working, you might recall that you're the one who sent me over there to do the installation for Mrs. Fowler. And I think I know why you did it too."

Vera stood up straight.

"Mrs. Fowler isn't exactly an easy client, but I did my best to make her happy."

"Apparently."

"And that's a problem?"

Vera made a huffing sound. "Call her, please."

"Okay."

Vera left and Megan imagined a puff of dark smoke going behind her. But she looked up Mrs. Fowler's number and dialed. Expecting the worst—like perhaps Mrs. Fowler had decided that she really did want red drapes, or even worse wanted everything removed from her parlor—Megan waited for Mrs. Fowler to answer. After about twelve rings, Megan was tempted to hang up. Except she knew the house was large and Mrs. Fowler was slow. Finally, she heard the crackling sound of the old woman's voice.

"This is Megan Abernathy from Sawyer & Craig Design," she said politely. "I'm the one who was at your home yesterday, and I was told that you needed me to call."

"Yes, yes, Megan. That's your name. I know you gave me a card, but I seem to have misplaced it. All I could remember was your pretty red hair. Did you know that I had red hair once … oh, about a million years ago?"

Megan chuckled. "No, you didn't mention that."

"Well, I did."

Megan wondered if that's why she called but wasn't going to ask. "I've never been too fond of my hair," she said instead.

Mrs. Fowler made a cackling sort of laugh. "Nor was I. But that was then. Now I wonder what on earth was wrong with me. Red hair is beautiful. You better enjoy it while you can, because redheads tend to go white early in life. Mine started turning white in my thirties."

Megan stood and nervously glanced into the decorative mirror that hung behind her desk, peering closely at her roots to see if there was any trace of white. "I'll keep that in mind," she muttered. "Now, Mrs. Fowler, what can I help you with? Is everything okay in your parlor?"

"I'm still getting used to it. But I have an idea."

"An idea?"

"Yes. I think that I would like to change the love seat for two chairs."

"Oh?"

"Yes. Do you think that would look nice?"

Megan considered this. "Actually, I do."

"And love seats are an awkward piece of furniture, I think," she continued. "Often two people do not like to share it. So two chairs seem to make more sense. Do you think you could take care of that for me?"

"I will do everything possible," promised Megan. "Let me check into it and call you back in a bit."

"That's fine."

As Megan hung up, she knew she needed to be careful with this. Vera was already on the defensive. Or was it the offensive? Megan wasn't sure. But she considered how to word this as she walked to Vera's office and tapped on the partially closed door.

"Come in," called Vera.

Megan stepped in with caution.

"Oh, it's you."

"Sorry to interrupt you, but Mrs. Fowler would like to change something."

"What?" snapped Vera.

So Megan explained. And Vera just sat there drumming her long fingernails on the surface of her desk. "So?"

"So, what do you want me to do?"

"You?"

"Or anyone."

"Don't forget that Mrs. Fowler is my client, Megan."

"Yes, that's why I—"

"I will handle it. Thank you."

"Okay." Megan backed up to the door. "Do you want me to call her and explain—"

"No, I do not need you to call her. Thank you."

Without saying another word, Megan left, but it was all she could do not to slam the door. She wished that Cynthia were in this morning. Megan knew that she'd understand, and perhaps she'd even say something to Vera. Cynthia was the senior partner in the firm, but why she put up with Vera's crankiness was beyond Megan. Except that Vera had "connections"—meaning she had wealthy friends. According to some people, people that Megan had yet to meet, Vera was a "brilliant designer." Still, she could be such a witch. For whatever reason, she seemed to have set her sights on Megan from day one.

As Megan returned to her office, she felt torn. She'd promised Mrs. Fowler a return call. And yet Vera had told her not to make it. Fortunately, it was almost her lunch hour, and Megan decided to figure it out later. She was supposed to meet her mother at Demetri's Deli at noon. Perhaps her mother would have some words of wisdom for her. But when she got to Demetri's, her mother wasn't there. Megan got in line anyway. Just as she was nearly to the counter, her phone rang.

"I'm sorry," said her mother breathlessly. "Louise drove down from Seattle yesterday, and she got here late last night, rather unexpected. Anyway, this morning we got to talking and the time just flew and suddenly I remembered my lunch date with you."

"Oh, that's okay, Mom," said Megan.

"I'm so sorry, I hate to forget something like that."

"Really, it's fine, Mom."

"Are you at the deli?"

"Yes. And I'm just about to order some soup."

"Oh, that sounds good."

"Tell Louise hi for me and we'll do lunch another day, okay?"

"Thanks for understanding, sweetie."

"No problem."

"How about Friday? I have to go to a dentist appointment at two that day."

"Sounds great." Megan moved up to the counter. "I'll have a bowl of corn chowder," she told the guy.

"See you then," said Mom.

Megan hung up and tried not to feel aggravated. Or was it jealous? Really, it was fantastic that Louise and Mom were reconnecting. They'd been best friends in high school but lost track of each other over the years. Louise had been very lonely and blue, and Mom went on the Caribbean cruise with her, and it sounded as if they both had a blast. Really, Megan was happy for her mom. Mom felt she was helping Louise, and Louise was actually helping to distract Mom from her own grief. Her mom needed that right now. Of course, Megan felt like she needed her mom too. Now she couldn't even ask her for advice on the Mrs. Fowler situation.

"Megan!" said a high-pitched voice.

Megan looked up to see her friend—make that her acquaintance—Gwen Phillips approaching her. "Oh, hi, Gwen," said Megan.

"Is that seat taken?" asked Gwen hopefully.

"No. Actually it's not."

"Great. Don't mind if I join you, do you?"

Megan shook her head.

"So, how are you doing? I haven't seen you since we were both trying to get a room in that house on Bloomberg Place. I assume you didn't get in either. That girl who owned the house was such a snob."

Megan smiled. "Actually, I did get in."

Gwen blinked. "Seriously? You live there? Isn't that girl, well, she seemed so … oh, I don't like to sound judgmental, but she seemed very worldly and very materialistic."

"Her name is Kendall and she does like things."

"And you're okay living with her?"

"It's been interesting."

"She's not a Christian, is she?"

Megan frowned.

"Not that it's my business." Gwen peered curiously at Megan now. "Come to think of it, I haven't seen you at church or the singles group lately. You haven't fallen away, have you?"

"I've been going to second service," said Megan.

"*Second* service?"

Megan shrugged. "Yeah. Is that a problem? I mean, it's pretty much the same sermon as first, isn't it? Or is that the remedial service?"

Gwen sort of laughed, but she still looked piously concerned. "But what about the singles group? You used to be a regular."

"I guess I've been busy."

Gwen nodded with interest. "A guy?"

"Sort of," admitted Megan.

"Who is he? Anyone I know?"

"No, you don't know him."

"So he's not from church or college?"

"No."

"Does he *go* to church?"

"Not really." Megan looked up to see her soup coming at last. She smiled as the girl set it on the table. "Thanks." Then she dipped in her spoon and started to eat.

"You forgot to pray," said Gwen.

"Oh, yeah." Megan bowed her head and murmured a quick, "Thanks, God." Then she took another bite.

"So, you're involved with a guy who doesn't go to church?" Gwen persisted.

"I don't know if I'd say *involved*. We're more like friends." Megan was trying to think of a way to change the subject.

"Then why don't you bring him to church?"

"Oh, I don't know."

"You know what the Bible says about being unequally yoked, Megan. You don't want to fall into that old trap."

"Like I said, we're really just friends."

"Right." But even as Gwen said this, Megan could hear the doubt in her voice. And Megan had to admit that Gwen might be onto something. To be honest, Megan wasn't always so sure about the "just friends" thing herself, but even so, she didn't need Gwen Phillips preaching at her about it. So before Gwen could say another word, Megan thought of a way to redirect their conversation.

"Hey, I could use some advice," she said as Gwen's lunch was set before her.

"Sure." Gwen nodded eagerly, then bowed her head to pray.

So, after a fairly long blessing, and after Gwen finally said "amen," Megan explained her dilemma at work, describing how she'd promised to call old Mrs. Fowler back and yet how Vera had explicitly told her not to. "I feel torn. What would you do, Gwen?"

"Wow." Gwen picked up her sandwich. "That's a tough one."

"I know." Megan took another bite of soup and hoped that perhaps she'd stumped Miss Spiritual Know-It-All.

"Here's what I think you do," said Gwen, still chewing her bite.

"What?"

"You appeal to your boss."

"Vera?" Megan frowned. "She's not my only boss."

"Yes, but she's the one in charge of this, right?"

"I guess."

"You appeal to her authority."

Megan refrained from rolling her eyes and just nodded, pretending to listen.

"You go to her and you say, 'Vera, I know you told me not to call Mrs. Fowler, but I feel that I need to keep my promise to call her, so if you don't mind, I'd like to do that.'"

"And what if she says forget it?"

"Why would she?"

"Because she's territorial about her clients."

"Well, if she says forget it, I suppose that's what you do."

Megan frowned. "That just seems mean."

Gwen shrugged. "You asked my opinion and I tried to give you a biblically sound answer."

"Right." Megan hurried to finish her soup, then glanced at her watch. "Sorry to run, but I need to get back to work."

"Hey, it was great seeing you."

Megan nodded and reached for her bag.

"By the way, we're looking for people to help out at the mission."

"The mission?" Megan paused.

"If you're around on Christmas Day. Our singles group has offered to serve food that day, but a lot of people are going to be gone. We really need some more hands. Do you think you could come?"

Megan remembered how she'd been one of the people who suggested their group do some kind of outreach program last year. How could she say no now? "Yeah, sure, I'd like to do that."

"Cool." Gwen smiled. "And feel free to bring friends. Your roommates or your boyfriend or whomever."

"Okay, I'll keep that in mind." Megan waved. "See ya."

"God bless!"

Megan never knew how to respond to that one. To say, "God bless!" back sounded a little phony to her, like she was parroting. Plus the phrase wasn't exactly within Megan's comfort zone. It wasn't that she didn't want God to bless her and everyone else for that matter, but a few years ago her whole church had gotten into this blessing thing—like they all expected God to do something special for each and every one of them. And not just within the spiritual realm either. Some people expected God to give them cars or houses or to pay off their credit card bills. Maybe it was lack of faith or something else, but Megan just hadn't been so sure. She still wasn't.

Megan headed back to work and, as often was the case, a homeless woman was waiting on the corner next to the design firm. Because it was a habit, Megan fumbled for a couple of bucks, tucking them into the woman's hand. And, as always, Megan said, "God loves you!" Now that was something that Megan was comfortable with—because she meant it.

"Thank you, dear!" The woman waved a dirt-encrusted hand and smiled broadly enough to reveal her rotting teeth. Megan smiled back and waved as she hurried on past. Okay, it was a done deal. She *would* help at the mission on Christmas Day. Maybe her mom would like to join her too.

Megan was about to go into the design firm when her phone rang. This time it was Marcus. "Hey, what's up?" he asked cheerfully.

She gave him the quick rundown about being stood up for lunch and then getting stuck with her zealous friend Gwen.

"You should've called me. I would've rescued you."

"I never had a chance." She sighed. "But Gwen did instruct me to invite you to help at the mission on Christmas Day."

"The mission?"

"You know, they serve dinner to the homeless people. They need help with servers."

"Cool."

"Cool?" She was surprised. "You mean you'd be interested?"

"Sure, why not?"

"Great." His response made Megan feel hopeful. "And how about coming to the singles group with me on Friday night?"

"Oh, well …"

She could tell by his tone that this didn't interest him.

"I was actually going to ask you to come with me to hear a jazz band on Friday night, Megan."

"Oh?"

"Yeah, they're only here this weekend, and a friend of mine plays sax for them. I thought it'd be fun."

"Where are they playing?"

"Zeke's."

Zeke's was a bar. And she wasn't that surprised. It wasn't like a secular jazz band was going to play in a church. Maybe because of her conversation with Gwen, or maybe because being in a bar presented such a stark contrast with being in the church singles group, Megan felt uncomfortable. Also, she noticed that Vera was rapidly coming up the walk toward her. "Can I get back to you on that?" she asked quietly. "I need to get to work now."

"Sure. Call me."

Megan gave Vera a quick nod, then hurried into the building and directly to her office. As she hung up her coat, she wondered if she was being too hard on Marcus, expecting too much from him too soon. But the next thing she knew, Vera was storming into her office and all thoughts of Marcus went sailing out the window.

Fourteen

Anna

"I almost thought you were going to blow me off tonight," said Edmond as he stopped by Anna's office after work.

"Blow you off?" she asked innocently.

"As in, 'See ya later, Edmond,'" he said as he helped her into her coat.

"Hey, I promised you dinner," said Anna. "I'm not backing out."

Edmond didn't look convinced. "But maybe you were thinking about it?"

"No, of course not."

"So, we're still on for six thirty then?" He still sounded like he expected her to bail on him.

"That's what I said." She buttoned her coat.

"And I'm picking you up?"

"Unless you'd rather meet there."

"No, I'm happy to pick you up."

She forced a smile. "Great."

"Do you need a ride home?" he asked hopefully.

"No," said Anna. "Thanks."

"But I didn't see your car in the lot."

"The weather wasn't bad, so I walked. And I plan to walk home. I wanted to stop by the store on my way."

"But it's dark out."

She gave him a warning glance. "Now you're starting to sound like my mother."

He nodded. "Okay. I get it."

"See you at six thirty," she said as she reached for her bag and headed toward the front door.

"See ya!"

Edmond was right, it was dark, and Anna wished that she'd taken him up on that ride. Not that she was afraid, exactly. But maybe a little uncomfortable. Growing up with her mother's constant phobias and dire predictions had left its mark on her. Anna knew it was time to grow up. Wasn't that one of the main reasons she'd moved away from home in the first place?

So, with renewed confidence, she marched down the sidewalk and stopped at the small grocery store, where she got a quart of milk and a box of cereal and a few other things. Then she hurried on home. Bloomberg Place was less than three blocks away, and the streets were actually well lit. Other pedestrians just like her were out and about, and no one seemed the least bit concerned about any of it. By the time Anna was in the house, she realized that she wasn't concerned either.

But as she was putting her groceries away, she knew what concerned her most was tonight's dinner with Edmond. He'd given her every opportunity to get out of it. It was as if he expected her to. And yet that had made her simply dig in her heels. She was determined to keep her promise to him, even if it meant she dumped him afterward.

Was she really going to dump him?

"You seem troubled," said Megan as she came into the kitchen.

Anna sighed and shook her head. "Flustered. I'm thinking of breaking up with Edmond tonight."

Megan frowned. "Too bad. He's a nice guy."

"I know."

"Then why are you breaking up?" Megan seemed genuinely curious.

"I'm not sure. I mean, he *is* a nice guy and I really like him. But there's Jake to consider now."

"Meaning you're choosing Jake over Edmond?"

"I don't know."

Megan put a hand on Anna's shoulder. "Maybe you should just take it one step at a time."

Anna thought about this, then nodded. "One step at a time. Okay."

So that's what she was telling herself when Edmond picked her up. And what was rumbling in the back of her mind as she made small talk with him on the way to the restaurant. But once they were there, she was worried this was a big mistake. Why was she going to the trouble of introducing him to her parents if she was about to dump him? Or maybe she wasn't about to dump him? And, really, *dump* was the wrong word. She would let him down gently.

"This must be Edmond," said her mother as soon as they entered. She had obviously posted herself as hostess so that she'd be the first to see him. Anna went through the formal introduction and her mother actually took Edmond's hand and smiled. "Very nice to meet you … *finally.*"

"Finally?" he peered curiously at Anna.

"Oh, our Anna's been telling us all about you," said her mother.

Edmond smiled. "She has?"

"Oh, yes. We've been looking forward to meeting you." She waved to Anna's dad, who was coming their way. "And this is Anna's father, Mr. Mendez."

Anna tried to look relaxed as her father chatted briefly with

Edmond. But the whole time she was asking herself why, why, *why* she had brought him here. It would only make everything harder in the end.

"This is a great place, Anna," said Edmond after they were seated. "Not at all what I expected."

"Thanks." Anna put her napkin in her lap. She glanced around the semicrowded restaurant, trying to see the usual round tables with white linen tablecloths, crystal votives, and fresh flowers with fresh eyes. Quiet Mexican music played in the background. "What did you expect?"

He smiled. "Oh, you know … bright colors, pottery, piñatas, that sort of thing."

She kind of laughed. "Well, you should've come here back in the old days. Gil has worked hard to change that image. He's trying to make this restaurant more upscale and elegant. Are you disappointed?"

"No, not at all. This is nice. And very romantic." He winked at her.

"Don't expect violins."

"Do your parents want to join—"

"No," she said too quickly.

"Oh?"

"I mean they have to work. That's all."

He nodded, but his brow was creased. "Are you okay?"

"I'm fine."

"Okay, then." He sighed and Anna could tell that he was suspicious. And why shouldn't he be? She was acting like a total idiot. She was a total idiot. What kind of fool brings her boyfriend to meet her parents and have dinner on the same night she's thinking of breaking up? So, to distract herself from this, and to somehow make it through this evening without losing it, Anna began to chatter away about the restaurant. She started with the linen napkins that she used to be in charge of, explaining how they couldn't afford to have them laundered, so it had been Anna's job to get them clean and pressed. She went on and on about how stubborn some stains could be and how monotonous it was to iron square after square after square.

"It was so wonderful when we got laundry service," she went on, knowing she probably sounded even more idiotic now than before. But somehow she managed to get them clear through dinner, and then they were eating flan for desert.

"Anna," began Edmond carefully. "I know that something is wrong."

"Nothing is wrong," she said quickly.

"No," he continued. "I can read you like a book." He sort of laughed. "Okay, maybe not quite that well yet. But I know that something is troubling you. Did I do something to offend you?"

She frowned and laid down her fork, then folded her napkin and set it on the table. "No, you haven't done anything wrong, Edmond."

He nodded. "Okay. What is it then?"

She looked down at her lap now.

"You don't want to talk about it here?"

"No, not really." She looked back at him and pressed her lips together.

"I understand." He glanced around to spot their waiter, one of Anna's cousins, who seemed to have totally disappeared.

"Do you need something else?" Anna asked, ready to pop up and get something, anything, just to get away from him for a few seconds. "More coffee?"

"No, just the bill."

She laughed. "Oh, there's no bill, Edmond. I told you it was my treat."

"You're sure?"

"Of course." It was actually her parents' treat, but that was pretty much the same thing. "Are you ready to go?"

"If you are." He quickly stood and helped with her chair—always the gentleman. She wondered if she'd miss that. Then he helped her with her coat and politely told her parents good-bye and thanked them for everything.

"It was a pleasure to meet you," said Anna's mother, winking at Anna.

"You kids be good now," called her dad.

Edmond gave him a thumbs-up and a smile that had a shadow behind it. Anna wondered if her parents could see. Finally they were back outside, walking silently to his car. In the car, Edmond turned to look at her, his face dimly lit from the parking lot lights. "Anna, what's going on?"

She felt her hands balling up into fists in her lap. Why was this so hard? Why didn't she just spit it out? Maybe it was because she knew how it felt. She knew how badly it hurt to be dumped. But Edmond was different from her. For one thing, he was a guy. For another thing, he always seemed to take life in stride. Easygoing and generally cheerful, he'd probably actually understand and get over it. Maybe he'd be happy for her. Maybe they could still be friends.

"Edmond ..." She looked directly at him. "Remember the guy I told you about?"

"The guy?"

"The guy I went with for a couple of years."

He frowned. "The dude who broke your heart?"

"Yes."

An uncomfortable silence settled in the car.

"You don't think …" he began slowly. "You don't think that's what I'm going to do, do you, Anna? Because if you do, you can just forget about—"

"No, no, that's not it," she said quickly.

"What, then?"

"Edmond, I'm so sorry, but that guy … his name is Jake. Jake Romero. And he was at the wedding last weekend and …"

"Oh." He nodded and put his key into the ignition, but didn't turn it.

"I never expected to see him at the wedding," she continued. "I didn't even know that he knew the couple. And I actually tried to run when I realized he was there. But he stopped me. And then we were talking, and he was saying how much he missed me, and I suddenly realized that I still had feelings for him. I wanted to tell you last weekend, but I just wasn't sure."

"Weren't sure?"

"About how I felt."

"And you're sure now?"

"I don't know."

"You *must* know, Anna." He stared at her with wounded eyes. "How do you feel? Tell me."

"Confused." She felt tears coming now. "And sorry. Edmond, I'm so, so sorry. I didn't want to hurt you."

"That's okay, Anna." Edmond turned the key.

"What do you mean, *that's okay?*" she demanded.

"I mean I know what you're saying to me. I get it. I think I actually knew yesterday."

"How could you know?"

"Because I know you, Anna."

She didn't say anything now. How could he possibly know her when she didn't even seem to know herself? He drove her back to the house in silence. And it felt like the longest twenty minutes of Anna's life. Still, she could think of nothing to say.

"Thanks for dinner tonight," he said as he opened the door and helped her out of the car.

"How can you say that?" she demanded.

He sort of shrugged, but she could see he was hurting. "It was a good dinner, Anna. And your parents seem nice."

"Edmond," she tried again, "I'm really sorry."

"You said that."

"But I am. And I know I've hurt you."

He paused halfway to the house. "I'll get over it."

"Don't be mad," she said.

"Mad?" He seemed to be thinking hard over this. "No, I don't think I'm mad."

"I'm really, really sorry."

"Good night, Anna." Then without saying another word, he turned and abruptly walked back to the car, got in, and drove off. He didn't swear or slam his door. He didn't even drive fast. Not that she'd expected him to do any of those things.

Anna went on up to the porch, telling herself that at least the hard part was over now. She didn't need to feel like she was leading Edmond on anymore. She had made her choice, and she'd been honest with him. Not only that, he'd taken it well. He wasn't even mad. And he'd politely said good night. She should feel totally relieved now. Instead, she felt like crying. And she felt just as confused as before.

Lelani

"What are you doing home in the middle of the week?" Kendall asked as she joined Lelani in the kitchen.

"I have the morning off." Lelani poured some cream into her second cup of coffee. She wanted to add that since she had the morning off, she had hoped to enjoy a bit of peace and quiet. She glanced at the kitchen clock. It was barely past nine. "What are you doing up this early, Kendall?"

"Oh, not much." Kendall's blue eyes twinkled with mischief as she reached for the coffee carafe.

Okay, now Lelani was curious. Kendall had been acting strange lately—even for Kendall. "Seriously, Kendall, what's up? Did you find a job or something?"

"Or something."

"What kind of something?"

Kendall adjusted the belt on her fluffy white bathrobe and smiled smugly. "Well, can I trust you?"

"Trust me?" Lelani wasn't sure. What was Kendall planning now? "I'm not sure what you mean."

"I mean I'm not ready for everyone to know what I'm up to."

"Meaning you don't want me to tell Megan and Anna?"

"I just don't want all three of you on my case all at once."

"On your case for what?"

Kendall took a slow sip of coffee, then pressed her lips together and smiled coyly. But she didn't say anything.

Lelani could feel herself being sucked into this—this whatever it was. And she decided she really didn't want to know, didn't want to be involved. Whatever Kendall was up to was her problem, not Lelani's. "Well, have a nice day." Lelani smiled as if speaking to an "I'm just looking" customer at the cosmetics counter. And then she started to leave the kitchen.

"Wait," said Kendall.

Lelani turned and looked evenly at her.

"Come on," said Kendall eagerly. She joined Lelani in the dining room and pulled out a chair. "I need someone to talk to."

With reluctance, Lelani sat down. She'd had her chance to make a smooth getaway and blown it. Maybe she deserved this. "Okay, Kendall, what's up?"

"So I can trust you then?"

Lelani shrugged. "I guess. I mean unless you're planning on doing something totally nuts or illegal or dangerous."

"None of the above." Kendall frowned slightly. "At least I don't think so."

"You don't think so?"

Kendall laughed. "Kidding."

"Seriously, Kendall. What's going on?"

"Okay." Kendall took in a deep breath then slowly exhaled. "I'm planning to go down to LA."

"So?" Lelani wondered what the big deal was here. Or was Kendall just a drama queen who could make anything into a personal premiere?

"So … I'm meeting Matthew down there."

Lelani slowly nodded as it sunk in. "Meeting Matthew, as in continuing your, uh, your little affair with him?"

Kendall looked uncertain. "You make it sound so skanky."

"Isn't it?" Lelani peered curiously at her now. "I mean, you know now that Matthew's married. Even if you didn't know before, as you claim, you don't have that excuse anymore."

"Unhappily married," Kendall corrected her.

"Even so." Lelani frowned at her. "Why are you doing this?"

"I'm in love."

"He's married."

"Unhappily."

Lelani just shook her head.

Kendall looked like someone had just popped her balloon. "I should've known better than to tell you."

"I'm just being honest."

"Honest from your perspective. Can't you even consider mine?"

Lelani thought about this. Little did Kendall know that Lelani hadn't only considered Kendall's point of view, she'd been there. She'd been the other woman. The problem was that Lelani honestly hadn't known Ben was married. He deceived her, then betrayed her. But of all the girls in this house, Kendall was the last one she'd trust with that story!

"I don't know how I got so lucky," said Kendall unhappily.

"What?"

"To end up with three goody-goody housemates." Kendall's lower lip jutted out. "I had hoped that maybe you were different."

Lelani kind of laughed. "I am different. We're all different. Look, I can understand how you feel, Kendall. I guess I'm just questioning your judgment. Are you sure that it's wise to go down there to be with a married guy?"

"I think he loves me too, Lelani. And I know that his marriage is in trouble. I've been reading about it online. And I've been reading about Matthew, and I think we have a lot in common. I think it could really work."

"Seriously?"

"I feel like I need to at least give it my best shot. I mean, what if I didn't even try, and what if his marriage *is* over with and some other girl jumps in before me? How would I feel? Matthew told me that I was special. He wanted to spend more time with me. How can I let that slip by?"

"You could get hurt."

"It's better to have loved and lost than never to have loved at all."

Lelani couldn't help but laugh at the melodrama. But even as she laughed, she could see the sensibility in Kendall's plan. And that scared her.

"Fine," said Kendall, standing. "Go ahead and laugh at me. I know you guys all think I'm just a joke."

"I'm not laughing at you." Lelani snickered.

"Then what?"

Lelani stood too. "I guess it's just life in general. And in a way I do admire you, Kendall."

Kendall blinked. "You do?"

"Yes. For going for your dreams—even if they do seem a bit crazy to me."

Kendall made a little half smile. "Well, thanks. I think."

"When are you going?"

"Friday morning. In fact, I was wondering if I could talk you into driving me to the airport. In exchange you can have the use of my car while I'm gone."

Lelani considered this. Not a bad deal. "What time?"

"Early. My flight's at 7:35 a.m."

"And you're supposed to be at the airport two hours early."

"Well, I was thinking an hour early would be okay."

"No," said Lelani firmly. "Holiday travel has already started, and I heard on the news that you really do need to be two hours early."

"Sheesh, maybe I should just stay in an airport hotel."

"No," said Lelani. "You'll just get to bed early and I'll wake you up in time to be at the airport by five thirty."

Kendall groaned.

"Unless you just want to forget the whole thing and just—"

"No," said Kendall quickly. "I'm going."

Now Lelani was curious. "Did you get your tickets already?"

"Oh, yeah. And booking a flight at the last minute is not cheap."

"So how could you afford it?"

Kendall smiled. "Mommy and Daddy."

"Huh?"

"Early Christmas present."

"So they're okay with what you're doing? Or do they even know?"

"They know. And they're totally on board. They just want me to be happy."

"And it probably doesn't hurt that Matthew Harmon has a pretty successful career and is making good money."

Kendall put her hand on her chest as if offended. "You don't think I'm after him for his money, do you? A gold digger?"

Lelani shrugged. "I'm just saying."

"Well, I'm not. Even if Matthew were poor, I'd still love him."

Lelani wasn't convinced, but she wasn't going there.

"Anyway, I need to get my wardrobe set," said Kendall.

"Your wardrobe set?" Lelani tried not to laugh.

"You know, for the warm weather down there. I've done a little shopping, but summer clothes are scarce this time of year."

"Don't you already have things?"

"Old things." Kendall's eyes lit up. "Hey, I'll bet you have a good selection of clothes from Hawaii."

Lelani shrugged. "I doubt there's anything there that you would—"

"Let's go check it out," said Kendall as she headed straight for Lelani's room. And the next thing Lelani knew, they were digging through her closet in search of "cool" clothes for Kendall's trip.

"This is awesome." Kendall held up a white gauzy top and looked in the mirror. "Diesel's not my favorite designer, but this one is great. Can I borrow it?"

Lelani studied the blouse. The last time she'd worn it had been with Ben. "You can have it," she said.

"Hey, thanks."

Lelani gave Kendall several things that she associated with bad memories. In a way it felt like a purging, like getting some skeletons out of her closet.

"This is going to be great," said Kendall. "I won't even need to shop much more. At least not until I get down there. But I feel bad that I've made a dent in your closet. You really don't have a lot of clothes, do you?"

"I have enough." Lelani frowned. "But what I really need is some ski stuff."

"Ski stuff?"

So Lelani told her about Gil's plan to take her up to Mount Hood.

Kendall grinned. "Hey, you're talking to the right girl. Come on up." She took off toward the stairs with Lelani trailing her.

Before long, Lelani was loaded down with some pretty cool ski stuff. Several items still had the tags on. "You're sure you don't want to return any of these new items?" asked Lelani for the second time.

"No, I got them last year. I'm sure they wouldn't take them back now."

"Maybe not. At least not without a huge markdown."

"So take them and have fun." Kendall heaped a sweater on top of Lelani's pile. "Maybe we'll both have fun."

"Maybe." But as Lelani took her pile back to her room, she wasn't so sure. Oh, she'd probably have fun with Gil. But she wasn't sure about Kendall. Should Lelani have been more forceful with her, more persuasive about the trouble she was getting into? But wasn't that a bit hypocritical considering Lelani's own past? And, as impossible as it seemed, what if Kendall was right? What if Matthew was done with his marriage? What if he and Kendall really did have a future? Why should Lelani attempt to stand in their way?

Lelani dumped the ski clothes onto her bed, and then systematically began trying them on. Most of them not only fit but were very nice. She knew she shouldn't be too thankful for Kendall's shopaholic ways, but at the moment she was. Hey, maybe Kendall would marry Matthew Harmon, and maybe he'd help her to pay off her bills. It could happen.

Although Lelani's shift didn't start until one, Mr. Green had planned several mandatory employee meetings throughout the day. Her plan was to attend the noon session. Who could complain about being paid for sitting and listening to someone drone on for an hour? As she went up the stairs to the employee lounge, she hoped they'd have food. Fortunately they did. She quickly filled a paper plate, then sat down at the big table with fellow employees.

"Thank you for coming," said Mr. Green in his usual formal voice. "You've probably heard by now that the purpose of this meeting is to address the increase of theft in our store. We have invited a small panel of experts to educate us." Then he introduced a security expert who began spewing out some staggering statistics.

"More than thirteen billion dollars' worth of goods are stolen from retailers each year," he said. "That's more than thirty-five million dollars per day." He went on to explain that most shoplifters were adults, but about a fourth were juveniles. Then he described various techniques of professional shoplifters—the ones who did it regularly—and pointed out that it took more than security cameras to catch them.

"Your employer relies on your eyes as well," he said as he wrapped up. "It's up to everyone to slow this train down."

The next expert was a police officer. Her purpose seemed to be to put the fear of the law into the employees' hearts. "Unfortunately, a fair amount of thefts are inside jobs." Then she went on to describe how some employees feel that they are owed something beyond their wages, how they justify that stealing from the workplace is acceptable.

Finally, a psychologist was introduced. He explained how many shoplifters were addicted to stealing, whether they needed the items they took or not. "They get an actual chemical high from their escapades," he said. "Without professional help, they're unable to resist the impulse to steal."

Lelani tried to appear interested in all this, but the truth was she knew it didn't apply to her particular job. Everything she sold was kept in a glass cabinet. When she showed various items, some quite expensive, to customers, she kept a sharp eye on things. So far she didn't think a single thing had been stolen from her counter. At least not on her watch.

"So, as you see, it's up to all of us to be alert," Mr. Green was saying now. "And we're implementing a bonus plan for employees who participate. If we can reduce the lost revenues from theft, we will reward employees who give assistance."

Did he expect them to act like bounty hunters now? Lelani didn't open her mouth to ask. Finally the meeting ended and Lelani went down to work. To her surprise, between busy times, she did find herself watching customers, wondering which ones were there to shop and which ones had stealing on their minds. Really, how could a person know for sure?

For instance, she spotted a woman whose clothing seemed a little shabby. The lady kept lurking around the accessories department, picking up scarves and examining them closely. Yet this woman looked as if she'd never worn a scarf in her life. Lelani tried not to appear to obvious as she puttered around, wiping down the glass surface of the case and straightening a display shelf, but the whole while she was watching the woman in the gray jacket. Finally the woman carried a pastel-colored scarf to the cashier and paid for it. Lelani felt foolish for being so suspicious.

Was it possible that some individuals, like her, for instance, had a natural inability to discern between well-intentioned people and those who were not? Take Ben. Lelani had assumed that because he was a doctor, he was honest. As it turned out, he was not. Then Lelani had trusted her aunt and uncle, but they ultimately betrayed her. Maybe Lelani was just a bad judge of character. Then she thought about Gil. Everything in her said that Gil was good and sincere and honest. But then she'd been wrong before—who could say if she'd be wrong again?

Lelani had been trying to do what Megan suggested. She had been trying to believe in God, to trust him, and even to pray. And to her surprise, this effort had been helping with some of her panic attacks. Or at least it seemed to be. But what if her judgment about that was impaired too?

Sixteen

Kendall

"So you're *really* going through with this?" asked Amelia.

"Yep. I leave tomorrow." Kendall had met Amelia for coffee again. For no explainable or rational reason, she felt the need to have someone support her decision to go to LA. As futile as it probably was, it seemed that Amelia was her best bet. Kendall wasn't even sure why she had this strong need for affirmation. Maybe it had to do with her last counseling session.

Her therapist, Marjorie Thorpe, had been encouraging Kendall to take advice from others, particularly from her sister Kate as well as her killjoy housemates, all of whom Kendall was avoiding. Well, other than Lelani occasionally, and even that had proven dicey. But Marjorie said that discussing her plans with others was a good way for Kendall to get a "reality check." So maybe that's what Kendall was attempting with Amelia now.

"I told my parents all about it," said Kendall, "and they're backing me."

"Seriously?"

Kendall nodded as she stirred her mocha. "They want me to be happy."

"Well, of course."

"And I can accept that you think I'm being stupid."

"I didn't say stupid."

"Well, something to that effect."

"I just want you to be careful, that's all."

"And it might interest you to know that I spent some time with Laura Stein."

"You called Laura?" Amelia looked stunned. "What did you say? 'Hey, Laura, I'm about to have an affair with a married guy and I'd like to get your perspective?' Did you tell her that I told you?"

"No, of course, not. I just happened to run into her at the mall. She was getting cruise clothes and we started to chat."

"Cruise clothes?"

"Yes." Kendall nodded. "She and her lover are taking a Caribbean cruise. If you ask me, she seemed perfectly happy."

"Being the other woman?"

"Well, I don't know about that part."

"What do you mean you don't know? That's exactly what you're planning on doing, aren't you?"

"No. It's not like that."

"Yeah, right."

"I did my research, Amelia. Matthew's marriage is already in trouble. Otherwise I wouldn't be going down to meet him."

"And he's okay with this?"

"What?"

"You being down there, on his turf."

"Of course." Kendall took a sip of her mocha. Okay, maybe that was a lie, but maybe it wasn't. And why should Amelia care anyway? The point was, Kendall was in love with Matthew. And she had a feeling he was in love with her too. Or he would be.

"Well, I still think it's a bad idea."

"Fine. I just thought that since you were my best friend, or so I supposed, you might want me to be happy. Even Lelani was more supportive than you." Kendall frowned.

"Lelani thinks this is a good idea?"

"She even gave me some great summer clothes to take down there."

"Well, then she's not as smart as I assumed. I thought you said she'd been in med school."

"She is smart." Kendall sat up straighter. "Actually she's both smart and beautiful."

"Whatever."

Kendall could tell that she'd hit a raw spot with Amelia. But she didn't care. Hadn't Amelia been running roughshod over Kendall's feelings?

"Well, I should probably go," Kendall said in a less-than-friendly tone. "I have a lot to get done. My flight is pretty early tomorrow, and I have an appointment for the works at Julien's, and then I have to pack."

"Lucky you." But even as Amelia said this, Kendall thought there was a trace of envy in her tone.

"Sorry," said Kendall. "But I thought you were my friend. And I thought friends wanted to be in on what's going on in their friends' lives. Guess I was wrong." She reached for her bag now.

"All right, Kendall." Amelia almost sounded like she was giving in. "I hope you have a fantastic time in LA. I hope that Matthew falls head over heels for you. And I hope that his marriage is over and you guys get married and live happily ever after."

Kendall beamed at her. "Thanks."

"Happy now?"

"A little."

"Keep me posted," said Amelia as they went out to their cars.

"It's a deal."

"And if you and Matthew do get married, you better invite me down there to soak up some sunshine." Amelia hugged her.

"Yeah." Kendall glanced up at the dark clouds overhead. "It looks like it's about ready to let loose. I'm definitely not going to miss this weather."

"I've been trying to talk Arden into taking me someplace sunny after the New Year," said Amelia sadly. "But he keeps reminding me that our honeymoon isn't even paid for yet."

As they both went in their separate directions, Kendall wondered if Amelia's whole attitude problem might simply have been jealousy. Of course, that had to be it. And why shouldn't Amelia be pea green with envy? After all, Kendall had it all going on. And she was going down to LA to sweep Matthew Harmon right off his feet and to live happily ever after. Kendall felt nearly ecstatic as she drove to the salon. She was going to have her highlights touched up, a pedicure and manicure, and finally she was going to get a spray tan, which she'd been told was satisfaction guaranteed.

Of course, she hadn't been told how cold the spray was going to be, or that the smell would cause a sneezing fit. But when it was all said and done, Kendall thought she looked hot.

It was close to five when Kendall finally got home. Before she packed, she tried on several outfits just to see how they looked with her new tan and highlights. She did her own little fashion show in her room and decided she didn't only look hot, she looked totally hot. There was no way that Matthew would be able to resist her. Sure, his wife was cute enough, in her own drab little brunette sort of way. But she was nothing like Kendall.

Finally Kendall put on her bikini and strutted back and forth in her room. The spray-on tan actually made her thighs look slimmer. Really,

Kendall couldn't remember any time in her life when she had looked this fantastic. She had it going on, and she knew it. Matthew would know it too, although he would not know that she'd come down there to see him. No, she had it all worked out in her head. She was simply in LA to interview for a job. And it was just a coincidence that she was house hunting in his neighborhood. Seriously, how could she have known where he lives? Don't celebrities keep those things top secret? Kendall laughed and did another spin. And maybe she *would* interview for a job while she was down there. What could it hurt? Maybe someone would scout her for a role. Seriously, it could happen.

Kendall tried on the new sundress she'd found last weekend. It was a sweet little strapless Nicole Miller number, and Kendall was tempted to trot downstairs and show off to her housemates. On second thought, she knew that would only stir up questions—questions she did not want to answer. Although she did plan to let them know *where* she was going and *how long* she'd be away, via Lelani, she did not intend to tell them *why* she was going. And Lelani better not either!

Finally Kendall had everything packed and was ready to roll. She almost wished she'd booked a red-eye flight. Except the last thing she wanted was to arrive in LA looking red-eyed and worn out. No, her goal was to look fresh and pretty and hot. To that end, she'd actually avoided drinking much this week. Of course, at the moment she could think of nothing she wanted more than a cosmo or two—just to help her relax and get some rest. Instead, she took a sleeping pill and hoped that she would wake up looking refreshed and lovely.

It seemed she'd barely fallen asleep when Lelani was tugging on her and saying it was time to get up.

"It's still nighttime," said Kendall.

"It's almost five in the morning. You need to be at the airport in thirty minutes."

"Why?" asked Kendall sleepily.

"You're going to visit Matthew Harmon in LA, remember? Or maybe you changed your mind." Lelani frowned at her, then started for the door. "In that case, I'll go back to bed—"

"No, no," said Kendall. She jumped out of bed. "I'm still going."

Somehow the two of them managed to get Kendall and her stuff together, and before long they were on their way to the airport.

"It feels like the middle of the night," said Kendall as Lelani exited toward the terminal.

"You're telling me." Lelani sighed. "At least you can sleep during your flight. And just think! When you get there, it'll be warm."

"Hmm. That does sound wonderful."

"You've got everything you need, right?" asked Lelani as she pulled up in front of the terminal. "Ticket? ID?"

"Yes, yes." Kendall blew a kiss. "Thank you, Mother."

Lelani rolled her eyes. "Just be careful, Kendall. Be smart."

Kendall grinned. "Sure. I won't do anything you wouldn't do."

Lelani looked surprised at this, but she simply nodded. "Yeah, well, I hope it all turns out the way you want it to."

But Kendall could tell by Lelani's expression that she doubted anything would turn out. Just the same, Kendall thanked her. It wouldn't be long before Lelani and Amelia and all of them were surprised. She couldn't wait to see their faces when she came back with an engagement ring and a wedding date. Okay, the truth was, Kendall would probably settle for a diamond pendant, the promise of a future relationship, and the breaking news of the impending divorce of Matthew Harmon and Heidi Hardwick. That would be victory enough!

Even though it seemed to take forever to get through check-in and security, Kendall still arrived at her gate forty minutes before her flight would leave. She put those forty minutes to good use in the bathroom, fixing her hair and carefully applying the makeup that she'd been too rushed to put on at home.

"Looks like someone's got a big date," said a woman who washed her hands at the sink next to all of Kendall's cosmetics.

"Uh-huh," said Kendall as she coated her lashes with another layer of mascara. "Very big."

Finally, the plane boarded, and Kendall was able to relax and close her eyes. Okay, she would've been a lot more relaxed in first class, but that would come another day. For now, coach would have to do. At least there were no fussing babies or fidgeting toddlers in her row. That was the absolute worst. As soon as the plane took off and the flight attendant made her way down the aisle, Kendall ordered a Bloody Mary. "Just to calm my nerves," she told the woman as she handed Kendall the drink. "I don't normally drink in the morning." The flight attendant nodded and smiled like she'd heard that line a few times.

But the drink did the trick, and Kendall woke up to the announcement about seats and tray tables needing to be restored to their upright position. Kendall turned to peer out the window but couldn't see much. Still, her apprehension was growing. This was her big chance. She would pick up her rental car, then check into her hotel and freshen up. And by later this afternoon, she might actually run into Matthew. It could happen!

Kendall could feel people looking at her as she strutted through LAX. She knew that she was the kind of girl who turned heads. Sometimes she was even mistaken for a celebrity—or at least that's what she told herself. And maybe someday soon she would actually be a celebrity, or nearly, or even a face in the tabloids. That would work too.

It was a little past two when she finally checked into her hotel. And by three forty-five, she'd showered and changed and primped and fussed until she knew that she was looking as good as it was going to get. She had on the blue and white Nicole Miller sundress, her new white D&G bag, and a sexy little pair of Marc Jacobs sandals. Perfect.

By five o'clock she was approaching the neighborhood where Matthew Harmon lived. Well, Matthew and the little woman. It was an older development not far from Beverly Hills. It wasn't quite as impressive as she'd expected, but the ranch houses looked fairly large and sprawling, and most of the views up here appeared to be pretty nice. She even stopped a few blocks away from Matthew's street to take the top down on the light blue Mustang. It wasn't an expensive car, but it was cute and fun, and anyway it was just a rental. Besides, it went with her dress.

But after slowly cruising down Matthew's street a couple of times, she realized that she might be looking a bit conspicuous. She also realized that there might be a flaw in her plan. What if Matthew wasn't around? What if he was off shooting on location? But that wouldn't be likely. He had told her that he was filming on the lots. And the research she'd done on him confirmed this. Still, she couldn't just keep driving up and down Matthew's street. Someone might think she was a stalker and call the police.

She considered driving over to the movie lots, since she knew where he was supposedly shooting, but she knew they wouldn't let her on. Instead, she got out a map and figured out which was the most likely route for him to use between the lots and his house. And then she parked in what she hoped was an inconspicuous place, in front of a convenience store, and waited. She knew from her research that Matthew had two vehicles he regularly drove. One was a bright yellow Hummer, which would be easy to spot. The other, a black Porsche 911, might be a bit harder to detect. It seemed that dark sports cars were fairly common down here.

By the time the sun went down, Kendall still hadn't spotted her man. She began to fear that her perfect plan might be flawed. Still, she wasn't ready to give up. The night was still young, and she knew some of the clubs where Matthew sometimes hung out. She just wished she had a friend to go barhopping with her. Why hadn't she considered bringing Lelani along? But then she remembered how much attention Lelani had gotten at that wrap party last week. Chances were, Lelani would come down here, strut her stuff, and walk away with a movie contract or marriage proposal. And Kendall would be left in her dust. Well, that wasn't going to happen. Kendall was determined to come out on top this time. She would do whatever it took, and when she was done, she would have her man. She just knew it!

Seventeen

Megan

"Yes, yes! Those chairs are just what the room needed," Mrs. Fowler gushed to Megan. "I knew that you would find the right ones, dear."

Megan tried not to look too pleased, since Vera was with her today. She wasn't sure why Vera had insisted on coming, especially after experiencing the wrath of Mrs. Fowler on Tuesday, when Vera showed up with her catalogs and sketches but without Megan. Vera had made sure that Megan heard all about that little fiasco, acting as if it too was all Megan's fault.

"You're sure these chairs are right?" asked Vera with a creased brow.

"Perfect." Mrs. Fowler beamed at Megan. "And much better than waiting for some silly custom chairs. Goodness gracious, at my age, I don't have time to wait for a delivery from halfway around the world."

"Well, I'm glad they work for you," said Megan. "We were lucky to find them." Okay, the use of the word *we* was a stretch. Megan had found them completely on her own, and only after Vera threw another hissy fit, then tossed the project back in Megan's lap. Of course, Vera had been certain that Megan would fail. Megan felt fairly sure that Vera hoped she would fail. But somehow this pair of plum-colored club chairs hit the target. And Megan thought they actually looked pretty nice. "They sort of cozy it up in here," she said as Mrs. Fowler sat down.

"And they are comfortable."

Megan scooted the plaid ottoman over for her. She had chosen it on a whim, since it had both the green and plum shades. "And you're sure you want to keep this, too?" she asked. "I can easily return it."

Mrs. Fowler put her feet up and smiled. "The ottoman stays. And so does Megan. Let's have some tea, dear."

Vera cleared her throat now but didn't say anything.

"I'd love to stay, Mrs. Fowler." Megan glanced at Vera. Her arms were folded across her chest and she was scowling. She had driven them over, and Megan was sure that she was ready to go. "But we have work to do. So we should probably take a rain check."

"Well, if you must." Mrs. Fowler nodded sadly.

"Maybe I could visit you on the weekend," offered Megan.

The old woman brightened. "Would you?"

"Sure. How about Saturday morning. Around ten?"

"I will look forward to it."

"Have a nice day," called Megan. "And enjoy your parlor."

"Have a nice day," mocked Vera as they walked to the car. "Good grief, I think I should start calling you Pollyanna!"

"What's wrong with being polite?"

"Polite? You're a brownnosing schmoozer, Megan."

"Thanks a lot," said Megan as she got into Vera's car.

"That might be okay for some lines of work, but when it comes to design, you need to take control." Vera sighed loudly. "Although I doubt that you'll ever have what it takes to be a good designer."

"And why is that?" Megan was accustomed to Vera's sharp jabs and insults, and usually she tried not to engage, but today Vera seemed thornier than usual, and Megan was fed up.

Vera laughed. "Because you are a wimp, Megan. You'd let the client push you around until the design ended up looking like a bad day at the flea market."

"I happen to like flea markets."

"Exactly my point."

Rude or not, Megan decided to interrupt with a call to her mom, just to make sure they were still on for lunch. If nothing else, it would end this frustrating conversation.

"I wanted to make sure you're still meeting me," she said after her mom answered.

"I'm just heading out to the car. I'll be there at high noon."

"Cool." Then, to prolong the conversation, Megan told her a little about Mrs. Fowler and her parlor. "It was fun to see her really pleased with how it turned out," she continued. "She lost her husband last year and it's been hard for her to face the holidays."

"Well, I suppose we know a thing or two about that, don't we?"

"I even invited her to the Christmas Eve party," continued Megan. "I thought it would be nice for her to meet you."

"Well, uh, let's talk about that at lunch, okay? I'm just pulling out of the driveway now, and you know how I can't drive and talk on the phone simultaneously."

"See you in half an hour." Megan closed her phone.

"You invited Mrs. Fowler to spend Christmas with you?" Vera's voice was a mixture of amusement and disbelief.

"Just for one evening."

"You *are* a brownnoser."

"I wish you'd quit saying that."

"Why?" Vera laughed. "Does the truth hurt?"

"For one thing, it's not the truth. I don't treat Mrs. Fowler any differently than I'd treat anyone. Well, anyone who's even slightly civil."

"Meaning me, I'm sure."

"You can be a little prickly, Vera."

"I simply like to keep the upper hand. Perhaps someday when you're older and more experienced, you will understand."

"Perhaps." Megan turned to look out the side window, then rolled her eyes. More than anything, Megan hoped she would never turn out like Vera. Cynthia told her that Vera had been in and out of several marriages, like that was supposed to explain everything. If anything, Megan suspected that Vera had driven her husbands nuts—what could be worse than being married to a temperament like Vera's?

"Everything all worked out for Mrs. Fowler?" asked Cynthia as the two of them entered the design firm building.

"Why don't you ask Little Miss Brownnose," said Vera as she swaggered off to her office.

Cynthia gave Megan a sympathetic smile.

"Mrs. Fowler was very pleased with the new chairs," Megan informed her. "She even liked the ottoman."

Cynthia patted Megan on the back. "Good girl."

"But I don't think Vera is too happy."

"And that surprises you?"

"No, I suppose not." Megan wanted to ask Cynthia if anything ever pleased Vera. But then Megan thought she knew the answer to that. As far as she could tell, only two things seemed to make Vera happy: money and adoration. Neither of which Megan felt she could spare.

⋈

To Megan's relief, her mom was already waiting for her at Demetri's Deli when she arrived. "So, you didn't stand me up again," said Megan as they exchanged hugs.

"I felt so bad about that."

"It's okay." As they stood in line, Megan told her about running into Gwen. "She actually gave me some good advice."

Mom looked doubtful. She knew Megan's sentiments toward her old friend.

"She told me to be honest with Vera about wanting to help Mrs. Fowler."

"And Vera was okay with that?"

"Actually, she was so frustrated with Mrs. Fowler by then that she was relieved to have me call, although, being Vera, she didn't show it. Even today, when everything was all smoothed out, Vera acted ticked and called me Little Miss Brownnoser."

Mom frowned. "That woman. I don't know how Cynthia puts up with her."

"Because she has rich friends?"

Mom laughed. "You're probably right."

They placed their orders and found an empty table. "So what did you want to tell me about the Christmas party?" asked Megan as she hung her coat on the back of her chair.

"Oh, that …"

Megan could tell by the way her mom said, "Oh, that," that she wasn't about to hear good news. "What's up?"

"Well, Louise is feeling lonely again. She's been trying to talk me into going down to Mexico for Christmas this year."

"Mexico? For Christmas?" Megan frowned. "Seriously?"

"She has a timeshare down there that she has to use before the New Year. And, well, we had such fun on the cruise, we really did manage to cheer each other up. I thought it might be nice."

"But it's Christmas, Mom." Megan felt a lump growing in her throat. How could her mother—her only living parent—suddenly decide to abandon her during their first Christmas without Dad?

"I know, I know." Mom nodded. "That's exactly what I told Louise. I said that you and I need to be together for Christmas, and that I couldn't even consider going to Mexico. I shouldn't have even told you about it, Megan."

But she had, and somehow Megan knew that meant something. It meant that Mom actually wanted to go to Mexico for Christmas!

"I'll call Louise as soon as we're done here and tell her it's impossible and that she should find someone—"

"No, Mom," said Megan. "Don't do that. Maybe it's a good idea. I mean, you did have a great time with her on the cruise. And you probably are good medicine for her. It's cool that you're getting reacquainted. I think you should go with her."

"Really?" Mom looked surprised but pleased. "You'd really be okay with that?"

"I'm a grown-up, Mom. Besides, we're doing our Christmas party, and that'll keep me pretty busy."

"You really won't feel bad?"

Megan firmly shook her head. "No. I'm fine, Mom. And I even promised Gwen that I'd help serve Christmas dinner at the mission on Christmas Day." Megan didn't mention that she'd hoped her mom would join them. "And I think that Marcus might come and help out too."

"That sounds great, Megan." Mom reached across the table and squeezed Megan's hand. "I don't deserve such a sweet daughter."

Megan shrugged.

"You should hear Louise talking about her kids. Oh, my. That woman has been through the wringer. I don't know how I got so lucky, but I give the credit and thanks to God." Mom smiled. "Oh, I can't wait to tell Louise the good news. She is even going to let me use her frequent-flyer miles for my ticket. Really, it'll be a very economical trip."

Megan forced what she hoped looked like an enthusiastic smile. "I'm sure you guys will have a great time."

"Yes." Mom sighed. "I hate to admit it, but I wasn't looking forward to being home … you know, in the house … without you and Dad … during the holidays."

Megan considered this. It probably would be hard being alone in the house. In fact, she suddenly wondered how her mom had managed to deal with it these past few months. It hadn't even occurred to Megan that her mom might be extra lonely, by herself day in and day out.

"So how are things with you and Marcus?" asked Mom when their order came.

Megan frowned. "I guess I'm still feeling a little unsure. I mean it's cool he's willing to help at the mission. But when I talked to him about coming to the singles group at the church, he said he wants us to go listen to his friend play jazz at a bar instead. And I'm not really sure how I feel about that."

"Can't he do the singles group another time?"

"I guess. I'm just not sure we're on the same page, Mom. I mean I have a feeling I could get him to do some church things with me, but I don't really like the idea of dragging him there, you know?"

Mom laughed. "Well, dragging him might be a bit extreme. But sometimes people need encouragement, Megan."

"Maybe. But I still wonder if it's a mistake."

Mom dipped her spoon into the Hungarian mushroom soup. "He seems like such a nice boy. I really like him."

"Yes." Megan nodded. "I like him too. But just because you like someone doesn't mean you need to be involved. Gwen was pointing out that dating a guy who doesn't go to church is asking for trouble."

"Since when did you start taking Gwen so seriously?"

Megan sort of laughed. "See what happens when you stand me up?"

Mom smiled. "Okay. I'm going to tell you a little story."

"A true story?"

"Yes. A story that your father didn't want me to tell you."

Megan grew concerned now. "Why?"

"Oh, I think he was afraid that I might corrupt you."

"Corrupt me?"

"Yes. You know how your father prayed for the man you'd one day marry? You know how he wanted you to hold out for that strong Christian man, do everything just right?"

"Yes. Of course."

"Well, that's not exactly how it was with your father and me."

"Really?"

"Yes. As you know, we met in college. And we dated off and on. I was involved in a college fellowship group, but your father, well, he was a bit of a wild guy."

"Dad was a wild guy?"

"Oh, not terribly wild. But he did smoke pot."

"Pot?"

"You know, marijuana."

"Weed? Dad smoked weed?"

Mom chuckled. "Yes. He and his buddies enjoyed a little weed now and then."

"Seriously?" Megan stared at her mother. "That does not sound like Dad."

"People change."

"I'll say."

"So, due to your dad's habits of smoking weed, as you say, and also his fondness for beer—"

"Dad was a beer drinker too?"

Mom nodded and laughed. "Yes, I'm sorry to destroy your perfect image of him, Megan, but I think it's for the best. Your father was a good, good man. But he did sow some wild oats in his early days."

"Wow."

"So, due to those habits, which I did not embrace, I finally broke it off with him. I told him we could be friends, but no more dating."

"And?"

"And we were just friends." Mom made a face. "Well, as much as possible. I suppose I blew it a few times. Your father was persuasive."

Megan held up her hands. "Okay, not too many details, please."

"During your dad's senior year, a friend of his died suddenly."

"Cliff?"

"Yes. You've heard him tell this part of the story."

"I know it was a real wake-up call to him spiritually."

"Yes. And he started going to church with me. And then he gave his life to God and, well, I suppose the rest is history."

Megan slowly shook her head, trying to take that all in. "So, Dad, my father, was actually a wild dude for a while."

"But he changed his ways."

"It's hard to imagine Dad smoking weed and drinking beer."

"I know. You see, my point is that Marcus may seem like a lost cause to you, but in reality I don't think he's nearly as lost as your dad was once upon a time."

"So, you're saying I should keep dating Marcus?"

Mom seemed to consider this. "I don't think I can tell you what to do, sweetie. I'm just saying that things aren't always black and white. I'm saying that just because the Gwens of the world want to draw a dividing line between Christians and non-Christians, well, I don't think that's how God looks at it."

"How do you think he looks at it?"

"I think he sees us all as his children. But some of us have figured it out and some of us haven't."

"Oh."

They talked a while longer, and Mom shared some crazy stories about stunts that Dad pulled, which still seemed strangely out of character, and then it was time for Megan to go back to work.

"So, you're really okay with me being gone for Christmas?"

Megan nodded, then they hugged, and she hurried on her way. The truth was that she wasn't that okay with it. But she hoped to get used to the idea. A part of her knew that it would be good for her mother to get away. But another part of Megan wanted to be selfish. She wanted to stomp her foot and insist that her mother remain at home and make cookies and cook a turkey and decorate a tree and do everything to make Megan feel at home. But as Megan walked up the steps to the design firm, she realized that would be like something Vera would do. Megan didn't want to end up like that!

Anna

"Three girls without dates on a Friday night." Anna reached for the remote as they all flopped down on the sectional with a big bowl of popcorn.

"It figures that Kendall would be the only one out tonight," said Megan.

"Actually, she's more than just out," said Lelani.

"What do you mean she's more than just out?" asked Megan as Anna flipped through the movie channels.

"That one looks good," said Lelani as Anna landed on *Sleepless in Seattle*.

"Yeah, I haven't seen that flick in years," agreed Megan.

"But what about Kendall?" asked Anna. "What's she up to, anyway?"

"She's in LA."

"LA—as in Los Angeles?" Anna muted the sound of the commercial and turned to stare at Lelani.

Lelani nodded. "Yep. She flew down there this morning."

"Why?" asked Megan. "Furthermore, *how*? She's broke."

So Lelani explained about Kendall's early Christmas present and how she was certain that Matthew Harmon was going to leave his wife for her.

"And you didn't try to talk her out of it?" asked Megan.

"I tried." Lelani sighed. "But it was useless."

"That girl is totally, unequivocally nuts." Megan reached for a handful of popcorn and just shook her head. "Someday they'll probably lock her up."

"I don't know," said Anna. "At least she's out having fun."

They both turned to stare at Anna now.

"Well, I'm just saying. Here we are in our jammies on a Friday night, watching an old movie and junking out. Kind of pathetic, don't you think?"

"Why aren't you out, Miss 'I Have Two Boyfriends'?" asked Megan.

"Actually I only have one now."

"Who did you dump?" asked Megan.

Anna swallowed hard. "Edmond," she said quietly.

"Edmond?" both Lelani and Megan said at once.

Anna nodded.

"But he's such a sweetie," said Megan.

"You must've broken his heart," added Lelani.

"Oh, I don't know."

"You don't know?" pestered Megan. "Don't you see him at work every day? How could you not know?"

"Actually, I think he's avoiding me."

"Poor Edmond." Lelani shook her head.

"Enough about my problems," said Anna. "What about you guys? Why are you dateless on a Friday night?"

"Gil and I are going to Mount Hood early in the morning," said Lelani. "I told him I wanted to get to bed early."

"What about you?" Anna asked Megan. "What's your excuse?"

"Marcus is at Zeke's listening to jazz," Megan said quietly.

"He didn't invite you?" asked Anna.

"Actually, he did." Megan glanced away like she was uncomfortable.

"Why didn't you go?" persisted Anna.

"I just didn't want to." Megan looked back at Anna. "You still haven't told us why you aren't out with Jake."

"That's right," said Lelani.

Anna shrugged. Why were they suddenly so interested in her love life?

"You guys are back together, right?" asked Megan.

"Yes, of course," said Anna. The truth was she had expected Jake to ask her out tonight. She wasn't even sure why he hadn't.

"I mean, how sad would it be if you broke up with a really sweet guy like Edmond and then Jake and you, well, you know ..." Lelani gave her a sympathetic look.

"Jake's called me every day this week," Anna said quickly. Okay, every day except for today, but she wasn't admitting that. She wasn't sure why he hadn't called today. Maybe he had a perfectly good reason. But she was not about to call him and demand to know why.

Halfway into the movie, Anna told them she was sleepy and headed up to her room. Actually, she wanted to check her phone in private. And although her mom had called, without leaving a message, Jake had not. Anna was tempted to call him, just to make sure everything was okay. But it went so against the grain. Her parents had drilled into her that a girl *never* calls a guy. A guy does the pursuing, the girl simply waits. And although she'd rebelled against many of her family's traditions, she'd held onto this one. Perhaps that would change tomorrow.

Why hadn't he called?

Something else was troubling her as she got ready for bed. Why had Edmond been so evasive this week? She had convinced herself that he was okay with the breakup. After all, it wasn't as if their relationship had been terribly serious. They hadn't even dated for long. And Edmond was so easygoing. Why was he taking this so hard? Or was he? Maybe his being upset was all in her imagination. Or maybe she secretly hoped that he was missing her. But why? Finally she picked up a thick manuscript that her boss, Edmond's uncle Rick Erlinger, had asked her to read, which was enough to put her to sleep in spite of all these nagging questions. Didn't he know she was a children's editor? Of course, he assumed that because this book was about parenting young children, she was the one to handle it. Like she knew anything about that!

The next morning she awoke to the sound of her cell phone ringing. Certain it had to be Jake, she eagerly answered.

"Anna," said her mother.

"Oh, hi, Mom." Anna couldn't help but be disappointed, and she knew it probably showed in her voice.

"Am I bothering you, *mija*?"

"Well, it's a little early. What's up?"

"I wanted to talk to you."

"Uh-huh?" Anna sat up and stretched her legs.

"I have some ... some news."

"News?"

"Yes. Not very good news, I'm afraid."

"What's wrong? Is it Dad?"

"No."

"Is it Gil? What's wrong?"

"No, it's not Gil and not Dad."

"What, Mom? Now you got me really curious."

"It's me, Anna."

Anna frowned. What was her mother up to now?

"I went to the doctor this week, Anna."

"Yes?" A cold wave of fear rushed through Anna.

"The results of my, uh, my mammogram came back."

"And?"

"And I seem to have breast cancer."

"Oh, Mama!"

Her mother was crying now. "I—I don't want you to be too worried, *mi'ja*, but I felt you should know."

"Oh, Mama," said Anna again. "I'm so sorry."

"The doctor says treatments are better than ever nowadays."

"Yes," said Anna. But all she could think is that her maternal grandmother had died of breast cancer back when Anna was five. History was repeating itself.

"I haven't told Gil yet."

"Why?"

"I was going to this morning, but he's gone."

"He took Lelani to Mount Hood."

"Oh."

"Do you want me to call him for you, Mama?"

"Would you, Anna?"

"Of course."

"I wanted you kids to come to the house for dinner tomorrow night."

"You're not working at the restaurant?"

"No. Your father said we need to take some time off."

"Yes, good for him."

"Can you come, *mi'ja*?"

"Of course."

"And bring your boyfriend, Anna. And tell Gil to bring Lelani."

"Really?"

"Yes. I want to see you all together. Like a big, happy family." Now her mother was crying even harder. "But tell Gil not to tell Lelani. I don't want her to feel sad or to treat me differently. Do you know what I mean?"

"Yes, I'll tell him to keep it to himself."

"Thank you."

"Are you sure you want others there, Mama? Not just Gil and me and you and Dad?"

"I need people around me. I need to feel the love of my family and their loved ones too. To hope for the future, Anna, do you understand? And we—we won't speak of this tomorrow night. *Comprende?*"

"Yes."

"Please, tell Gil not to worry. Everything will be okay."

"I will, Mama."

"Thank you."

"I love you, Mama."

"I love you too, *mi'ja.*"

Anna called Gil as soon as she hung up. But he must've been out of range, and so she left a message. "Call me as soon as you get this," she told him. Then she went downstairs, hoping that someone was there to talk to. But she remembered that Lelani was with Gil. Kendall was still in LA. And it seemed that even Megan was gone. Anna paced in the kitchen as she waited for the coffee to brew. Finally, feeling desperate, she called Jake.

"Hey, Anna," he said in a tone that sounded like he'd just woke up.

Before she could stop herself, she spilled the whole story.

"Oh, I'm sorry, Anna," he said. "That's got to be hard."

"My mother wants us to come to dinner tomorrow night." Jake didn't say anything, and Anna wondered if she needed to be more clear.

"She asked for Gil to bring Lelani and I'm supposed to bring you. She thinks that having family around is going to make her feel better."

"But I'm not exactly family, Anna."

"I know. But I think it's her way of accepting things." Anna considered this now. Her mother had been acting differently lately. Maybe this was why. "But if you don't want to come—"

"No, no, I want to come."

"Good."

"How are you doing with all this?" he asked.

Hearing the kindness in his voice made her lose it now. She started crying and could hardly speak. "I just feel so sad," she blurted. "And everyone is gone."

"Do you want me to come over?"

"Yes!" she said eagerly. "I don't want to be alone."

"Give me enough time to catch a shower, and I'll be there in about an hour, okay?"

"Thanks, Jake." Then Anna hung up and went to take a shower too. Her tears ran freely in the water, and she even prayed out loud. "I know it's been a long time since I've spoken to you, God," she began, "but I need you to send a miracle." Then, with sincerity and all the faith she could muster, Anna asked God to make her mother well. Because as much as Anna complained about her mother and her demanding ways, Anna still needed her. And she wasn't ready to lose her.

Anna spent the rest of the day with Jake. They walked to town and ordered a huge bouquet of flowers and had them delivered to her mother. They had a light lunch and finally went back home to watch a football game. But as Jake was absorbed with the game, all Anna could think about was her mother. Anna had called her about an hour ago, but her call went straight to the answering machine. Anna hoped that meant her parents were having a nap.

"Thanks for hanging with me today," Anna told Jake when he finally got up to go home. "I really appreciate it."

"No problem." He leaned down to kiss her.

"I'll let you know what time dinner is tomorrow."

He nodded, then patted her on the head and left. As she watched him drive away, she realized that her mother had said to bring her boyfriend, but she hadn't said which one. She wondered if her mother would be disappointed to see that Anna asked Jake and not Edmond. Or maybe she didn't care.

Nineteen

Lelani

"This is totally amazing," said Lelani as they stood at the foot of the mountain watching the chairlifts slowly moving up. "It's so white!"

Gil laughed. "Yeah, that's one way of putting it."

Lelani watched as a couple of snowboarders whooshed down. "You know, that doesn't look much different from surfing."

"Want to give it a try?"

Lelani giggled. "Do you think I'll hurt anyone?"

"Are you a good surfer?"

She gave him a sly glance. "Not bad." In truth, she was pretty good, but she wasn't tipping that hand. Just in case.

"I've ridden a few times."

"Ridden?" Lelani was confused now.

"Snowboarding—they call it riding."

"Oh, yeah." She nodded. "So, are you game?"

"Why not?"

It took about an hour to rent snowboards and, just to be safe, they signed up for a beginner lesson on the bunny hill. But by their second run, the instructor was impressed. "You said you haven't done this before?" he said to Lelani.

She shrugged. "I've done some surfing."

"She's obviously been holding out on us," Gil joked to the instructor.

"She probably competed in last year's Winter Olympics."

Consequently, it was Lelani who wound up coaching Gil. "Just relax," she said. "Bend your knees. Use your arms for balance."

Around noon, they finally went up the chair to the beginner slope. "You going to be okay?" she asked as they got off the lift.

He grinned. "Here goes nothing." Then he took off and after about fifty feet crashed.

"Are you okay?" she asked as she stopped, then sat down beside him.

"I think so."

"Is that your phone?" she asked, hearing one ring.

He reached inside his parka and removed his phone, then flipped it open. "Yeah?"

Lelani tried not to eavesdrop, but she could tell it was Anna.

"Are you sure?" he finally said. He frowned and shook his head as if something was wrong. "Yeah. I understand." He nodded now. "I guess so. Sure, we can talk later. Are you okay?" He listened with a troubled expression. "Yeah. It's tough. I know." He tossed Lelani a hard-to-read look. "Sure, I'll ask her. Tomorrow night?" He waited. "Okay. You take care, Anna. I'll call you later." Then he closed his phone.

"Is something wrong?"

His brow was creased, but he forced a smile. "Oh, you know Anna. She can get a little worked up sometimes."

Lelani nodded as if she understood, although she felt slightly lost. "I do know she broke up with Edmond this week. Do you think she's sorry about it now?"

"She should be," said Gil as he slowly got back to his feet, balancing himself on the board. "Edmond is a good guy."

"I know. I hope getting back with Jake isn't a mistake."

"My guess is that it is a mistake. But you can't tell Anna that."

"So, are you ready to ride?" asked Lelani.

"I guess."

Gil seemed to be doing better, but when they were nearly to the bottom of the slope he took a hard tumble. By the time Lelani joined him, he was sitting up, but rubbing his left arm.

"Are you okay?" she asked.

He frowned. "I'm not sure."

"Does it hurt?"

"Yeah."

"Do you think it's broken?" She was unbuckling his boots from the snowboard. Clearly, he couldn't ride with an injured arm.

"You're the doctor."

"Yeah, right." She glanced over her shoulder. "Want me to flag down some help? They have rescue guys—"

"No," said Gil quickly. "Just help me up." He extended his right hand.

"Easy does it," she said as she helped him to his feet. "Let's go to the lodge and see what the problem is."

With the assistance of a couple of riders who offered to carry their boards, Lelani finally got Gil settled into a chair by the fireplace and helped him to remove his parka, then took a good look at his arm.

"What's the prognosis, doc?" he asked with a charming smile.

"It doesn't feel broken," she said as she ran her fingers up and down his forearm. "This is the radius," she explained. "And this is the ulna."

"Ooo, I love it when you play doctor."

She laughed. "My guess is that you've injured some ligaments. Hopefully not too seriously."

"So what do I do about it?"

"For starters, you're done riding for the day." She unzipped one of her many pockets on the parka Kendall had given her, then retrieved a small bottle of Advil and handed it to him. "And you should take a couple of these. Then we should get some ice on your arm, and a wrap might help. And you need to keep it elevated."

"You really do know medicine, don't you?"

"That's like beginner's first aid."

"Oh."

"You stay here and I'll go see what I can find."

After asking around, Lelani was directed to the first-aid center, where she was able to purchase an ice pack and an Ace bandage. She also picked up a couple of cocoas, then returned to Gil. Before long she had his wrist wrapped and the ice pack applied.

"Should I go get the boards?" she offered.

"Why?"

"To turn them in at the rental place."

"You mean you're done riding?"

"Well, yeah."

Gil frowned. "You were doing so great, Lelani. Why don't you go and ride a few more times? I'm fine now that the doctor has taken care of me."

"Oh, I couldn't—"

"Yes, you can. And you'll add insult to injury if you don't."

"Why?"

"Because I'll be blaming myself for ruining your day."

"You didn't ruin—"

"Seriously, Lelani. It'd make me happy to see you enjoy this." He waved his wrapped arm toward the big window.

This was very tempting. She had been enjoying herself, and she hated for it all to end. "Are you positive?"

"Absolutely."

"And you'll be okay?"

He grinned. "Hey, I can still walk. And if I need to, I can always go get this cocoa spiked with something to help relieve the pain."

She laughed. "Okay. I'll do a couple more runs and then we might want some lunch anyway."

"Sounds great."

Lelani felt a little guilty as she made her first run. But by the second run, she was totally enjoying the adventure. This was the first time since coming to the mainland that she had actually felt like she was having fun. Riding reminded her of surfing, but in some ways it was almost better. You never got to have such long rides on a wave. Although it was colder. Definitely colder. And she didn't mind returning to the lodge to check on Gil.

"How's it going?" she asked.

He set down the *Popular Mechanics* magazine that he'd been reading and smiled. "Not bad, all things considered. I've had a couple of chicks stop by and offer me their sympathy."

"What a surprise. Cute guy, incapacitated. You're like a real chick magnet."

"But I told them my girlfriend was a doctor and that seemed to scare them off."

She laughed. Then they went to have some lunch. And after they were seated, she told him just how wonderful the day was. "Well, other than your injured wrist." She frowned. "I feel terrible about that."

"And I feel terrible that I've abandoned you." He popped a fry into his mouth. "But I'm glad you're having a good time."

"And we can go whenever you like."

"I think you need to get in some more rides."

"It's so magical up there." She looked out the window to where the slope met the blue sky with pine trees all around. "It's like I feel connected to the earth again. I know that probably sounds weird. But it's a feeling I get when I surf—like I belong. And it makes me think of God, too."

"Of God?" Gil cocked his head slightly. "How so?"

She wasn't sure how to explain it. "Kind of like I'm thankful that God created such a spectacular planet."

"I didn't know you were into God."

"Well, Megan was telling me that I needed to trust God. I was sort of having one of those panic attacks. Like I just couldn't go through another day. The stuff with my parents ... with Emma ... like I was never going to figure it all out."

"And God helps with that?"

She nodded. "I don't even totally understand it myself. But there is something to it. I know there is. Because when I think about God, and when I sort of give my troubles to him, well, I begin to feel better. Like someone—I mean God—has lifted this heavy thing from my shoulders. I know it probably sounds strange. But it's real. It's tangible. And when I was riding up the lift and then down the slope, it's like I felt that reality even more. Do you think that's weird?"

He shook his head. "No. Not at all. I mean, I've never been too into church or God. We were raised Catholic. Well, until we refused to go to Mass and confession. Both Anna and I are a great disappointment in that regard to our mom, although our dad doesn't participate either. But my mom takes her religion very seriously." Gil frowned now.

"And that's not good?"

"No, I'm not saying that. I think it's very good for her. She needs something like that to hold onto. I'm just not sure about myself."

"So, you don't believe in God?"

"I'm not saying that, either."

"Oh."

"I guess I'm saying that I haven't given it much thought. I suppose I do believe in God. But that's about it."

"Okay."

"But I think it's great if the whole God thing is helping you, Lelani. And I don't mean that as a putdown. I'm just being honest. I don't totally get it."

"But you're open?"

He nodded. "Sure. Why wouldn't I be?"

Lelani smiled. She wasn't even sure why it mattered, but for some reason it did. And she was relieved to know that Gil didn't think she was foolish for getting interested in God. She knew that wasn't the case with some of her old med school friends. The science world that she'd been exposed to seemed fairly antagonistic toward God. Certainly Ben had been so. She cringed to remember how he insisted she have an abortion, or how irritated he'd been when she refused. He'd even accused her of being a religious fanatic who was disguising herself as something else. Of course, that was ridiculous. But it hurt just the same.

As Lelani rode down the slope for the last time of the day, she paused midway down to look up at the sky. She took in a long, deep breath and felt strangely strong. But perhaps most surprising was that she felt truly hopeful. She couldn't even remember the last time she'd felt hopeful. And she suspected it had to do with God.

"Thank you," she whispered up to the sky. "Thank you!"

Because of Gil's wrist, Lelani drove them home. And she wasn't sure if he was just worn down from his injury or if she'd somehow offended him, but Gil was strangely quiet. Perhaps she shouldn't have continued to ride through the afternoon. Or maybe his arm was actually hurt worse than she'd suggested. Maybe she should've checked it before they left.

"How's your wrist?" she asked as she entered the freeway.

"It's aching, but not too bad."

"Sorry."

"It's not your fault."

"Well, it sort of is," she pointed out. "I was the one who wanted to go up there, and I was the one who wanted to try snowboarding."

"I was totally on board," he said. "You didn't force me into it."

"Anyway, I can still feel sorry, can't I?"

"Sorry, but not responsible. You know that you do that, don't you?"

"What?"

"Blame yourself for a lot of things that aren't your fault."

"Oh."

"It's because you've got a kind heart, Lelani. But sometimes you're way too hard on yourself."

"Yes. I'm trying to figure that all out," she admitted.

Then Gil got quiet again and Lelani decided that maybe he was just tired. She knew enough about medicine to know that an injury could wear a person out. Finally, they pulled back into town. "Hey, should I drop you at your house or what?"

He straightened in his seat. "Oh, I can probably make it okay from your house. Why don't you just head home?"

"You're sure?"

"Yeah. My wrist is actually feeling a little better. I think that last dose of Advil kicked in."

"Well, remember to keep it iced and elevated," she said. "And make sure that bandage isn't too tight. You don't want to cut off your circulation."

"Yes, Doctor." He chuckled.

"Sorry."

"Don't be."

She pulled up in front of the house on Bloomberg Place. "You're sure you can drive?"

"No problem. It's only a few miles."

They both got out of the car, and Lelani gathered up her stuff. "Thanks for everything, Gil. It was really a fantastic day. Well, except for your wrist."

"Oh, I almost forgot," he said before she headed up the walk. "My mom has invited us for dinner tomorrow night. Anna and Jake are coming too. Can you make it?"

Lelani considered this. A part of her was excited to go, happy to become a bigger part of Gil's life. But another part was cautious. Or maybe just nervous.

"It's not like you're making a life commitment," he said as if reading her thoughts. "My mom just wanted to have family around and she asked Anna and me to bring a friend."

"Bring a friend?" She frowned.

He gave her a goofy grin. "You're more than a friend, Lelani. At least from my point of view. But I don't want to push you."

She smiled now. "I'd love to come."

"I'll call you with the details later, okay?"

Then he leaned over the stuff she had in her arms and, totally out of character, gave her a quick peck. She blinked but tried not to look too surprised. After all, hadn't she known this was coming? Still, it caught her off guard. She thanked him again and, eager to get away, she dashed up to the house.

Kendall

"Are you lost?" A pretty brunette paused on the corner with her dog by her side. It was one of those little dogs, not a Chihuahua, but a small, fluffy white one. One of those yippy breeds, and it was wearing a blue collar with rhinestones that sparkled in the sun. It was Saturday morning, and Kendall had driven down Matthew's street several times, hoping to spot him, although that hadn't been the case. And now, just her luck, Kendall thought she'd been spotted by his wife.

"I noticed you've driven down the street a couple of times," said the woman, who had to be Heidi or her twin. "Are you looking for something?"

Kendall considered stepping on the gas, but knew that would only draw more attention. "I, uh, I was just looking for a house."

"What house?"

"A house to buy, you know," lied Kendall. "I thought there was one for sale on this street."

"Oh?" The woman's brow creased. "You know, there was a house for sale, that gold stucco down there, but it sold a couple weeks ago."

Kendall nodded. "Yeah, that sounds like it."

"I don't know of any other homes for sale." The little dog was lunging on his leash now, barking and acting as if he wanted to jump onto the rental car.

"Cute dog," said Kendall. Another lie.

"His name is Finley. He thinks he's really a Doberman trapped in the body of a Westie."

Kendall couldn't help but laugh.

"Sorry about the house being sold. Do you have a realtor?"

"No." Kendall shook her head. "A friend had told me about the house. I don't live down here, but I'm relocating for a job."

"One of my best friends is a realtor."

"Oh, that's okay." Now Kendall was getting worried. What if Matthew popped out of the house and saw her talking to his wife?

"No, it's fine. If you have a minute, I can write down her number for you." She pointed to the house—the same house Kendall had been driving past since yesterday. "I live over there. You can pull into the drive."

So, not wanting to make more of a scene, Kendall slowly drove around and pulled into the circular driveway, stopping short of the security gate.

"I'll be right back," called the woman.

Kendall's heart was racing now. Should she just make a fast break and get out of there? Or wait and see what happened? Part of her was curious and, she had to admit, starstruck. As much as she had pooh-poohed Heidi Hardwick and her fledgling career, which maybe was or wasn't rising, she could see this woman had something. Still, maybe that proved that her marriage was in trouble. How could two celebrities survive that kind of pressure?

"Here it is." Heidi jogged back out and handed a slip of paper to Kendall.

"Are you"—Kendall frowned as if trying to think of something—"Are you an actress on that new Fox series?"

Heidi nodded and pushed a shiny lock of hair out of her eyes. "Yeah. That's me."

Kendall feigned surprise, then smiled. "Well, that's cool."

"Yeah. Anyway, give Kellie a call, and I'm sure she can help you find something. Maybe even in this neighborhood. Sometimes houses are listed without for-sale signs."

"Thanks!" Then Kendall waved and pulled out of the driveway. She felt silly, but she also felt hopeful. Maybe this would be the key to connecting with Matthew. She drove a few blocks away and dialed the number.

"Hey, this is Kellie," said a cheerful voice.

"Your friend Heidi Hardwick gave me your number," Kendall began. "I'm house hunting and she thought you could help me."

"I'm sure I can."

So they arranged to meet at a Starbucks about a mile away. Over coffee, Kendall manufactured a story about coming down for an executive job in the film industry.

"Which studio?" asked Kellie eagerly.

Kendall put a finger over her lips. "It's kind of top secret right now."

"Oh." Kellie nodded. "I get you."

Kendall let Kellie show her several houses. The whole time they chatted away, and Kendall knew she was making Kellie think she was somebody—somebody she wasn't, but somebody that she might be someday.

"So, you're probably coming to the birthday party tonight," said Kellie as they were walking around a sprawling ranch house.

"Oh, yeah." Kendall smacked her forehead. "I almost forgot. Now where is it again?"

"You're obviously not a local," said Kellie. "No one around here would forget Spago."

"Oh, yeah. Of course." Kendall wanted to ask what time, but knew that could be pushing it. Besides, it was tonight. How difficult could that be? Kendall glanced at her shiny Cartier watch. "Oh, wow, I didn't know it was so late. I have to meet up with some, uh, associates, you know. I'm going to have to take off if I'm going to make it on time."

"Sure, no problem. Did any of these houses interest you?"

"I totally loved the second one," said Kendall as Kellie locked the front door. "That pool area was awesome."

"Great, I'll e-mail you some more details on it, and you can get back to me at your convenience. Although I'll warn you, houses in that particular neighborhood don't remain on the market for long."

"I'll keep that in mind."

"Great to meet you, Kendall," said Kellie. "See you tonight!"

Kendall smiled and waved and got back into the rental car. Her plan was to head to her hotel, get a little sun, take a little nap, and then make sure she had the perfect party outfit. The hotel boutique seemed to have possibilities. After that, she'd spend her remaining time primping for the party.

Okay, she was a little curious about whose birthday she was crashing but felt fairly certain that Matthew and Heidi would be there. Maybe it was Matthew's birthday. What a surprise she would give him.

Her conscience was bothering her a little. It hadn't helped matters to meet Heidi, or to find out that she seemed fairly nice, although looks could be deceiving. Just because Heidi was friendly to a perfect stranger didn't mean she was a good wife to her husband. Plenty of wives were witches behind closed doors. She had a feeling that was Heidi's little secret—and the reason their marriage was in trouble. At least that's what she told herself as she changed into her bikini. Then she admired her reflection. That spray-on tan was still looking good. It was a shame that Matthew wasn't around to see her looking this good.

Kendall was careful not to get too much sun. No way did she want to show up at the party looking like a lobster. On her way back to her room, she decided to stop at the boutique, just in case they had something really special—something that would jolt Matthew back into her reality.

"I'm going to a party tonight," Kendall told the saleswoman. "It's sort of unexpected and I'm not sure I have the right outfit."

The woman looked Kendall up and down, then nodded. "I have the most delectable little Vera Wang."

Kendall considered this as well as her credit-card limit. She certainly didn't want history to repeat itself with her being thrown out of this hotel. "Well, I am on something of a budget."

"You're in luck, then. I marked the dress half-off this morning. It's really more of a summer color, but I think it would be perfect on you. Honestly, the color is almost the same as your gorgeous blue eyes. Do you want to see it?"

Kendall smiled. "Sure."

The woman went to find it, and Kendall tried not to get her hopes up. In all likelihood the dress would be too expensive. But it wouldn't hurt to look.

"Here it is," said the clerk. She held out a scrumptious little beaded dress in sparkling robin's-egg blue. Kendall wasn't too sure about it matching her eyes, but the color was amazing.

"Wow, that's really pretty."

"Let's go try it." The woman led the way to the dressing room, then handed Kendall the dress. "And don't even look at the price, let the dress speak for itself."

So Kendall did as she was told, and when she saw the dress hugging her body, the spaghetti straps showing off her golden tan, well, it was a no-brainer. "So, how much is it?" she asked as she stepped out of the cubicle.

"Oh, my!" the clerk clapped her hand over her mouth. "You look fabulous." She turned her head and called out. "Marilee! Come here and look at this."

Another woman came and scrutinized Kendall, then smiled and nodded. "That dress was made for you."

"Really?" Kendall turned in front of the mirror to get a better look.

"Are you an actress?" asked the woman named Marilee.

Kendall feigned embarrassment. "No, not really."

"Well, if you're spotted in that, you may want to rethink your career choice."

Kendall giggled. "Okay, you guys, just break it to me gently. How much is this little number?"

"Like I said, I just marked it down this morning," said the clerk. "Originally it was $680."

Kendall attempted the math. "So, that's like three hundred and change?"

"Three forty," supplied Marilee. "And a steal."

"Especially for you," said the other one. "Because, believe me, you look like a million bucks."

Marilee nodded. "This is the kind of dress that could change your life."

Kendall was hooked now. "Okay."

"What about shoes?"

"I have some gold sandals—"

"Not gold," said Marilee. "This dress screams for silver. Do you have silver?"

Kendall shook her head.

"Well, we do. We have just the shoes."

By the time Kendall left the boutique, she had managed to max out two credit cards, but she knew that the purchases were worth it. Marilee was right. This was the kind of outfit that could change her life. Also, she had come up with a revision to her original plan. Really, she couldn't believe she hadn't thought of it sooner. Instead of appearing to crash someone's party, she would simply be at Spago on a dinner date. Surely this party wouldn't be using the whole restaurant. And when she ran into Matthew, she would act extremely surprised. She would explain how her date had *just* called to cancel due to a—a what? Perhaps his mother had died. Anyway, she'd come up with something. It would be all downhill after that.

⋈

Kendall felt nervous as she climbed out of the taxi. She knew she looked fantastic, but she also knew she was on foreign turf. But as she walked up to Spago, she could tell people were looking. She could tell they thought she was someone. And she *was* someone—or about to be—once it became known that she and Matthew were an item. She wondered if her photo might show up in some of the celebrity magazines.

"Kendall," said a woman's voice.

Kendall paused in front of the door in time to see Kellie and a guy approaching her. "Oh, hi," said Kendall nervously.

"This is my husband, Glen," said Kellie. She smiled at the short, dark-haired man attached to her arm. "This is the woman I told you about. She's house hunting in Matthew and Heidi's neighborhood. She's an old friend of Heidi's."

"Nice to meet you," said Glen.

"You look fantastic," said Kellie as they walked into the restaurant together.

Kendall tried to remember if she'd really said she was an old friend of Heidi's. Never mind. It was time to regroup. She either needed to break free of these two or somehow cook up a plan to pretend to be their friends. That was it. She'd cling to Kellie and hope that the realtor would hold up her end for her new client. Glen spoke to the hostess, and she pointed toward a sign that said "Happy Birthday, Heidi." So it was Heidi's birthday party. Just great.

Kendall was about to make a fast break for the bathroom when suddenly she found herself face-to-face with both Heidi and Matthew.

"Look who we brought," said Kellie happily. Then she hugged and air-kissed the birthday girl. "Happy birthday, dahling!"

"Oh?" Heidi kind of blinked at Kendall, then made what seemed a forced smile. "Uh, nice to see you again."

"Happy birthday," said Kendall in a cheerful voice, putting on a confident smile as she stood straighter. She could feel Matthew staring at her. Was he as excited about this as she felt?

But Matthew's face actually seemed to grow pale and he didn't say a word, just stared.

"Kellie's been fantastic," Kendall directed this to Heidi. "She's shown me lots of great houses with loads of potential."

"You—you're looking at real estate?" asked Matthew in a strained voice.

"Oh, yeah," said Kendall. She smiled directly at him.

"I thought you knew all about it," said Kellie.

"Well, it was Heidi who recommended you," said Kendall lightly. Then to her relief, some other guests arrived, and Heidi and Matthew were distracted. Kendall followed Kellie and Glen over to where drink orders were being taken. Kendall ordered a double green apple martini and took in a deep breath. She remembered the salesclerks at the boutique and how they thought she might be an actress. Well, maybe she was. And if she could continue pulling this off, she might even win herself an Oscar!

Just as her martini arrived, so did Matthew. "I want to speak to you privately," he said in a serious voice.

"Sure."

"Meet me outside in about five minutes."

"You got it."

Then he walked back to where Heidi was greeting some of her friends. Hollywood, celebrity-type friends—the kind of friends Kendall would have before long. Kendall told Kellie she was going to powder her nose, then slowly meandered through the crowd and out toward the bathrooms.

Her heart was beating with excitement as she went out the front door. But where was Matthew? Certainly he didn't expect her to stand out here on the street and just wait for him. Someone might think she was a hooker. So instead of standing, she strolled down the sidewalk. Just before she turned around, she felt a hand on her elbow and looked up to see Matthew by her side. "Come on," he said as he escorted her on down the street, waving to a taxi parked nearby. "Let's take a ride." Then, before she could say a word, he practically pushed her inside and then ducked in beside her.

"Well." She adjusted her dress and composed herself, then smiled.

"Where to?" asked the driver.

"Just go," commanded Matthew. And the driver took off.

"It's nice to see you—"

"Don't start," he snapped at her.

"What?"

"What the—" He stopped himself, then glared at her with clenched fists. "What are you doing here?"

"I just came down to—"

"Don't give me any bull, Kendall. I know why you're here."

"But I just—"

"There's a word for what you're doing, you know."

She blinked. "What?"

"Stalking. You are a stalker, Kendall. And if you don't get out of town and out of my life, I will press charges. And it won't be the first time, either."

"But I just wanted to see—"

"I told you I'm married. I don't need this from you."

"But, Matthew, I only—"

"Seriously, Kendall. Get out of town. Get out of my life. And don't ever come back. Do you understand?"

Kendall couldn't believe it. She felt like Cinderella just now—except that she'd been thrown out of the ball without one single dance.

"I love my wife, Kendall. Sure, I've made some mistakes. But we're working on it." He swore now. "I can't believe you crashed her birthday party." He stared at Kendall like she was some horrible monster. "What kind of a person are you?"

She didn't know what to say.

"Drive back to Spago," he spat at the driver. "Drop me off there and then take this—this woman back to wherever she came from. But whatever you do, do not bring her back to Spago. Understand?"

"Got ya."

Soon they were back in front of the restaurant. Matthew threw a twenty at the driver, then turned to glare at Kendall. "If I ever see you around my house or my wife or me again—I swear I'm calling the police and then my lawyer. Don't mess with me, do you understand?"

She nodded without speaking. A huge lump was growing in her throat, and tears were burning in her eyes.

"Good riddance!" Then he jumped out and slammed the door.

"Rough night," said the driver.

Kendall just nodded, and her tears spilled over.

"Where to, little lady?"

She told him the name of her hotel.

"You know, you're a real pretty girl," he said in a way that she suspected was a come-on.

"Thanks," she said with no warmth. The last thing she needed right now was to be hit on by a middle-aged taxi driver.

"You shouldn't let that guy get you down," he said kindly.

And now she just started to bawl. The taxi driver said a few more things, something about love and life and relationships, but she couldn't really hear him, couldn't take it in. She just wanted this night to end. How could she have been such a complete fool? As she paid the driver and got out of the cab, she wondered if there was a twelve-step program for idiots. Maybe she could join Stupidolics Anonymous.

Twenty-one

Megan

Megan picked up the coffee carafe and took a sniff. It smelled stale and acidic, probably the same batch she'd made earlier.

"Did you go to church this morning?" asked Lelani as she came into the kitchen and got a bottle of water from the fridge.

"Yeah." Megan shoved the carafe back and turned the coffee-maker off.

"For someone who just got home from church, you seem a little bummed." Lelani peered curiously at her.

Megan shrugged as she filled the teakettle with water.

"Is something wrong?" asked Lelani.

Megan put the kettle on the stove and turned it on. "I guess I'm just having second thoughts."

"Second thoughts?"

"I broke up with Marcus yesterday."

"Really?" Lelani studied her. "Why?"

"Oh, we got into an argument."

"Yeah?"

"Well, Friday I wanted him to come to the singles group with me."

"And he refused?"

"He wanted to go to Zeke's."

"Yeah, you mentioned that. To hear a jazz group?"

"A friend was playing …" Megan frowned.

"And that's why you broke up?"

"Well, I'd had a rough day with Vera the day before. And I said some things to Marcus that I might not have meant. At least I didn't mean them completely. Or I said them wrong. Anyway, it's over. And it's probably for the best."

"What did you say to him?"

"Like if I was dating someone, I wanted that person to be supportive of my faith, and I wanted us to have similar values. Stuff like that."

"And he didn't agree?"

"He sort of agreed. But he didn't really get it. He told me that we did have similar values and that I needed to lighten up."

"Maybe you do."

Megan frowned at Lelani. "Meaning I should compromise my beliefs?"

"That's not what I—"

"Meaning it would've been better for Marcus and me to spend an evening in a smoky bar instead of going to a fellowship group at my church?"

Lelani's brow creased, like she wasn't going there. Megan didn't even blame her.

"I probably handled it all wrong."

"You really think it's over?"

Megan nodded. "I told him it wasn't worth it, and that we should call it quits before we got even more involved."

"Did you mean it?"

Megan considered this. "You know, I think I just wanted Marcus to jump in and say something like, *I want what you want,* or *I'm willing to give up some things.*"

"Oh."

Megan sighed. "It probably is for the best."

"So you're really not going to see him anymore?"

Megan shook her head. "Guess not."

"And you're okay with that?"

"Not really, but the alternative ..."

"Maybe you've just reached a new stage of the relationship," said Lelani hopefully.

"You mean the we're-not-together-anymore stage?"

Lelani kind of laughed. "That's not exactly what I meant. But maybe God is doing something."

Megan blinked in surprise. She wasn't used to hearing Lelani talk about God. "What do you mean?"

"I've been thinking about what you told me the other night. Actually, I've been doing more than just thinking about it. I'm trying to live it. I've been praying, Megan. And I've been trying to trust God with things. Maybe that's what you need to do about Marcus."

"I have been." Now Megan considered this—had she really? "Or maybe not so much. I'm not sure."

"But it's not too late."

"It might be too late as far as Marcus is concerned. I think I hurt him."

"But if it's meant to be, if God wants you to be with him, then it can't be too late, right?"

"I suppose not. I'm just not sure it was meant to be."

"How do you feel about losing him?"

"Not so great." Megan frowned as she moved the whistling kettle from the heat. "But at the same time, I'm sort of relieved. It's like one less stressful thing in my life."

"So maybe it was the right decision after all."

"Maybe, but I think it's kind of a chickenhearted relief." Megan poured hot water over her tea bag and watched as it steeped. "Do you know what I mean?"

Lelani nodded. "Actually, I do. Like sometimes we stop something just because we're feeling nervous, but not because it's the best thing to do. Sometimes I feel like I did that with med school."

"Why don't you go back?"

"I don't know."

"What if God wants you to go back?" challenged Megan. Actually, she was relieved to get the spotlight off of her.

"I guess I'd have to go back, then." Lelani smiled. "But hopefully he'd make it very clear if that was the case—and then send money."

"Where's Anna?"

"I don't know. She took off earlier. I didn't even see her in the house, but I heard her car leaving."

"Any word from Kendall?"

"No." Lelani just shook her head. "But I'm really curious as to how this insane plan of hers is going to turn out."

"Do you think she and Matthew really have a chance to get together?"

"If Kendall has her way."

"So what are you up to today?" Megan took a sip of tea.

"Just hanging."

"Well, I have an idea. I mean, if we're still having our big Christmas Eve party."

"As far as I know, we are. I've already invited a few people."

"So have I." Well, Megan had only invited old Mrs. Fowler so far, and she doubted the old lady would come.

"So what's your idea?"

"Well, it's what my mom used to do. She'd bake sugar cookies a couple weeks before Christmas and—"

"Won't they be stale?"

"Not if you freeze them. She'd put them between sheets of waxed paper and store them in the freezer. Then she'd take them out a couple days before Christmas and we'd frost and decorate them."

"That's a great idea. Do you have a recipe?"

Megan thought about this. "Not really."

"Why don't you call your mom?"

"Okay." Megan picked up the phone.

"Maybe she'd like to come over and help us," suggested Lelani.

"She might." Megan paused before dialing. "But I don't want to tell her about breaking up with Marcus, okay?"

"Why not?"

"My mom thinks he's a nice guy."

"He *is* a nice guy."

"Yeah, yeah," said Megan as she dialed her mom's number. "But that's not the main issue right now."

As it turned out, Megan's mom was game. Not only did she come over with her recipe, but she brought her cookie cutters too. And the three of them made dozens of shaped cookies.

"This has been so much fun," said Lelani as Megan's mom was packing up her things to go home. "Thanks so much for helping."

"I wish I could come to your party."

"You're not coming?"

"No," said Megan. "She's off to Mexico to sit on a beach and drink margaritas."

"Oh, it's not like that," said Mom.

Megan patted her mom on the back. "It's okay. I think it's a great idea."

"Not me," said Lelani. "I've had more than enough beachy Christmases. Nothing would make me happier than having snow."

"I hate to disappoint you, but that's probably not going to happen." Megan's mom pulled on her coat. "I can count white Christmases in Portland—and I mean in *my* lifetime—on one hand. And that's not counting my thumb."

Lelani laughed. "Well, anyway, it's not like Maui."

As Megan's mom left, Anna came in. "Smells good in here," she said as she peeked into the kitchen. They had saved out one plate of slightly deformed cookies to eat, and Megan offered this to Anna.

"A one-legged reindeer?"

"Yes," said Lelani. "Those are the rejects."

"Right."

Just then the landline phone rang. Megan answered it and was surprised to hear Kendall's voice. "How's it going down in sunny Southern California?" asked Megan cheerfully.

"Not well."

"Oh. Anything seriously wrong?"

"I need a ride from the airport," snapped Kendall.

"Sure. Okay. When do you—"

"Tonight."

"When tonight?"

"My flight gets in late. Is Lelani there?"

Megan just shook her head. "Hang on." She nodded to Lelani now. "It's Kendall dearest, and she wants to speak to you."

Lelani frowned and took the phone. "Hey, Kendall, what's—" But she was obviously cut off by a grumpy Kendall.

"She sounds mad," Megan whispered to Anna.

Anna frowned. "Her big plans must've fallen apart."

"Ya think?" Megan rolled her eyes.

"So now she'll probably come home and be a big old grouch."

"The Grinch who's going to steal Christmas?"

Anna nodded. "Just what we need."

They waited until Lelani hung up. "Wow," she said. "Kendall does not sound like a happy camper."

"What did she think was going to happen?" asked Anna.

"She was slightly delusional when she went down there," said Lelani. "But she's had a huge reality check."

"I wonder what happened," said Megan.

"She said Matthew told her to get lost. Or something like that."

"Poor Kendall," said Anna.

"You feel sorry for her?" asked Megan.

"Okay, maybe I feel sorry for me," said Anna. "I'm the one who shares a bathroom with her. I get more of her wrath than you guys."

"Don't be so sure about that," said Lelani. "She seems to think I'm her best friend in this house. And when I let her down, she lets me know."

"And she still seems to hate me," said Megan.

"She doesn't hate you," protested Lelani.

"Maybe not," Megan admitted. "But I'm pretty low on her food chain."

"Anyway, I'll use her car to pick her up. Her flight doesn't get in until ten fifteen," said Lelani. "And it sounds like she's broke."

"Big surprise," said Megan.

"It also sounds like she's pretty brokenhearted and discouraged." Lelani seemed to direct this comment to Megan. "And I think she could use a little warmth and support from her housemates."

Suddenly Megan felt guilty for being so mean and judgmental toward Kendall. Seriously, what kind of Christian was she anyway? "Yeah," Megan said slowly. "I'm sure you're right about that. I'll try to be nicer, okay?"

Lelani brightened. "Who knows? Maybe God is working on Kendall."

Anna seemed surprised by this. "What do you mean?"

"Megan's been talking to me about God lately. And I'm starting to take him seriously. Maybe Kendall needs to do the same."

Anna stared curiously at both of them. "So, you guys really believe in God?"

"Sure," said Megan. "Don't you?"

Anna shrugged. "I'm not sure."

"But aren't you Catholic?" asked Megan.

"I'm also Hispanic," pointed out Anna. "But, if you haven't noticed, I don't exactly embrace all those customs either."

"Gil was telling me that you guys haven't gone to Mass or confession since you were kids."

"Well, that could change any minute," said Anna. Then she pointed to Lelani. "Speaking of Gil, he asked me to tell you he'd pick you up at six for dinner tonight, if that's okay."

"Sounds good."

Then the three housemates went their own ways. Megan couldn't help but feel somewhat corrected, albeit gently, by Lelani. She knew Lelani was right; Megan did need to try harder with Kendall. She'd actually tried to be a better friend a few weeks ago, back before Kendall had fallen for Matthew Harmon. But the truth was Kendall's stupid choice to hook up with her celebrity crush—a married man—disgusted Megan.

It was just so wrong. Still, it would be even more wrong for Megan to kick Kendall while she was down. Okay, it would be wrong to kick Kendall even if she was up. But sometimes Megan wished she could smack some sense into that girl!

Anna

"Let me help you with that, Mom." Anna slipped on the oven mitts and stepped in front of the oven to remove the hot baking dish of enchiladas.

"I'm not an invalid," said her mother. "At least not yet."

"Even so." Anna set the dish on the tiled countertop and turned to look at her mother's face. Flushed from the heat of the stove, her cheeks looked rosy and healthy, but there was fear in her eyes. As if she was bracing herself for the worst.

"That smells yummi-licious," said Jake as he leaned over the breakfast bar and sniffed loudly. "I haven't had homemade enchiladas in ages."

"Doesn't your mother make them?" asked Anna in surprise. Hardly anything was simpler than enchiladas.

Jake laughed. "My mom only cooks the kind of food that comes prepackaged, canned, or frozen."

"I'm back from my tour," said Lelani as she and Gil joined them in the kitchen. "You have a lovely home, Mrs. Mendez."

"Thank you." Her mother smiled, but Anna heard the stiffness in her voice.

"Do you need any help in here?" offered Lelani.

"No, everything's just about ready," said Anna quickly. "Why don't you guys go check on Dad, Gil?"

"Yes," said their mother. "Tell him dinner will be ready in about ten minutes."

Once again, it was just Anna and her mother in the kitchen. "So, what do you think of Lelani, Mom?" asked Anna.

"She's a very pretty girl." Despite this observation, Anna couldn't help but notice her mother's frown.

"Yes, I know she's pretty." Anna sighed impatiently. "But what do you really think of her?"

"She's polite."

"Come on, Mama," persisted Anna. "Tell me what you really think."

"I think that Gil is in love with her." She sighed sadly.

"Tell me something I don't know."

"Fine," she snapped. "You want to know what I know, Anna?"

"What?"

"I wasn't going to say anything." She glanced over her shoulder as if to see whether anyone was listening.

"What is it?" demanded Anna.

"You must not speak a word. And do not say I told you this."

"What? *What?*" Anna was growing extremely curious.

"Well, you know your cousin Brad and his wife, Camille, were expecting a baby, right?"

"Yes, of course."

"And you know that Camille had her baby."

"Oh, really? What was it?"

"A boy, but that's not what I'm saying."

"What are you saying?"

"Camille's mother was in the restaurant last night. And she mentioned that Camille had seen Gil and Lelani shopping for baby things."

"So?"

"So?" Her mother's voice got slightly shrill, and then without warning she started speaking in Spanish. A clue that something was very wrong.

"What are you saying?"

"What more do I need to say, Anna? Gil and Lelani ... shopping for—for baby things ... *together.*"

Anna considered this. She knew what her mother was thinking, but she also knew it was ridiculous. "Oh, no, Mom. I don't think so."

"But you do not know, do you?"

"Are you suggesting that Gil and Lelani are ..." Anna couldn't even bring herself to say the word.

"An unmarried couple, shopping for baby things. What do you think it means, *mi'ja?*"

"That they were buying a gift for someone? Camille and Brad maybe?"

"No, they were looking at *girl* things. Everyone knew that Camille was having a boy."

"Mom, even if Gil and Lelani are, uh, expecting ... how would they know it's going to be a girl? I mean so soon? And they've only been going out a couple of months, so how would they even—"

"Hush!" Anna's mother tossed her a warning glance.

"Is dinner about ready?" asked Mr. Mendez. His brows were arched slightly as if he'd been listening to their conversation.

"Yes," snapped Anna's mother.

Anna gave her dad an empathetic smile, and he just nodded in a sad way. "Go ahead and tell the others." Anna picked up the hot dish of enchiladas and carried it out to the dining room.

"Your mama," whispered Dad. "She is so upset."

"Yes." Anna nodded. "It's understandable."

Dad put his hand on her shoulder. "We're going to need you, Anna, more than ever."

"I'm here for you guys," she assured him. Of course, she wondered what this promise would entail. Would they expect her to move back home now? Maybe it was the right thing to do. Still, Anna felt disappointed to think she might lose her freedom. And then she felt angry at herself for thinking like that. Not to mention guilty.

Soon the six of them were seated at the table, and Anna couldn't help but stare at Lelani. Was it possible that she was pregnant? And if so, did that mean that she and Gil would be getting married soon? Anna couldn't imagine Gil not wanting to do the honorable thing. Still, Anna felt sure that her mother must be wrong. It just seemed impossible. Unthinkable.

So much was going through Anna's mind as they sat around the large dining table, all attempting to make small talk and get to know each other better, or at least appearing to try. But the conversation seemed strained and unnatural. She knew that she and Gil and Dad were distracted and concerned about their mother's condition, whereas Lelani and Jake were oblivious. Consequently, it seemed the two of them were bolstering most of the chitchat. Right now they were discussing Lelani's home in Maui. And since Jake had been there once, a surprise to Anna, it seemed he thought he was an expert. It also seemed that Lelani was being overly nice to him, putting up with his presumptions and even laughing at his rather lame attempts to remember how to pronounce some tricky Hawaiian words.

As they ate dessert and drank coffee, Anna couldn't help but notice that Jake was paying way too much attention to Lelani. At first, she had assumed he was simply being polite. And she even appreciated that he'd kept the conversation moving along while she and her family silently suffered. But now she felt worried. Why was Jake so interested in

Lelani? Was it her looks that captivated him? And if so, what did that say about Jake?

She didn't want to, but she started comparing Jake to Edmond—and she wasn't too pleased with what she saw. In some ways, she felt like she was reliving a blast from the past. A bad blast. Edmond had spent plenty of time with and around Lelani, but never once had he acted like this. And even around Kendall, a consummate flirt, Edmond had simply been polite. He somehow managed to keep a safe distance, and it seemed his attention was primarily focused on Anna. Why hadn't she noticed this before?

Or maybe she was being too harsh on Jake. Maybe Lelani was encouraging him. Maybe she was enjoying all this attention. And there was Gil ... hardly taking notice. He had taken the news of his mother's health even worse than Anna.

"I can't believe you don't want to go home for Christmas," Jake said loudly to Lelani. "Man, if I had parents in Maui, I'd be on the next flight out of here."

Lelani laughed. "Maybe you would. But not me. I think it's that old grass-is-greener thing. You always seem to want what you can't have."

Jake grinned. "Like forbidden fruit."

Gil cleared his throat. "That was a great meal, Mama. Can I help you clean up?" Before she could protest, Gil was using his one good hand to clear the table. And Anna jumped up to help him.

"Let me help too," said Lelani, but Gil stopped her.

"You're a guest," he said firmly.

"Yes, but you've got a bad wrist," she pointed out.

"It's actually feeling a lot better."

"Still, you're not supposed to use it," Lelani reminded him.

"And I'm not, see." He balanced a small stack of plates with one hand. "Really, Lelani, we don't allow guests to help. Especially on their first visit."

"That's right," said Anna. "We'll hurry and get this cleared up, then maybe we can play a game of pool." She smiled at Jake. "Jake's been begging to get beaten."

"I'm sure I can beat him with one hand tied behind my back," teased Gil.

"That's a good idea," said their mother in a tired voice. "You kids go downstairs and play some billiards. And the old folks will go put their feet up."

"And Lelani and I can go warm up the pool table," suggested Jake.

"Great," said Gil.

Anna wasn't sure it was so great as she watched Jake tugging Lelani toward the stairs. Then once she and Gil were alone, she turned to face him. "What is going on with Lelani tonight?" she demanded.

"What do you mean?" Gil looked surprised.

"Why is she coming on to Jake like that?"

"Lelani coming on to Jake?" Gil shook his head as he put a plate in the dishwasher. "I don't think so."

"Because you're oblivious."

"If anyone is doing the coming on thing, it's Jake."

Anna just frowned. Okay, part of her agreed with him.

"I don't know why you're back together with him," continued Gil.

Anna didn't say anything.

"Edmond was a nice—"

"Yes. Fine. Edmond was a nice guy. He is a nice guy. Whatever. It's over, okay?"

"Just saying."

"Like it's any of your business."

"I happen to like Edmond."

"Great. It seems everyone does."

"Why are you so angry, Anna?"

She tossed her towel onto the counter. "Why? Well, for starters, my boyfriend seems to think your girlfriend is hot. And then there's the fact that our mother has cancer. And I think our father expects me to move back home to take care of her. And, oh yeah, Mom's worried that you and Lelani are expecting a baby."

"What?" Gil's eyes grew huge. "Why?"

So Anna told him what Camille's mother had told her, and Gil seemed relieved. "Oh, is that all?" he said.

"Well, you have to admit it's a little suspicious that you guys went out shopping for baby things together."

"We were doing Christmas shopping. Lelani has nieces, you know."

Anna nodded. "Yeah, I forgot."

"So, do I need to speak to Mom?" Gil looked truly worried now. "And what do I say? 'By the way, Mom, I'm not about to become a daddy'?"

"Maybe we can talk to her together," offered Anna.

"Thanks." Then Gil put an arm around her shoulder. "Let's not forget we're family, Anna. We're in this thing together."

Anna frowned. "What about Jake and Lelani? Do you suppose he's down there throwing himself at her?"

"Maybe we should go check."

So without finishing the kitchen cleanup, they went down to the basement to find that Jake was shamelessly flirting with Lelani. And while she looked uncomfortable, it was hard to tell whether it was because Anna and Gil popped in on them or what.

"You know," said Gil slowly. "There's something going on with my, uh, our parents tonight. And Anna and I just really need to sit down together to talk to—"

"You want us out of your hair?" asked Jake a little too eagerly.

"Well, not exactly," said Gil. He seemed to be eyeing Lelani with some uncertainty now. "But we—"

"How about I drop Lelani home?" offered Jake. "And we'll catch up with you guys later."

"Are you sure you don't mind?" asked Gil.

"Not at all," said Jake. "I have an early morning meeting anyway. Might as well call it a night."

So they all went upstairs, where Lelani and Jake thanked and said good-bye to everyone. Then it was just the four Mendezes sitting in the living room.

"Jake seems to be fond of Lelani," observed their mother.

"Jake likes beautiful women," said Anna in what she knew was a sour tone.

"You are a beautiful woman," said her father with a genuine smile. Of course he thought she was beautiful. She was his little girl. What else could he think? Or say?

"Thanks, Dad," she said.

"I encouraged them to leave together," said Gil, "so we could have some privacy. We need to talk. As a family."

"No, no, no," said their mother, holding up her hands to stop him. "That is not what I had planned for tonight. I do not wish to discuss my illness or—"

"Not just that, Mom," said Gil. "Anna told me that you think Lelani is pregnant."

Mrs. Mendez looked surprised, but simply nodded.

"She isn't pregnant."

"But why were you—"

And so Gil told her the same thing that he'd told Anna.

"Still," said their mother. "It was suspicious."

"Lelani loves children," he assured her. "She adores her nieces and nephews. And you should've heard her encouraging Camille about her baby. She sounded just like a real doctor."

Anna could hear the pride in her brother's voice, and she could see the love in his eyes. Then she remembered how Lelani and Jake had left together, how they were together right now, and her stomach twisted. What a mistake.

"She is also very beautiful," said their mother sadly.

"You keep saying that as if it's a defect," said Gil.

"Beautiful women can be dangerous."

"But Dad just said I was beautiful," said Anna. "And I know he thinks you're beautiful too, Mama."

"Yes, but ours is a different kind of beauty—deeper."

"You're saying Lelani isn't beautiful on the inside?" challenged Gil.

"I'm saying she might break your heart."

"How can you know that?" demanded Gil. "You've barely met her."

"Yes ... and where is she now, Gil? Why is she not here?"

"Because we needed to talk," he insisted. "Just the four of us."

But their mother was not going to cooperate. Instead she continued to jab Gil about his choice in women. And as she did this, Anna couldn't help but feel that much of what her mother said was meant for her as well. Still, she didn't want to argue. And neither did Gil. So they both just sat there and listened to her pontificate about what makes for a good spouse, a good marriage, good children ... and in the meantime their father fell sound asleep.

Lelani

"So, what do you think of those Mendezes?" asked Jake. He was driving Lelani back home now. And it seemed to her that he was taking the long route.

"What do you mean *those* Mendezes?" She tried not to sound as irritated as she felt, but something about the way Jake referred to Gil's family sounded wrong, almost like a put-down.

He laughed. "Don't get defensive. And to be fair, I've known them longer than you. Remember, Anna and I dated for nearly two years."

"Before you broke her heart?"

"I think that's overstating things a bit."

"Not according to Anna."

"Well, she's forgiven me."

Lelani wasn't so sure. She felt certain she'd seen fire in Anna's eyes tonight. Whether it was aimed at Jake or Lelani, she wasn't totally sure. But it had definitely been there, and it looked like jealousy. In Anna's defense, Jake had been a jerk, and Lelani couldn't blame Anna for reacting. Not that Lelani had the slightest interest in Anna's boyfriend. Oh, sure, he was good-looking and almost charming at times, but from the moment she met him, something about his smooth ways and easy manners made Lelani uncomfortable.

The way Jake had behaved tonight was inexcusable. Lelani had

purposely not attempted to stop him in front of the Mendez family—
that would have embarrassed Anna. She'd managed to keep a cool
distance from him while they were playing pool, although being with
him felt like a cat-and-mouse game. Still, her hope was that Jake had
revealed his true colors to everyone. Lelani seriously hoped that Anna
would rethink getting back together with him. Perhaps Jake's behav-
ior would help Anna to see Edmond in a whole new light.

Lelani glanced over at Jake. He looked so smug, so confident, like
he really thought she was interested in him. Hopefully no one else had
gotten that message. Hopefully she hadn't allowed things to go too far.
She hated to think that she had sacrificed her friendship with Anna in
the process of exposing Jake. She'd have to set Anna straight when she
came home.

"Why so quiet?" asked Jake as he finally exited the freeway.
Seriously, had he even been going the speed limit?

"I guess I'm just tired," she said in a flat tone. "Long weekend …
long work week ahead."

"Anna told me you work at Nordstrom. That must be brutal during the Christmas season."

"It's pretty bad."

"So, tell me, how serious is it between you and Gil?"

"What?" Lelani gave him a sharp look. What nerve!

He smiled in a way that he probably thought was attractive, a way
that had probably worked for him in the past. "You can't blame me for
asking, Lelani. I know you guys have been dating for a few weeks. But
I get the impression you're not that serious."

"What gives you that impression?"

"You."

"Well, you know what they say. Looks can be deceiving."

"Meaning you really are into old Gil?"

"He's the nicest guy I know." She said this with such a force that surprised her. But Jake's laugh surprised her more.

"Nice is nice, but it doesn't always come with fire, Lelani, if you know what I mean."

"And fire can burn you," she shot back, "if you know what I mean."

He chuckled. "Hey, some kinds of burns can feel pretty good."

She turned and glared at him. This guy was so full of himself, so conceited—how could Anna stand him?

"Sorry if I'm making you uncomfortable, Lelani." His voice softened now. "I've been accused of being a little too straightforward at times."

"I guess."

"But I have to lay my cards on the table. Ever since I met you, well, you just sort of take my breath away."

"I'm sorry." Her tone was even sharper now, almost hostile. "Maybe you should open a window."

He laughed. "See, there you go again."

"Look," she began carefully. "Anna is my friend and I wouldn't do anything to hurt her, do you understand?"

He nodded. "Yeah, I get you. And I totally respect that. The truth is I don't want to hurt Anna either."

"How can you say that and act like—*like this?*"

"I've already decided to break it off with Anna. Not that there's much to break off, really. I mean when I saw her at the wedding, well, I was feeling pretty down and lonely. And the truth was I had been thinking about her. So it seemed like fate to run into her there. But then after I spent some time with her, and especially being back around her family again, well, it seems clear that Anna and I are a mistake. I have a feeling she sees it too."

"I hope so."

"But how about you and Gil? I hate to be blunt, but am I wrong to think that your relationship is not that serious?"

"To put it bluntly, our relationship is none of your business."

He chuckled. "Oh, yeah, I so like a feisty woman."

She pressed her lips tightly together and began to count slowly in her head. They were less than five minutes from the house now, if she could just last that long without totally letting him have it. The only reason she wasn't letting him have it was for Anna's sake. She felt certain if she didn't blow him off completely, he might follow through with his plan to break up with Anna. Really, wouldn't that be in Anna's best interest? Lelani kept her mouth shut.

"Well, here we are." He turned and smiled at her as he pulled into the driveway.

'Thank you for the ride, Jake." Her tone was no-nonsense and she reached for her bag.

"I meant what I said, Lelani. I'd really like to see you again."

"I meant what I said too." But she smiled at him. Just to throw him off.

He looked slightly confused, but then he smiled back. "Cool."

"Good night." Then before he could say another word, she hopped out of the car and ran up to the house. "Jerk!" she said as she went inside.

"Thanks a lot," said Megan. She was standing by the door with a surprised expression and a cup of tea.

"Not you." Lelani let out an exasperated groan. "Men!"

"What's wrong? Did Gil do something?"

"No, not at all. I'm not talking about Gil." Lelani peeled off her coat and hung it. "I'm talking about Jake—*Jake the Snake,* as Gil has called him, although I think it was Mrs. Mendez who first came up with that fitting little term of endearment."

"You mean Anna's Jake?"

"Hopefully he won't be Anna's Jake much longer."

"Huh?"

So Lelani gave her a quick explanation.

"Eeuw. That is so slimy," said Megan.

"You're telling me. I feel like I should go take a shower. He is such a sleazeball. How can Anna stand him?"

"Well, he's very good-looking." Megan frowned. "Not that it means anything when you're a slime bucket."

"I just can't believe that Anna could fall for someone like that."

"Love is blind."

"I guess." Lelani just shook her head.

"Poor Anna."

"Yes. And I'm afraid she's really mad at me now. I just don't want her to think that I have the slightest interest in that creep."

"Can't you just tell her?"

"I'm not quite sure how to go about it. I mean how do you tell a friend that she's dating a jerk, especially after he's hit on you?"

"Very carefully?"

"That's what I'm thinking. I plan to stay up and talk to her when she gets in. Hopefully it won't be too late."

"Hey, what about Kendall?" asked Megan. "Isn't she getting in late tonight?"

Lelani slapped her forehead. "Oh, no, I totally forgot." She looked at the clock. "And her flight will be landing in about half an hour."

"Do you want me to go get her?" offered Megan. "I could drive her car."

"I'd love for you to go," said Lelani. "But she'd probably be ticked."

"Well, I know she's not crazy about me, but a ride is a ride."

"Except that I made a deal with her. A deal is a deal." Lelani reached for her coat again. "And as it is, I'm probably going to be late."

"She'll have to go to baggage claim," pointed out Megan. "That might slow her down some, especially this time of year."

"Even so, I better get going." Lelani so wished she hadn't agreed to pick Kendall up. Not only did it mess things up with Anna, but Lelani really did feel exhausted. More than anything else, she just wanted to go to bed. Who knew having housemates could be this much trouble?

"What about Anna?" asked Megan as Lelani headed for the garage. "Do you want me to say anything to her?"

Lelani considered this. "It might just complicate things to hear it secondhand. But thanks anyway."

"You're probably right. This is a pretty sensitive issue." Megan yawned. "Besides, I was on my way to bed with a good book."

"Lucky you."

"Hang in there."

It started to rain as Lelani drove toward the airport. She turned on the wipers and to her surprise, found herself wishing that she was back home in Maui—not under present circumstances, but the way things were years ago, back when she was still a kid and life was uncomplicated. She sighed and cut short her own longing. She'd heard the old quote "You can never go back home again." The older she got, the more she understood its meaning. You can't turn back the clock. You can't undo what's been done.

Just as Lelani pulled into the terminal, her cell phone began to ring. She hoped that it was Gil. The sound of his voice would be soothing. Instead, it was Kendall.

"Where are you?"

"I'm heading toward the passenger-pickup area right now. Three minutes."

"Good. I'll meet you outside."

Sure enough, there was Kendall in a short skirt, a lightweight cotton sweater, and high-heeled strappy sandals. She was tan and barelegged. If she'd been on a street corner, she might've been mistaken for a hooker. As it was, it looked like she was freezing.

Lelani hurried out of the car and started to help Kendall with her luggage. Without saying a word, Kendall got into the passenger seat then slumped down like she'd been deflated. Lelani realized that she was expected to load the luggage alone. She shoved in the last bag, then slammed the trunk closed.

"How are you doing?" asked Lelani as she started to drive out of the terminal.

"Don't ask."

Lelani nodded. "Okay." Actually, that suited Lelani just fine. She was getting fed up with people's problems and messed-up romances. A little silence was welcome.

"I wish I were dead," muttered Kendall.

Lelani felt a serious stab of concern and glanced over at her. Kendall's expression was totally dismal, as if the life had been drained from her eyes. Beneath the veneer of that golden tan, Kendall looked pale and drawn. Or maybe it was just the cold. Kendall was shivering, so Lelani turned up the heat. "Oh, you'll be okay, Kendall."

"Okay?" Kendall sat up straight, then turned and glared at Lelani. "How can you say that? How can you possibly know how I feel?"

"Because we've all been there, Kendall. Everyone gets their heart broken at least once in this life."

"Right!" Kendall swore. "I'll bet *you* never did."

"Don't bet on it." For a very brief moment Lelani considered telling Kendall her story. But in the next instant, Lelani knew that would be a big mistake. Some stories weren't meant to be shared—not with certain people, anyway. Maybe Gil was the only one who would ever know the truth.

"Whatever."

"Just give it time," said Lelani.

"Yeah, right. The old time-heals-all-wounds thing." Kendall cussed again.

"Or maybe time wounds all heels."

"Very funny."

Lelani shrugged as she entered the freeway. It was raining even harder now, so she turned the wipers onto full blast.

"I can't believe he didn't love me," sobbed Kendall. "I really thought we had something—something special."

Lelani wanted to ask her why she thought that. Why, after a drunken one-night stand, would Kendall assume that Matthew Harmon should be in love with her? Of course, Lelani wasn't about to say this. Kendall was in enough pain already. So Lelani just listened as Kendall went on and on about how hard she'd tried, how she would never love another man, how Matthew was only pretending to love his wife because they were such a "Hollywood" couple and everyone expected them to stay together.

"Someday he'll wake up and smell the coffee." Kendall blew her nose loudly. "Matthew will realize what he missed out on with me—a woman who'd be devoted to him, who'd do everything possible to make his life nothing but bliss. His little Heidi Hardwick will be too busy, too famous, and too self-absorbed to take care of him the way I could've.

Someday he'll figure it out. And then he'll be sorry."

Without saying anything, Lelani nodded, pretending to agree. However, she suspected that Matthew Harmon was probably rejoicing over the fact that he'd just dodged a very big bullet.

Twenty-four

Kendall

Kendall slept for most of two days. If it were possible, she'd sleep right up through Christmas. Maybe even through New Year's. Her plan was to keep a low profile around the house for a while. Hiding out in her room, she imagined herself to be a bear—a wounded bear who had crawled off into her den to hibernate. It might be a good way to lose weight too.

By Tuesday afternoon she was ravenous. So she sneaked out to forage in the kitchen. So what if she hadn't bought any of the food in there, but this was her house, wasn't it? These girls were getting off pretty cheap on their rent. Certainly, she should be entitled to some privileges.

But as soon as she heard a key in the front door, she scurried up to her room again. The last thing she wanted right now was to be caught pillaging someone's leftovers, not to mention that she hadn't bathed or shampooed her hair in days, plus she had a huge zit on her chin. Besides that, she still felt embarrassed for confessing the whole humiliating mess to Lelani on the way home from the airport Sunday night. She cried and blubbered and had been absolutely pathetic. Honestly, Kendall felt like she didn't have a single shred of dignity left.

By Thursday, Kendall had a serious case of cabin fever. And she was seriously hungry. But it seemed that her housemates had discovered her foraging ways, and now there wasn't much to pick from. Or else it was bagged up and marked with their names and warnings like "Do not touch this!" or "Hands off, Kendall!" Like she couldn't take a hint. She'd go out and get her own groceries if she weren't broke. She still had one credit card with a few hundred dollars. But she thought she better hang onto that for emergencies. The way she saw it, this wasn't exactly an emergency. At least not yet.

Someone like Megan or her sister Kate would tell her to get off her hind end and go find a job. But who gets a job just a week before Christmas? And even if she did manage to get hired, she wouldn't get paid for—what—a couple more weeks? Really, it hardly seemed worthwhile. January would be here before long, and her housemates would have to pay their rent. And this time she'd be more careful with her money.

Still, she was hungry. And that meant she'd have to go out and get some food. And that meant she'd have to clean herself up. And for some reason that seemed as daunting as climbing a mountain.

Somehow, perhaps it was the hunger, she managed to put one foot in front of the next, and at a little past noon she was ready to face the world. Or at least Nana and her nursing-home friends. She couldn't remember when lunch was served, but as she sped across town, she hoped that she'd get there in time.

⋙●⋘

"Kendall," said one of the old guys that she'd met last fall. He paused to catch his breath from pushing his walker down the hallway. "It's good to see you again." He grinned, then winked. "I've been missing your pretty face."

She gave him a quick smile. "Is it lunchtime?"

"Lunch is over and done with," he told her. "They start serving at eleven and if you're not finished by twelve thirty, you can forget about it." He chuckled. "Sometimes that's the best thing to do. Like today. I don't know what they called it, but I've had C rations with more flavor."

Kendall frowned.

"Are you looking for your grandmother?"

Now Kendall brightened. Sometimes Nana kept food in the tiny kitchenette of her room. Nothing too substantial, just crackers or cookies or snacks. But at the moment, that sounded lots better than nothing. "Yeah," said Kendall. "Have you seen her?"

"Not since lunch, but I suspect she's in her room. Everyone seems to take naps after lunch." He shook his head in a gloomy way. "It's sure not easy being stuck here with a bunch of worn-out old people." He smiled. "But now you're here. Want to play a little rummy?"

"Not unless you have a little rum to go with it," she teased.

He shook his head. "We're not allowed to imbibe here. Darn shame too. I think some of these folks might brighten up with a nip of something good in their Ovaltine."

"You're probably right." She patted him on the shoulder. "Catch you later."

"You won't have to run too fast to catch me," he called as she took off toward Nana's room.

When she arrived, she knocked eagerly on the door.

"Why, Kendall," said Nana as she opened it. "What are you doing here? I hope you're not going to beg for money, because Kate told me to tell you no."

"I just came to say hello," said Kendall. She flopped down on her grandmother's love seat and smiled.

Nana eased herself into her recliner and narrowed her eyes, studying Kendall carefully. "Something's wrong, isn't it?" she finally said.

Kendall shook her head. "No. Nothing's wrong. But I had hoped to make it here in time for lunch. I'm starving."

"I've got some graham crackers in the cupboard," said Nana. "And a few other things. Help yourself, although it's not much. I haven't been to the store in a while."

Kendall found what was left of the graham crackers and took a bite. "Oh, Nana," she said in disgust. "These are stale." Then she got an idea. "Why don't I take you to get some groceries?"

Nana looked surprised. "Right now?"

"If you want. I could pick up some things too."

"Well, I usually take my nap, but I wouldn't mind getting out." Nana pushed herself up out of her chair. "What are we waiting for?"

Before long they were cruising the aisles of a nearby Safeway. With Christmas music playing in the background, Kendall happily filled the cart with all kinds of things that Nana seemed to want. Of course, Kendall knew these wouldn't fit into Nana's cupboards, but Kendall could relieve her of the surplus.

"Goodness," said Nana as they waited in the checkout line. "How did we manage to gather up all that?"

"I guess we just like to shop." Kendall laughed. "Or maybe you're planning to entertain over the holidays."

"Your sister Kate invited me to her house for Christmas." Nana made a face. "But I don't know that I'll go."

"You could come to my house," offered Kendall. Although she felt fairly sure that Nana would decline this invitation too. "We're having a Christmas Eve party."

Nana seemed to consider this. "A Christmas Eve party? At my old house?"

Kendall nodded.

"I'd love to come."

"Well, okay then."

"I'll have to remember to sign up for shuttle service," said Nana as the clerk began to ring up their purchases. "Unless you want to come get me."

"Oh, shuttle service would be nice," said Kendall. "I mean since I'm helping with that party. I should probably stick around, you know?"

Nana smiled. "A Christmas party at my old house. I think I'll enjoy that."

"With real eggnog," said Kendall.

"I hope I can find something festive to wear," said Nana. Then, without even looking at the total, Nana handed the cashier her debit card. Kendall was actually surprised to see that groceries cost so much. But then she didn't usually shop for them herself.

She felt slightly guilty as she loaded the bags into the car. But then she rationalized that she'd done Nana a favor by bringing her to the store. Surely that was worth something in return.

"Oh, look at the cute doggies in the window," said Nana as they were about to get into the car. She pointed to the pet shop next to the grocery store. "I just love little dogs, don't you?"

Kendall looked over to see a brown Chihuahua along with another small dog—a white fluffy one that looked kind of like Kendall's bedroom slippers, but not pink. She paused with her hand on the car door, staring at the dog and trying to figure out why it seemed familiar. Then she remembered Heidi Hardwick's little white dog, the one with the blue rhinestone collar. "Want to go look at the dogs?" she asked Nana.

"Oh, could we?" Nana sounded like a little girl now. But then Kendall knew that Nana had always loved dogs and cats. One of the hardest parts of moving to the nursing home was leaving her pets behind. Kendall didn't like to think about that. Part of the deal for taking on her grandmother's house had been to look after the last of Nana's pets, an old cat named Clara Belle. But Clara Belle had a serious incontinence problem and, after numerous accidents, Kendall took her to the vet and was informed that Clara Belle had some kind of kidney disease. The kindest thing, it seemed for both Kendall and the cat, was to put her down. Naturally, Kendall didn't tell Nana about this until months later. She reasoned that it would only make Nana's transition to the nursing home more difficult. When she finally told her about Clara Belle, she said the cat had died in her sleep. And wasn't that true?

"Oh, you little darlings," gushed Nana when the pet shop girl put the two little dogs down in a contained play area where they could look at them. "Oh, I'd take both of you home with me if I could get you past the security guard."

"She lives in a nursing home," explained Kendall. Then she reached down and picked up the white fluffy dog. She was surprised at how soft the dog's coat felt. Sure, the dog smelled kind of funny, but it probably hadn't been bathed recently. "What kind of dog is this?" she asked the girl.

"Maltese."

"Maltese?" Kendall considered this. Was that anything like the *Maltese Falcon*? She had really liked that movie but couldn't quite make a connection between the dog and it. "Boy or girl?" she asked now.

"Female. She's about six months old, and she's already had her shots and been spayed."

"Spayed?" Kendall frowned.

"That means she can't have puppies," said Nana as if Kendall should know this.

"Yes. The breeders have a policy. They will only sell us dogs that can't reproduce," explained the girl. "To keep the competition down."

"Oh." Kendall nodded like she understood. But the truth was she'd never owned a dog or a cat besides Clara Belle.

"I know, I know," said Nana. "I will get the dog for you for Christmas."

"Really?" Kendall considered this. She imagined herself walking this dog down the street with a rhinestone collar. Not blue, of course, but pink. And, okay, if she couldn't be Matthew Harmon's wife, she could at least have a dog like Heidi's.

"And you can bring it to the nursing home to visit me," continued Nana. "And I can come visit her." She rubbed the dog's head. "Wouldn't you like that, little puppy-wuppy? Wouldn't you like to go home with Kendall for Christmas?"

And so, just like that, Nana bought Kendall the little white dog.

"Thanks," said Kendall.

"I'm tired," said Nana. "I need to sit down and rest."

"Do you need anything for the dog?" asked the girl. "Do you have dishes or toys or a bed?"

Kendall considered this. "Well, yeah, I guess I do need those. And a collar, too. Do you have anything in pink rhinestones?"

"You go ahead and get what you need," said Nana in a weary voice. "I'm going to wait in the car. My feet are killing me."

So Kendall unlocked the car for Nana, then returned to the pet shop to pick out all sorts of cute things, including a pink rhinestone collar and matching leash, as well as a little pink raincoat and several other doggy outfits. By the time the girl rang up the purchases the total came to a little more than $250. Kendall handed her the only credit card that wasn't maxed out and prayed that it wouldn't go over. Fortunately it didn't. Then she loaded all these things, including her dog and the adorable pink carrying case, into the backseat of her car.

"What are you going to name her?" asked Nana as Kendall drove back to the nursing home.

"I'm not sure yet," said Kendall. "Do you have any suggestions?"

"I always liked Clara Belle," said Nana wistfully.

"But that was your cat."

"Yes, but it was a very nice name."

"Uh-huh." Kendall had an unpleasant flashback to cleaning up the carpeting and not being able to get the smell to go away.

"You could just call her Belle. That's a pretty name."

"I could." Still, Kendall wasn't convinced.

"Suzie Belle? Cora Belle?"

"How about Tinkerbell?" said Kendall.

"Tinkerbell!" exclaimed Nana. "From *Peter Pan*." She clapped her hands. "Yes, that is perfect. Little white Tinkerbell."

So it was settled. Kendall wondered what her housemates would think of this new addition to the family. If nothing else, it seemed that Tinkerbell might be a good distraction for them. Instead of focusing on Kendall's messed-up life, they would have a little dog to talk about. Yes, Tinkerbell would make a perfect smokescreen.

Twenty-five

Megan

"Stinkerbell has done it again," declared Megan as she came into the house to find a petite pile of dog poop by the front door.

"Done what?" demanded Kendall as she emerged from the kitchen with her little white pooch cradled in her arms like a baby.

"That," said Megan pointing to the little pile.

"Oh, Tinkerbell," scolded Kendall. "You didn't tell me you needed to go out."

"Well, she did it by the door," said Megan. "Maybe she was trying to tell you, but you just weren't listening."

Kendall frowned. "Having a puppy is harder than I thought it would be."

"And expensive, too," said Megan.

"Thank you for pointing that out—for like the hundredth time."

"Just saying." Megan checked the floor carefully before walking across the living room. Last night Lelani had stepped into a puppy puddle with bare feet. Eeuw. "Did you get the puppy potty pads like Anna told you to do?"

"I haven't been out of the house today," said Kendall.

Not a surprise. Kendall was still in her bathrobe. Even so, Megan was trying to take it easy on her. Lelani had told her how upset Kendall was after the California incident. And then she'd hidden in her room all week. Really, Megan knew she should be more patient.

"Tell you what," said Megan. "If you let me use your car, I'll run to PetSmart and pick the pads up for you."

"Really?" Kendall brightened.

"Yes. My treat, since I got paid today."

"Hey, thanks, Megan. I'd appreciate that."

Megan wanted to add that everyone in the house would appreciate it. Especially if Tinkerbell could actually learn how to use the pads. But she didn't want to sound too negative. She was actually relieved to get away from the house for a little while. Not just to escape the yippy little dog with needlelike teeth that liked to chew on everything, including people's ankles, but Megan hoped to avoid her housemates for a while as well. It was Friday night, but there wasn't much chance that Megan would be going out. Marcus hadn't called, and she didn't expect him to. For that matter, Anna would probably be spending the evening at home too.

Right now Anna and Lelani seemed to be stuck in a silent war. Lelani had tried to talk sense to her, but when Jake broke up with Anna, she blamed Lelani for everything. Finally, Lelani just gave up. Now they avoided each other. Megan couldn't imagine the strain this must be putting on Lelani's relationship with Gil.

It was sad seeing everyone so miserable with Christmas less than a week away. In fact, no one had even mentioned the Christmas party lately. Maybe it would be best to simply cancel the whole thing. But she would leave that to Lelani to decide. The party had been mostly her idea anyway.

Megan picked up the puppy pads, then noticed a craft store nearby. In the window a large sign announced that all Christmas decorations were marked down fifty percent. They'd already put up some decorations, but there was room for a lot more.

Megan was inspired by the spontaneous thought that she might be able to get everyone together by bringing home some really great Christmas decorations that they could all put up. And maybe they would bake some more cookies this weekend. Really, it could be fun. Also, it would be a distraction from the fact that Megan's mom was flying down to Mexico on Sunday, leaving Megan with no family on Christmas for the first time ever.

"You're really okay with this?" her mom had asked her just today when they'd met for lunch at the deli. Her mom had been running last-minute errands, getting everything all ready for her big trip.

"I'm fine," Megan had assured her. Like what was she going to say? *No, Mom, please cancel your vacation and ruin Louise's plans and stick around where it's cold and rainy just so you can stay home and babysit me?* Like that was going to happen.

"I just keep thinking I shouldn't have agreed to this," said Mom. "I'm worried it's a mistake."

"Why?" Megan felt concerned now. "You're not having any bad premonitions about the flight or anything?"

"No, nothing like that."

"No traveler's advisories in Mexico?"

"No. Not at all."

"Then why are you worried?"

"For *you*, sweetheart. I hate leaving you … alone. You know. It's our first Christmas without Dad."

"I'm not alone, Mom. I have my roommates. And we're having our big party. Really, it's going to be a fun Christmas."

"I hope you're not just saying that to make me feel better."

"I'm not." Okay, that was sort of a lie. But on the other hand, it was also a bit of positive thinking. She was being hopeful. It *could* be a fun Christmas.

And maybe reindeer could fly too.

Anyway, Megan decided to hit the craft store, and she hit it hard. She would shop the bargains and, like glad tidings of great joy, she would bring home some happy decorations to cheer everyone up. And why shouldn't she? She loved to decorate and she was good at it. She'd organize a baking party too, and lots of other things. If these women needed someone to pull them out of their doldrums, well, why shouldn't it be Megan? After all, Christmas was the celebration of her Savior's birth—she of all people should be ready to go all out.

After about an hour of gathering up decorations and baking supplies, Megan made her way back home. It was nearly seven and she was hungry but thought maybe she would order a pizza that they could all share while they decorated. She could just imagine how great the garland and bows would look going up the banister with battery-operated candles placed artistically along the way. Then more for the fireplace, and all sorts of wonderful things.

"I thought maybe you'd stolen my car," said Kendall as Megan came in carrying several bags.

"Sorry," said Megan. "I did some shopping."

"That's okay," said Kendall. "I'm not going out tonight anyway."

"Great. Because I got some very cool decorations on sale. And I thought we could all put them up for the party."

"All? As in Anna and Lelani?"

"Are they home?" Megan handed Kendall the puppy pads.

"Oh, yeah, they're home. In their rooms."

"Meaning?"

"Meaning you just missed the fireworks."

"What's going on now?"

"Anna just blew up. Lelani was trying to talk to her and Anna totally lost it. She called Lelani some really bad names." Kendall made a tsk-tsk sound. "Who knew sweet little Anna had such a vocabulary?"

"Poor Anna."

"Don't you mean poor Lelani?" asked Kendall.

"I mean both of them." Megan set the bags down on the dining room table. "So maybe it's not a good night to decorate?"

Kendall shrugged. "Unless you're a magician and can somehow make those two girls get past this."

"Maybe we could put Christmas music on and order some pizza?"

Kendall smacked her lips. "Pizza sounds good."

"Why don't you call it in while I get the rest of the things out of your car?"

"It's a deal."

After Megan brought in her packages, she knocked on Lelani's door.

"Come in," said Lelani in a defeated-sounding voice.

"Want to talk?" asked Megan.

Lelani shrugged, and Megan sat down in the chair across from her bed. "Kendall told me about the fireworks."

"Anna is so angry at me that I don't believe she can even think straight. It's like she blames me for absolutely everything."

"Everything?"

"Well, Jake, for starters. She's convinced I stole his affections and that they'd still be happily together if it weren't for me."

"That's ridiculous."

"And something at work went wrong and she blamed that on me too."

"How is that even possible?"

"She said she's been so distraught over the breakup that she hasn't been focusing on work."

"And that's your fault?"

"Apparently."

"And now she and Gil are in a big fight—over me."

Megan nodded. "You are in a tough spot."

"So I told Gil that I thought we shouldn't see each other until this is ironed out. I encouraged him to speak to Anna, but he told me that's not going to happen. He's willing to talk to her, but she won't listen."

"What a mess."

Lelani nodded sadly.

"Kendall and I ordered pizza—enough for everyone."

"I'm not leaving this room."

"But—"

"No way. If Anna wants to join you guys, great. But I'm not coming out."

"How is that going to help?"

"I don't know. But I'm sorry, I just can't take it anymore." Lelani looked up at Megan with tears in her eyes. "I've never felt such hatred from anyone, Megan."

"Kendall said it was pretty bad."

"I feel like I'm barely hanging on here. I mean, seriously, I'm thinking about going home—and how crazy is that?"

Megan didn't offer an opinion.

"Can you imagine how much the airfare would be right now?"

Megan nodded. "Like a thousand dollars or more?"

"Oh, yeah."

"Maybe you and Kendall can entice Anna to come out and talk to you guys. You know?"

"Maybe so."

"And maybe you can help her to see that I didn't steal Jake from her. The truth is I can't stand him, you know that. But I can't say that to Anna. She still thinks he's so great, that they were a great couple." Lelani held up clenched fists. "I feel like my back's against the wall."

"Well, don't think about it too much. Anna is obviously a little out of control right now."

"I feel bad for her. I really do. But I can't help her."

"Maybe I can."

"I hope so."

"And I'll bring you some pizza when it comes."

Lelani made a weak smile. "Thanks."

"Do you work tomorrow?"

"Oh, yeah. Every day from now until Christmas. It's crunch time."

Megan's attempt to talk to Anna didn't go nearly as well as it had with Lelani. Finally, after Anna told her to leave several times, Megan gave up. "I'm sorry you're having such a hard time with this," she said before she closed the door. "But being angry isn't going to help anything."

"If I need the emotion police to tell me how I should be feeling, I'll be sure to let you know."

Megan quietly closed the door and sighed. So much for the big decorating party. But as she went downstairs, she prayed that God would somehow bring peace and healing to this house.

Ironically, it was Megan and Kendall who shared pizza as they put up decorations together. And, surprisingly, Kendall was actually fairly congenial.

"You're really good at this." Kendall nodded her approval as Megan put the finishing touches on the arrangement over the fireplace. "That looks awesome."

"Thanks. I think decorating is fun."

"Too bad Lelani and Anna didn't want to join us."

"Yeah."

"Seems crazy to go nuts over guys."

Megan peered curiously at Kendall. Hadn't she been freaking over Matthew Harmon a few days ago? Still, Megan wasn't going there. Instead she went to the dining room and tweaked the candle arrangement on the table.

"I mean, look at us, Megan. You kind of stole Marcus from me a few months ago." Kendall took a bottle of red wine out of the wine rack and started to open it.

"Stole?" Megan frowned.

Kendall popped the cork, then set two goblets on the table. "Okay, that's a little strong. The truth is I wasn't really into him."

The rest of the truth was that Marcus hadn't really been into Kendall either. But, once again, Megan wasn't going to point that out.

"But I didn't really hold that against you, did I?"

Megan shrugged. "Well, we haven't exactly been best friends."

"But that could change." Kendall filled both glasses of wine, then held one out to Megan. "Here's to a good Christmas despite everything."

Megan wasn't so sure. Even so, she took the goblet, then held it up. "And here's to peace on earth, and goodwill toward men—and women."

Twenty-six

Anna

Anna got up early on Saturday. It was clear what she needed to do. She pulled out her suitcases and quickly packed them. Then she lugged them downstairs, trying not to be too noisy but at the same time not caring. Why should she? Megan appeared with a cup of coffee as Anna was rolling her two suitcases across the living room.

"Are you taking a trip?" asked Megan.

"No." Anna scowled as she parked her bags by the door.

"Oh." Megan looked confused.

"If you must know, I'm going home." Anna pulled on her coat, buttoned it up, then looped her purse strap over a shoulder with a sense of finality.

"Home? As in back with your parents?"

"Yes."

"For good?" asked Megan. "I mean, are you really moving out?"

"I'm not sure. All I know is I can't live under the same roof as—a certain person who shall go nameless."

Megan rolled her eyes. "Save the drama. We know who you mean."

"Yeah," said Kendall as she came down the stairs. She had on her bathrobe and was carrying the little white dog that had been keeping Anna awake at night with its never-ending whining. "Nobody likes a drama queen, Anna."

Anna felt her temper bubbling to the surface again. Still, she was determined not to lose it. Gil had already told her that he'd sign her up for anger management counseling if she didn't get a grip. That's why she was going home—to get some control and, more importantly, to help her mom. She probably should have told her housemates all about her mom's illness by now, if nothing more than to get a little sympathy. But her mother had sworn their immediate family to silence until after Christmas, when her treatments would begin, her hair would fall out, and she would need Anna's help. Anna was even considering quitting her job. The way things were going at work, they'd probably be relieved to see her go. Still, she didn't want to think about that now.

"So you're running out on us?" asked Kendall after she let her dog out into the backyard. "You do remember that you signed a lease, don't you?"

"That lease didn't include a noisy dog," Anna pointed out. "A dog that's been keeping me awake at night."

Kendall blinked. "Tinkerbell keeps you awake?"

"Yes," snapped Anna. "Don't tell me you can sleep through that constant whining?"

Kendall smiled and reached into her bathrobe pocket, then pulled out what looked like earplugs. "With these I can. Want me to give you a pair?"

"No." Anna just shook her head. "I've had it with this house. And, as far as the lease goes, well, you may be hearing from my lawyer."

Kendall laughed. "Oh, come on, Anna. Don't be such a—"

"Don't tell me what to be!" Anna shouted at her.

Kendall held up both hands. "Calm down."

"Don't tell me to calm down either!"

"Want me to help with your bags?" offered Megan.

"I can get them."

"It's okay," said Megan as she picked up the larger of the suitcases and went out the door.

"Stay in touch," said Kendall lightly. Anna wanted to hit her. She honestly wanted to walk right up to her, take a big swing, and just let her have it. And why? Because her dog was a pest? Because she was sloppy in the bathroom? Because she was Kendall, a spoiled, self-centered, shallow mess of a person?

Anna turned and without saying a thing, grabbed her bag and headed out the door. She slammed it on the way out. But how could she not?

Megan was waiting by Anna's car. "I'm sorry you're feeling so bad, Anna."

Anna pressed her lips together as she unlocked her car and stuffed her bags inside. They barely fit, and she struggled to get the door closed, hoping that Megan might just go back into the house. But she was still there, just looking at Anna with what seemed a sympathetic expression—something else that Anna didn't need right now.

"I hope things get better," said Megan. "And I'm sorry if I wasn't very understanding. If I don't see you before next week, have a good Christmas with your family." It almost looked as if Megan was close to tears.

Anna didn't even know how to respond or what to say. In fact, she didn't trust herself to say anything. She was a nuclear warhead about to explode in every direction. Maybe Gil was right. Maybe she did need anger management. Or maybe she just needed to get away from this nuthouse, make her big escape from Bloomberg Place. She looked up at that house with a lump in her throat and then simply nodded at Megan. "Thanks."

Anna got in her car and slowly drove toward home. It's not that she didn't want to get there, but it was hard to let go of that tiny bit of independence she had gained, in spite of its headaches. But she knew her mom would be thrilled to see her. She would assume that Anna was coming home for good. Maybe she was. Maybe that would be the best for everyone. After all, Anna had struggled a lot, living away from home. She'd managed to alienate herself from all of her housemates. Even Megan seemed bewildered by Anna. She'd made a permanent enemy of Lelani and had even tried to drive a wedge between her and Gil. She knew it was wrong, but she couldn't help herself.

Maybe it was true that pain loves company. Or maybe she was just a drama queen like Kendall had said.

To be fair, sometimes Anna had to admit that she was relieved when Jake broke up with her. Well, relieved and furious. She knew that made no sense, so she'd clung to the furious part, turning on anyone who questioned her, which was just about everyone. Well, everyone except her mother. Mama understood. Mama comforted her.

"What are you doing here?" asked Gil as Anna dragged her bags into the house.

"What does it look like?"

"Like you're losing it?"

She narrowed her eyes at him.

"Seriously, Anna. What are you doing here?"

"Obviously, I'm moving back home." She closed the door behind her.

"Anna?" He frowned down at her and shook his head like he was questioning her sanity. "Why?"

"You know why."

"Because you're enraged at Lelani?"

"No, because of Mom."

"Yeah, right."

"I want to be here for her treatments, Gil."

"Which don't start until after Christmas."

"I want to be home for Christmas."

"Right. And this has nothing to do with Lelani?"

Anna pressed her lips together. Somehow she had to keep her temper controlled. Somehow she had to contain this rage. She'd never been like this, never been the one to fly off the handle, to lose control of her emotions. But that was before.

"If it makes you feel any better," Gil said, "Lelani refuses to see me until this thing with you is resolved."

Okay, that was it—the trigger. "How dare you lay that on me, Gil?"

"Lay what on you?"

"Blame me for Lelani not wanting to see you. *How dare you?*" She was seething now. "Lelani shamelessly flirts with Jake—right here in our home in front of our parents—and then she decides to quit dating you and you have the nerve to blame me!"

"Shh!" He put his finger over his lips. "Keep it down."

"Don't tell me to keep it down after you blast me with something like that, Gil! I'm sure Lelani is telling you all sorts of lies about—"

"Lelani hasn't said one bad thing about you."

"Yeah, right."

"She's told me a thing or two about Jake and—"

"See, that's how sneaky she is. She's trying to play the victim. She's turned everyone against me. Back at the house and even in my own home!" Now Anna was sobbing.

"What is going on out here?" demanded their mother. She came into the foyer looking sleepy and disheveled, pulling her robe on and peering curiously at her children. Anna was sure they probably looked like they were about to engage in a fight like they sometimes had as kids. She wasn't even sure that she wasn't about to lunge at her younger brother and pummel him with her fists.

"Anna is losing her mind, Mom."

"What is wrong, *mi'ja*?" asked Mom as she put her arm around Anna and pulled her close.

"I'm moving back home," sobbed Anna. "And Gil is trying to make me feel bad—he's blaming me for—for whatever's happening between him and Lelani. Everyone is blaming me for everything."

Her mom patted her head. "It's okay, Anna. This whole mess with Jake and Lelani, well, you know it's hard on everyone. Let's not speak of it. It's very upsetting to me, too."

Anna stepped back and looked into her mother's face. "Do you blame me too?"

"No, of course not." She looked at Gil now. "I think we all know who is to blame here. But, please, let's not speak of it."

"Right," said Gil in a sharp tone. "We won't speak of it. We'll just pretend that it's Lelani's fault, even though we all know that Jake is a total jerk, even though everyone except our mixed-up little Anna here is happy to see him go."

"Gil!" Their mom's voice held a warning tone.

"And since Anna is moving back home to help out, I think it's a good time for me to look for someplace else to live." Gil put a hand on his mother's shoulder. "Just to keep the peace around here."

"Oh, Gil," said their mother sadly. "Don't do this."

"I think it's for the best," he told her. "I'll see you at the restaurant, and if you ever need me, you know how to reach me." He was avoiding Anna's eyes now. And she knew he was mad at her. She also knew she probably deserved it. But it was like she was on this runaway train, like she wouldn't be able to get off until it wrecked.

"I'm going to my room," she told her mom. To her chagrin, Gil grabbed both her bags. Before she could stop him, he lugged them up to her room, dumped them on the floor and, without saying a word, left.

Anna closed the door and looked around her room—or what used to be her room. She'd taken all her bedroom furniture to Bloomberg Place, and Mom had refurnished this barren space to serve as an additional guest room. Though it was spacious and attractive, well, in that over-the-top way that Anna's mother was famous for, it didn't feel like Anna's room anymore. She didn't feel at home. She hadn't felt at home in Bloomberg Place either. Maybe she wasn't going to feel at home again ever.

She flopped down on the bed and cried herself to sleep.

The weekend passed quietly at the Mendez house. Gil had, as promised, moved out. As far as Anna knew, he was staying with a friend until an apartment became available. Her parents quietly went about their normal activities, and by Sunday evening, Anna almost felt like she'd been through a time warp: like she'd never moved out, like her mother wasn't sick, like she and Gil still got along. That might've been a good thing, except that it felt like going backward.

Anna reminded herself that this was different, that it had been her choice to come back home, that she was only here to help with her mom, and that she was still an independent woman with her own life, her own career, her own autonomy. And yet she felt somewhat trapped.

So when Monday finally came, despite the stresses that waited for her at the office, Anna was actually relieved to go to work. She tried not to think about the Ramsay Rowan project as she drove to work, tried to block out the fact that Ramsay, the wild child fresh out of rehab, had decided she hated the children's book that Anna had been "helping" her to write. "It's unoriginal and unauthentic," Ramsay's agent had informed Anna's boss. Her day had gone downhill from there.

"How are you doing?" asked Edmond with concerned eyes. It was the first time he'd said anything even slightly personal to her since their breakup.

She shrugged. "Not so great."

"Sorry. Still feeling bad over the Rowan train wreck?"

"That and life in general."

He nodded. "Well, I was sorry to hear the Rowan book fell apart, Anna. I told Rick that it wasn't your fault."

"You did?"

"Yeah. That's the truth. You did everything you could to make that book fly. It was doomed from the get-go."

"Maybe." Anna didn't really want to think or talk about it.

"Anyway, I just wanted to say I'm really sorry."

She peered curiously at him now. It was almost as if he knew more than he was saying. Was he trying to clue her in on something? "Do you think I'll be fired?"

He looked like he didn't want to answer that question. Or maybe he just didn't know. But he simply shrugged. "No, I don't think so, Anna. They wouldn't do that. Not just a few days before Christmas, anyway."

"That's not too comforting." She wanted to say something more. In fact, she wanted to apologize to him. But for what? She'd already told him she was sorry for hurting him when she'd broken things off. Now she was sorry that she'd let him go. What had she been thinking? How could she have chosen Jake over Edmond? What was wrong with her? As he slowly walked away, she watched. She liked the way his loose khaki slacks were a little too long. She liked his tweedy jackets and nubby sweaters. She even liked his dark-rimmed glasses and shaggy hair. Why had she given that up? Edmond was good for her. She'd been happy with him. And then she'd thrown it all away for Jake. Jake the Snake. She was such a little fool!

Twenty-seven

Lelani

"Two more shopping days until Christmas," said Megan as she rinsed her coffee cup and set it in the sink.

"Thanks for the reminder," said Lelani. "Like I needed it."

"Sorry." Megan made a sheepish grin. "Couldn't resist."

Lelani sighed as she filled her mug with coffee. "I guess I should be glad. I mean, two days and the madness will be over."

"Well, then you have returns day," Megan reminded her.

"With friends like you—"

"Sorry," said Megan. "I think that Vera is rubbing off on me."

"You mean the Wicked Witch of the West?"

Megan nodded. "Yes, I saw a bumper sticker that I'd love to sneak onto her car."

"What's that?"

"It said, 'I haven't been myself since that house fell on my sister.'"

Lelani laughed so hard that she nearly inhaled coffee into her nose. "Thanks, Megan, I needed that."

"Has Gil said anything about Anna?" Megan put on her coat. "Like whether she's ever coming back?"

"No." Lelani added a little more cream to her coffee. "Actually, I still haven't heard from Gil this week."

"So he's taking your ultimatum seriously?"

269

"Either that or he's fed up with me too."

"Are you still up for the Christmas Eve party?"

Everything in Lelani wanted to say no as she followed Megan out through the dining room. But she'd already invited Mr. Green and a few other loners from work. Not that she knew whether they were coming. "We might as well do it," she said. "I mean, the house looks great and we've already gotten some food and things. Besides, what else would we do for Christmas Eve? Just sit around and feel sorry for ourselves?"

Megan slipped the strap of her bag over her shoulder and nodded. "And it'll probably be a lot of fun. We'll make a big fire in the fireplace and sing Christmas carols and drink eggnog and the works."

"Yeah." Lelani forced a smile for Megan's sake. "It'll be great."

"Uh-oh," said Megan as she opened the front door. "Here comes Stinkerbell, the escape artist dog."

"I'll take her out back." Lelani snagged the little white fluff ball as Megan went out the door. "Come on, you silly dust mop," she said as she carried Tinkerbell through the house. "I don't know why your mommy doesn't get up and let you out herself, but at least you're trying to be a good dog." Lelani opened the back door and Tinkerbell shot out. Lelani watched as the dog attended to her business, and then she let her back into the house. "I'll bet you'd like some breakfast, too," said Lelani. Tinkerbell wagged her tail, which wagged her whole body, and Lelani followed her to the kitchen, where the doggy feeding station was set up.

"Oh, there you are, Tinkerbell." Kendall walked groggily into the kitchen, then let out a long yawn. "Did you let her out already?" she asked Lelani.

"Yes. And she did her thing."

"Thanks. I was coming, but I had to do my thing too." Kendall poured a cup of coffee, then smelled it and made a face. "Does this smell bad to you?"

Lelani sniffed her own mug, then shook her head. "No. I was actually enjoying it, but thanks for pointing that out."

"Oh."

Lelani waited for her toast to pop up, then buttered it and even put on a thick layer of pineapple marmalade. She took it to the dining room to eat it with her vanilla-bean yogurt. She had exactly thirty minutes before she needed to leave the house and she planned to enjoy every second of it.

"Pretty busy at work this week?" asked Kendall as she joined her.

"That's an understatement."

"I hate to keep bugging you," began Kendall, "but have you heard anything from Anna?"

"I don't know why you guys think that I'd hear from her. She hates me more than anyone right now."

"Well, it's because of your relationship with Gil. I just wondered if I should put an ad in the paper for her room. I mean, I really do need that rent money."

"There's nothing I can tell you, Kendall. Why don't you call Anna yourself?"

"Yeah. I'll do that."

Just then Tinkerbell dashed through the dining room and begged for Kendall to pick her up and put her on her lap. The pooch sat across from Lelani with what looked like a canine smile across her furry face. "Hey, little girl," cooed Kendall. "Did you eat all your breakfast?"

Lelani couldn't help but smile at Tinkerbell. "She's really a good dog," she told Kendall. "But if you don't get up when she gets up, you can't blame her for making a mess."

Kendall groaned. "Yeah, I'm working on it. I just didn't sleep that great. And then I really had to make a run for the bathroom myself."

Lelani nodded. Actually, she thought that it was good for Kendall to have this dog to take care of. Maybe she'd become more responsible and grow up. At least she was getting out of bed a little earlier now, but Kendall still had a ways to go.

"I think we'll dress you up in your lavender outfit," said Kendall to her dog. "And then we'll take a little walkie."

"Sounds like you girls have a big day ahead," said Lelani as she finished her last bite of yogurt and the final sip of coffee. "Have a good one." Then she headed back to her room to enjoy her last few minutes of solitude and silence. She also used this time to meditate on God and to say a little prayer. She'd been trying to do this every day for the past couple of weeks. And on the days when she forgot, she regretted it. She knew that she needed that time—kind of a centering of her spirit.

Today she asked God to give her extra patience with those last-minute Christmas shoppers. Then, as she'd been doing the last few days, she asked God to help iron out the conflict between her and Gil and Anna. Then she took in a long, deep breath and said, "Amen." She wasn't sure if anyone else would think that her prayers were "real," but they felt real to her. Besides, prayer gave her hope—not just for her day, but for her life in general.

✠

"It's going to be a busy day," said Mr. Green after Lelani closed her locker.

She pinned her employee nametag in place. "Yes, but that's good, right?"

He smiled. "Of course. But we might need you to double up some, Lelani. If you see accessories getting swamped, you might pop over and lend a hand."

"Absolutely." She nodded as if this was an original idea, but the truth was she'd been doing this for about a week now.

"Have a good day."

She echoed this back at him, then headed to the floor, where the store was already buzzing like a beehive. The best part about the busyness of the holiday season was that it helped to pass the time more quickly. Lelani's least favorite part of this job was standing around on a slow day—watching the minutes tick by like hours and wondering why she was working in a department store instead of attending med school. But when it was busy, she didn't have time to wonder or think.

Before she knew it, it was nearly time for her lunch break. She was just getting ready to leave the floor when she noticed a middle-aged blond woman in a corner of the accessories section. Lelani blinked and looked again. It looked like the woman had just shoved something inside of her jacket. Was it possible that the woman was shoplifting? The weird thing was the woman was nicely dressed, had what appeared to be an expensive bag, and didn't really seem like a needy person. But then Lelani remembered the profiles of shoplifters. They weren't always as they appeared. So she moved near a post where she could watch the woman without being seen. Sure enough, this woman was shoving belts and scarves inside of her jacket and purse. With shaking hands, Lelani dialed security, then from her concealed position described the woman and waited. But before security showed up, the woman began making her way toward an exit. Lelani decided to cut her off.

"Excuse me," said Lelani with a nervous smile. "Can I help you?"

"I don't need any help," said the woman. "I'm on my way out."

"No," said Lelani. "I think you do need some help."

The woman narrowed her eyes. "And I think you are an obnoxious young woman."

They were nearly to the door now, but Lelani put her hand on the woman's arm. "Please, wait a—"

"Get your hands off me!" shouted the woman.

Lelani stepped back. "But I just—"

"I'm going to report you to the manager," snapped the woman with one hand on the door. "I'll file a complaint against you and—" She stopped when a security guard stepped between her and Lelani. The woman knew her game was over.

"Please, come with me," he told her.

"But I—"

"You can come quietly or we can do it the hard way," he said in a no-nonsense voice. "The police are on their way."

The woman glared at Lelani now. It was a hateful, evil kind of stare, like this whole scene was Lelani's fault.

"It's okay," the guard told Lelani. "I'll handle it from here."

Lelani nodded and backed away. But her knees were shaking so badly that it felt like she could barely walk in a straight line.

"Good job," said Mr. Green as he joined her. Then he peered curiously at her. "Are you okay?"

"Just shaken."

He actually put his hand under her elbow now, guiding her along. "It's a nasty business catching a thief," he said. "But unfortunately it's becoming part of the retail business."

"Right."

Back in the break room, she still felt uneasy and her stomach was tied in a knot, although she wasn't shaking so much. It was hard to forget that horrible look the woman had given her. Lelani looked around the crowded break room. Everyone was chattering, acting like it was just another ordinary day, but all Lelani could think about was that she'd sent a woman to jail just two days before Christmas.

She needed to get out of there. She grabbed her bag and coat and headed out, pressing through clogs of stressed-looking shoppers until she was finally outside and able to breathe. She walked down the street, trying to get her bearings, trying to remember why she'd come to Oregon, why she'd taken a job at Nordstrom, why her life made sense. Finally, she knew she just needed to pray again.

She stood in line at a deli and ordered a cup of vegetable-beef soup, which she ate standing because the place was so crowded. Just as she was finishing up, her cell phone rang. To her relief it was Gil.

"Oh, Gil!" she exclaimed happily. "You can't believe how good it is to hear your voice."

"Really?"

"Are you nuts?" She sighed as she tossed the disposable soup bowl into the trash, then went outside. "I have missed you so much."

"Does that mean we can talk … even if Anna is still mad at you?"

"Is she?"

"To be honest, I don't know. But I do have some good news."

"What?"

"Well, it was good news to me, but I think you need to hear the rest of the story first." Then he quickly told her how his mother had thought she had cancer and how their whole family had been derailed by this news. "I found out about it the day you and I went up to Hood."

"Oh, no," she said. "That's horrible. Your poor mother. I'm so—"

"But wait. That was just the backstory. The good news is that it was a mistake."

"What?"

"When my mom went back to the doctor, he told her that some-how the lab reports were wrong or mixed up or something. Anyway, she doesn't have cancer. She's perfectly fine."

"Really?"

"Yes. Of course, it would've been nice if she'd told us about it sooner."

"But how could she? I mean if she didn't know."

"She found out last week. And she didn't tell anyone. Not Anna or me or even our dad."

"Oh." Lelani frowned.

"I think she was enjoying all the attention."

"But it must've been so stressful for everyone. Maybe that's why Anna was, well, you know, kind of overreacting about the thing with Jake."

"You could be right. The fact is Anna has been under a lot of pres-sure from every direction. Not just from Jake and Mom, but according to my dad, her job's been stressful too."

"Poor Anna."

"Well, at least she should be feeling a little better about our mom now."

"Yes. That must be a huge relief."

"And we're speaking again," he said. "That's a relief too."

"For me, too." She wanted to talk longer and to tell him all about the shoplifter episode, but she knew it was time to get back to work. "I have to go, Gil. But it's great hearing your voice."

The store was even busier when Lelani returned. And she hadn't been on the floor for more than twenty minutes when she saw another suspicious-looking woman in accessories. But as she studied the woman, she thought maybe she was imagining things. Just because the woman was dressed somewhat shabbily didn't mean she was stealing. Lelani had seen a similar woman before, who had turned out to be a genuine shopper. On the other hand, Mr. Green had just informed Lelani that the shoplifter she'd turned in this morning had nearly two thousand dollars worth of merchandise on her. Unbelievable!

Still, Lelani couldn't help but watch as the woman slowly meandered around the accessories department. And it seemed she was looking over her shoulder occasionally. Finally, Lelani decided to go check it out.

"Can I help you?" she asked the older woman. She was probably in her sixties, with kind eyes and faded brown hair tinged with gray.

The woman blinked. "Oh, I'm just looking, dear."

Lelani smiled. "Well, let me know if I can help you." Then she straightened up a stack of scarves and slowly walked away. Maybe the old woman was legit. Lelani went back to help a customer who was standing at her counter. She nearly forgot about the old woman, but just as she was handing the customer her bag, Lelani saw it. The old woman had slipped something—it looked like a wallet—into her purse, then glanced furtively around and started to make for the door.

Everything in Lelani wanted to pretend she hadn't seen this. But she knew she needed to do her part. So Lelani cut the old woman off at the exit.

"Excuse me," she said quietly.

The old woman looked scared now, her hands clutching her handbag nervously. Lelani was about to escort the woman directly to customer service, but stopped as the woman looked directly into her eyes. In that instant, Lelani felt this woman's desperation, her fear, her regret, her sadness.

And somehow Lelani knew she was not dealing with a habitual thief.

"I—I'm sorry," stammered the woman. "I knew it was—"

"I just noticed that you may have accidentally picked up something that you forgot to pay for," said Lelani. She knew this wasn't what she was supposed to do, but it felt like the only thing she could do.

The woman nodded with wide eyes. "Yes, yes—I think you're right."

Lelani cleared her throat. "And if you'd just like to put it back, well ..." She glanced over her own shoulder now, then turned back to the woman with a smile. "I think it would be okay."

"Yes—yes—I would like to do that. Thank you!"

So Lelani followed the woman back to the wallet section, and she pretended to be showing her something as the woman fumbled to remove the stolen wallet from her purse and set it back down. Lelani could see that there was no other merchandise in the woman's purse.

"I feel so ashamed." The woman looked up at Lelani with tears in her eyes. "But my daughter-in-law Vivian ... she has such expensive taste, and she always goes on about how Nordstrom is the best store. I could never afford anything from a place like this, or anything fine enough to suit Vivian. And this Christmas, well, money is so tight, and I'm on my own with only my Social Security."

"And I'm sure you'll never do anything like this again."

"Oh, no." The woman solemnly shook her head. "I've never stolen a thing before and I don't even know what made me do it now. Besides desperation." She sighed. "I thought if I had a lovely present to take to her, perhaps I would be more welcome in her house for Christmas. And it's hard being alone, at Christmastime especially."

Lelani felt shocked by this. "You mean you're not welcome in her house if you don't bring an expensive gift?"

"My daughter-in-law is, I hate to say it, but a bit of a snob." The woman pulled a handkerchief from her purse and blotted her eyes.

"Well, she sounds foolish to me," said Lelani. "And if you have nowhere to go for Christmas, I will invite you to my Christmas party."

The woman looked stunned. "Really? You don't even know me."

"I can see that you're a good person." Lelani stuck out her hand now. "I'm Lelani Porter. And we're having a Christmas Eve party over on Bloomberg Place."

"I know where that is." The woman still looked shocked. "I'm Frances Miller. And if you really mean it I would love to come. You seem like such a dear, sweet girl."

So Lelani gave her the details, which weren't many. "Now I should get back to work."

"And I should get out of this store," said Frances. "It's far too expensive for me."

"Me too," admitted Lelani.

Twenty-eight

Kendall

"So tomorrow's the big night," said Kendall in a flat voice. She and Megan and Lelani were sitting around the dining room table. They'd just finished dinner—a mishmash of leftovers and Kendall's sorry attempt to make macaroni and cheese from a box. Now Megan wanted them to discuss the Christmas Eve party as well as make a guest list, which Kendall thought was a little ridiculous.

"Who do we know is coming for sure?" asked Megan as she picked up a pen.

"Besides Nana, who said she plans to be here, I don't have anyone to put on the list. Everyone I invited seems to have other plans," admitted Kendall. Okay, she didn't admit that she'd lost all interest in this party. But at least she was trying to be a good sport for Megan's and Lelani's sakes.

"I invited Mr. Green, who would like to come, as well as a couple others from work, although they haven't confirmed yet," said Lelani. "And, oh yeah, a shoplifter named Frances."

"A shoplifter?" Kendall felt alarmed. "You've invited a thief to my home?"

"She's a sweet lady. She'd never stolen anything before, and she didn't even steal anything today. She just needs a friend."

"I invited Mrs. Fowler," said Megan, "one of my clients who's alone at Christmas."

"I didn't invite Gil yet," said Lelani, "or reinvite him. But I will."

"What about Anna?" asked Kendall. "I left her a message, but she hasn't called back."

"I don't know what's up with her," said Lelani. "But I don't think we can count on her coming to the party, if that's what you mean."

Kendall frowned. What she really wanted to know was whether she could she count on Anna to pay her January rent. More and more Kendall felt like she was on a sinking ship, steadily going down. Losing Anna's rent money wasn't going to help. Besides this, she had no idea what she'd tell her parents. So far, she'd held her mother at bay by acting mysterious. But that couldn't last forever.

"There's this homeless woman I see on my way to work every day," said Megan, "I was thinking of inviting her."

"Are you serious?" Kendall couldn't believe this. "Shoplifters and homeless people—you have got to be kidding."

Megan shrugged. "Maybe I'll just invite her to the mission on Christmas Day. I'm helping to serve dinner there."

"Why do you want to do that?" asked Kendall. All she could imagine was dirty, smelly people lined up for a free handout. Of course, she realized that at the rate she was going, she might be eating there too before long.

"Because it's a good thing to do," said Megan.

"And you are such a good girl to do it," said Kendall. "Maybe Santa will put something extra special in your stocking."

Megan sort of rolled her eyes, but didn't respond.

"So is that all of our guests?" Lelani frowned. "Doesn't seem like much."

"Let's see," said Megan. "There's Nana, Mr. Green, the shoplifter

lady, Mrs. Fowler, and possibly Gil—counting us, that makes a whopping total of eight."

"Wow," said Kendall sarcastically. "We're gonna rock the house."

They all just sat there looking at each other.

"Oh, come on," said Lelani. "It's not that bad."

"And maybe we can all be on the lookout for others to ask," said Megan.

"Like more homeless people and shoplifters," suggested Kendall.

"It reminds me of a parable."

"Huh?" Kendall frowned. "A pair of what?"

"A parable, a story that Jesus told."

"Go for it," said Lelani.

"Well, a wealthy guy is throwing this big party and he invites all his
important friends to come, but no one shows up."

"Some friends," said Kendall. She had friends like that herself.

"So, he sends his servants out to ask other people to come, not just
important ones, but they don't come either."

"Maybe the guy throwing the party is a big jerk," suggested
Kendall. "And no one really likes him."

Megan frowned. "I'm not sure about that. Anyway, the guy then
sends his servants out to the streets to find street people, you know, like
homeless people and shoplifters and down-and-outers."

"And?" Lelani leaned forward with interest.

"And they came."

"So?" said Kendall.

"Is that supposed to mean something?" asked Lelani.

"It means that the people on the streets really appreciated being
invited, because they were down on their luck and they liked getting a
good meal," said Megan.

"So we should go invite street people to our party?" asked Kendall.

"No, I'm not saying that. I'm just saying this situation reminded me of that parable."

"But what does it mean?" persisted Lelani.

"The parable?" Megan seemed to consider this. "Well, I think it means that God has really great things in store for us—like the best party ever—but maybe it's just the people who realize they're poor and needy and hungry who will have the sense to come to his party."

"Wow," said Lelani. "That actually makes sense."

"It does?" Kendall frowned. It didn't really make sense to her. "Are you saying that God only likes poor, needy people?" Of course, even as she said this, she couldn't deny that not only was she poor and needy, she was going down.

"God loves everyone," said Megan. "But it means that we have to realize we need God—that we're like poor, homeless people without him—and then we get to go to his party."

Lelani nodded. "That's cool."

"But back to our party," said Megan. "How about if we all do what we can to think of other people to invite. Sometimes people change their minds at the last minute."

So they all agreed, but Kendall knew for a fact she was not inviting anyone. How could she? Her friends would think she'd lost her mind if they showed up here to find shoplifters, homeless people, and old ladies. No, it was better to just get this thing over with. When no one was looking, she would spike the eggnog and pour brandy over the fruitcake.

Megan

"Here you go," said Megan as she handed the homeless woman a booklet of McDonald's coupons and a five-dollar bill. "Merry Christmas."

The woman grinned. "Thank you!"

"And there's Christmas dinner at the mission tomorrow," said Megan. "I'm going to be there. I hope you'll come too."

The woman nodded as if she was considering this. "Merry Christmas to you too, dear," she called out. "God bless you!"

Cynthia handed Megan a Christmas bonus and told her to go home at noon. "There's nothing we can do around here anyway." So Megan's plan was to help get things ready for the party. Not that there was much to get ready.

"You're home early," said Kendall when Megan came in.

"Looks like someone slept in," said Megan as she hung up her coat. Kendall was still in her robe and slippers, sitting on the sectional with Tinkerbell in her lap.

Kendall made a face. "I'm having a slow morning, okay?"

"Except that it's afternoon now," pointed out Megan.

"Thanks for setting me straight on that."

Megan went to her room, quickly closing the door when she heard the sound of Tinkerbell's feet tapping down the hallway after her. That mischievous dog had already sneaked into Megan's room and chewed up a paperback book. No way was Megan letting her in now. Megan flopped down on her bed and let out a deep sigh. This was going to be one lousy Christmas. She wondered if her mom was having fun down in sunny Mexico with Louise. And why *wouldn't* she be having fun? Why *shouldn't* she? Really, Megan wanted her to have a good time. She wanted her to come home happy and refreshed.

Still, Megan couldn't help but feel envious. And lonely. And sad. Then she remembered the parable she'd told her housemates last night. Well, at least she should be welcome at God's party. She was like one of those needy street people. Maybe not financially, but emotionally. She closed her eyes and tried to imagine what God's fabulous Christmas celebration might be like—probably far more incredible than anything she could dream up. At least that was something to look forward to.

❮●❯

"Wake up, sleepyhead," said Lelani.

Megan sat up and blinked. "Huh?"

"It's Christmas Eve, remember. We need to get things ready for our party."

Megan nodded. "Oh, yeah, the big party. What time is it?"

"It's just past four. But we have things to do."

So Megan trudged out and followed Lelani to the kitchen, where the countertops were covered with various serving dishes—and far more food than eight people could possibly consume. Kendall, now dressed in sweats, was glumly arranging cheese and crackers on a red platter, and Christmas music was playing in the background. Oh, so festive.

"Merry Christmas," said Kendall in an unenthusiastic voice.

"Let the fun begin." Megan picked up a bag of veggies and dumped them in the colander to wash.

"Come on, you guys," urged Lelani. "It's Christmas. You're supposed to be merry."

"Yeah," Kendall directed this to Megan. "She's all giddy because Gil is coming tonight."

"Well, I'm glad someone is happy," said Megan.

They worked quietly together in the kitchen. And although Lelani made several attempts to cheer them up, the general feeling was not jolly. And by the time they were arranging the food platters on the dining table, Megan felt like this whole party idea was not only a waste of time and money, but an exercise in futility.

"At least we have food," said Kendall as she popped a deviled egg into her mouth.

"And we're sure to have leftovers," added Megan.

"Fine," said Lelani, shaking her finger at Megan. "Kendall can be the Grinch and you can be Scrooge. Have at it."

"I'm sorry," said Megan. "I'll try harder."

"Why don't we all go change into party clothes?" suggested Lelani. "I mean we can at least look like we're having fun, right?"

"Sure," said Kendall without a speck of cheer. "We can do that."

"And dress Tinkerbell up too," said Lelani.

"Yeah. Whatever."

Megan was starting to feel guilty as she went back to her room. Here Lelani was trying so hard, and Megan was acting like a spoiled brat. It even seemed like Megan's bad attitude was rubbing off on Kendall. And not that long ago, Kendall had been enthused over this little event.

As Megan brushed out her hair and applied some lip gloss, she decided it was time to put on her party face as well. No more pity parties, feeling jealous of her mom or missing her dad. No more questioning whether Marcus was thinking about her or not. She needed to buck up, and somehow she'd get through this. It wouldn't be long before the Christmas holidays were just a memory and life would go on. Besides, she reminded herself, this is what came from having high expectations.

As Megan headed back out she heard someone at the door, but it was too early for guests. Then she saw that it was Anna, and that she'd let herself in. With her luggage in tow, it appeared that Anna planned to stay.

"Hey, Anna," said Megan happily. "What are you doing?"

"Making amends," said Anna. "Is Lelani around?"

"Yeah." Megan hurried back to find that Lelani was already coming out of her room.

"It's Anna," whispered Megan. "She said she's come to make amends."

Lelani's eyes lit up. "Really?"

Megan walked back through the living room to make herself scarce in the dining room, but Anna stopped her.

"Please stay, Megan. I think everyone should hear this."

"Even me?" asked Kendall. She'd been lurking in the kitchen.

"Yes." Anna nodded. "I want to apologize to all three of you. I'm really sorry for the way I treated everyone. I was just very confused and I believed some things that weren't true. And I hope you'll all forgive me."

"Of course we will," said Lelani.

"Absolutely," agreed Megan.

"Not so quick," said Kendall. "I want to hear the rest of the story."

So Anna explained about her mother's cancer scare. Anna had been so terribly worried, which was why she'd moved home. "But it was only one reason," she told them. And then she explained about how enraged she'd been with Lelani. "It was so undeserved, Lelani. I'm so sorry. It's as if I was delusional or something."

"You were worried about your mother," Megan pointed out. "It impaired your rationale."

"Maybe, but I can't believe I actually thought Lelani was trying to steal Jake from me." Anna shook her head. "Jake the Snake. Why would Lelani even want him? Just the same, I blamed her for the breakup. And then I got mad at Gil—I think I was mad at almost everyone—and mostly myself." Anna looked at them with damp eyes. "It was like I was digging this deep dark hole in my parents' house, and I couldn't get out. I was so miserable."

Lelani patted Anna's arm. "I'm so sorry."

"The whole while, I was making a slave of myself for my mother," continued Anna. "I was so worried about her. And she could see I was miserable, but she wouldn't even tell me the truth. She'd known almost from the start that there'd been a mix-up in lab reports." Anna was crying now. "My mother's health was perfectly fine, she was just taking advantage of me, holding me hostage, and the whole time I felt like I was dying."

Soon they were all hugging. "It's like every single part of my life was a mess." Anna wiped her eyes. "I wanted to hold things together, but everything was falling completely apart."

Megan patted her on the back. "I think we've all been there."

"I'm so glad you came home!" cried Lelani as she hugged Anna again. "I've missed you so much."

"Does that mean you're moving back in for good?" asked Kendall. She was eyeing Anna's heap of luggage with what Megan thought was a hopeful expression.

"If it's okay."

"Hey, it's better than okay," said Kendall. "We all missed you."

"My mom is furious," said Anna. "Not that I care."

"I was worried about the cancer scare too," said Lelani quietly. "I'm so glad she's okay."

"Me too. But I'm still really mad. It's like she had us all under her thumb because of her big, fat lies—her narcissistic need for attention."

"Wow," said Kendall, "that's pretty extreme."

Megan bit her tongue to prevent reminding Kendall about the time she had lied and disappeared and strung all her housemates along just for the sake of attention. After all, it was Christmas. Bygones should probably remain bygones.

Soon the other guests arrived. And while everyone was cordial and seemed to enjoy the food and drinks, it was a very strange mix of people. Mrs. Fowler and Lelani's shoplifting friend, Frances, seemed to hit it off and were happily visiting over on the sectional. But Mr. Green seemed clearly uncomfortable with the small group and only stayed long enough to sample a few appetizers before he politely made an excuse to leave. It was barely seven thirty when the shuttle service picked up Kendall's Nana and returned her to the nursing home, where Megan suspected that a much merrier celebration was taking place. Shortly after that, Mrs. Fowler offered Frances a ride in her taxi, and then it was only the four housemates and Gil.

"I feel like odd man out here," said Gil. "Not that I mind being with you lovely women."

"Quite the party, isn't it?" Kendall set aside her eggnog and yawned. Megan was surprised that Kendall hadn't imbibed more tonight. But she hadn't really seemed much like her party-girl self lately. Maybe she was still grieving her lost romance. Or maybe she was starting to grow up.

Anna got up and tossed another log onto the fire, then sighed. "Maybe this party was a flop, but it's good to be back just the same."

Lelani nodded. "And good to have you back."

"Anyway, I hate to be a party pooper," continued Gil, "but I told the parents that I'd stop by before it got too late."

"Well, it's certainly not too late," teased Megan.

"Give them my best," said Anna firmly. "Because there's no way I'm going home tonight or anytime soon."

"That's okay," said Gil as he patted her on the head. "I think you've paid your dues, Sis."

"And then some." Anna refilled her eggnog glass and took a swig.

"Merry Christmas," called out Megan as Gil got his coat. Lelani walked him to the door, then out to the porch. The rest of them stood around the dining room table as if unsure what to do next, with only the sound of Christmas music and the wood crackling on the fire.

"So that's it, then," said Kendall when Lelani rejoined them. "Our big, whopping Christmas party."

"It was sweet," said Lelani.

"Sweet for you, maybe," said Kendall. "Since you're the only one with a guy around."

"You don't need a guy around to have a good time," argued Megan, even though she'd been missing Marcus just moments earlier. Despite her resolve not to, she was wondering why she'd broken it off with him. Was it because of what silly Gwen Phillips told her? Even Megan's mother had questioned that advice.

"Right!" Kendall laughed sarcastically as she slapped Megan on the back. "And just look at you, Little Miss Sunshine, why you're just the life of the party tonight."

"That's not why I'm feeling low," said Megan.

"Then why?" demanded Kendall as she filled a glass of eggnog and handed it to Megan.

"Well, if you must know, there are several reasons," began Megan. "For one thing, this is my first Christmas without my dad." Megan paused as the impact of those words slammed into her. Still, she didn't want to start crying. "And that's—that's not easy. My dad and I were close. I miss him." Her housemates gathered around Megan, and she could feel their empathy as they nodded and patted her on the shoulder. So she decided to tell them everything, just spill the works. "And for another thing, I'm feeling slightly envious of my mom, who's down in Mexico, and I guess I'm missing her too." She started to cry now and her voice grew raspy. "And … I can hardly stand to admit this, but I'm missing Marcus too. And I-I'm thinking maybe I was stupid to break up with him—just because of something this dumb girl said to me." Anna and Lelani looked at Kendall now, like it was her fault. "No one here," said Megan quickly. "Just someone I shouldn't have listened to. And now I'm feeling sad that I did."

They all circled her in a group hug, and she felt loved and a little bit better. Anna handed her a reindeer napkin to blow her nose on.

"Okay, if we're confessing what's making us blue, I have some things to say too," declared Anna.

"Go for it," said Lelani.

"Yeah, you go, girl," urged Kendall.

Anna refilled her eggnog glass and took a big sip as if it was going to strengthen her. "Well, as you all know, I'm fairly enraged at my mother, and that does not feel very nice—especially at Christmas when families are supposed to be together. Sure, I'm relieved she's okay, but I can't believe she tricked me like that. And then besides all that mess"—Anna took a deep breath—"I may be getting fired right after the holidays."

"No way," said Megan. She knew how seriously Anna took her job. Of the four of them, Anna was the only one with the sort of career that she'd actually planned.

"Seriously?" Kendall looked genuinely concerned too. Or maybe she was simply calculating the potential of lost rent money.

"Yes. I blew a really important project at work. So it's possible there'll be a pink slip for me early next week. I might have to move back home after all." Tears were spilling down Anna's cheeks now, and Megan handed her a Santa napkin.

"That's really rough." Megan placed a hand on Anna's shoulder.

"But you know what the worst part is?" blurted Anna. "I mean the thing that has me the most bummed? It's that I really *do* care about Edmond. He's the greatest guy. And I-I'm the one who dumped him— I let Edmond go for—for Jake the Snake!" Her voice cracked. "Oh, how could I have been so stupid?"

Now they all gathered around Anna as she sobbed, assuring her that it was going to be okay. "Edmond is crazy about you," said Lelani. "We've all seen it in his eyes."

"And even if you lose your job," said Megan, "I'm sure you'll find something else that's even better. You're so smart, Anna."

Anna attempted a shaky smile as she blotted her tears with the napkin. "Thanks, you guys. I'm so glad I have friends."

"Okay," said Kendall loudly. "It's my turn to spill my guts and, trust me, you guys better brace yourselves."

They all turned to look at Kendall, and Megan figured that she was about to go into drama queen mode, crying about how heartbroken she was over Matthew Harmon not leaving his wife for her—yada yada blah blah blah. In fact, that's how Kendall started, saying she'd done all she could, but it just didn't work. But then she started to cry, sobbing really loudly like she'd just had her leg amputated or something.

Lelani was the only one showing much mercy. She put a hand on Kendall's shoulder and nodded. "Yeah, that's hard," she said quietly.

"But that's not the worst part—not the worst thing," Kendall burst out. "The worst thing is that I think I'm pregnant."

Everyone got very quiet. The only sounds came from the fire, the Christmas music, and Kendall's choking sobs. They were gathered around Kendall with wide, concerned eyes, but no one spoke. Megan couldn't think of a single thing to say. What could she possibly say that would make Kendall feel better?

"Are you sure?" Lelani finally said quietly.

"I haven't taken a test. But my period is always on time and this time it's late, very late. And my body feels different. I mean my boobs are sore and I have to pee all the time. And all I want to do is sleep. Okay, that's not so different. But the smell of coffee—it makes me want to hurl."

"Oh, man," said Lelani. "That sounds like the real deal to me."

Anna handed Kendall several napkins, then just shook her head. "I'm sorry."

Kendall broke into fresh sobs now, and they gathered around her in another group hug. As Megan patted Kendall's back, she couldn't help but remember how Kendall had complained so bitterly about kids not long ago. Megan remembered how Kendall had sworn she'd never have children—and now this?

"It's going to be okay," said Anna in a voice that sounded more confident than her expression. "We're your friends, Kendall. We'll help you."

"And you'll get through this," Lelani assured her. "I know it seems scary right now, but you'll get through it."

"How?" demanded Kendall with red-rimmed eyes and smudged mascara. "How can you possibly know that?"

Lelani cleared her throat. "Because … I've been through it myself."

"Okay. I need to sit down!" Anna shook her head, then headed toward the living room. "This is making my head spin and I don't think it has to do with the eggnog, which I'm pretty sure Kendall spiked."

Megan followed her, and soon they were all sitting around the sectional, including Tinkerbell, who had hopped onto Kendall's lap and snuggled down into a small white fluff ball. And they were all looking at Lelani.

"I've been trying to think of a way to tell you guys," she began slowly. "But it's not exactly easy …" For the next several minutes, Lelani poured out an incredible story of how she'd been involved with a doctor and how he'd pretended to be single but wasn't. She became pregnant, and he wanted nothing to do with her. It all made no sense and yet it made perfect sense. All the mystery surrounding Lelani, her unexplainable sadness, her quitting med school and working at a low-level job at Nordstrom…. Suddenly Megan got it—Lelani had been running from her life.

"Does Gil know about this?" demanded Anna. Her dark eyes flashed with fiery anger again, and Megan was worried they were about to go straight back to where they'd just come from.

Lelani nodded somberly. "I've told him everything."

Anna seemed to soften a bit now. "Is that why you guys were shopping for baby things?"

Lelani looked puzzled. "How did you know that?"

"My mother found out from a friend who happens to be our cousin Brad's mother-in-law." Anna shook her head. "That's how our family works, Lelani, and if you're serious about Gil you better get used to it." Then Anna slapped her forehead. "Oh, mama mia! Wait until my mother hears about *this!* She was freaking over the possibility that you and Gil were expecting—"

"Gil and me?" Lelani looked shocked.

"I'm sure Gil will explain it all later."

"But your baby, Lelani," persisted Kendall. "Where is it?"

"My baby's in Maui with my parents. She's seven months old now," Lelani spoke calmly, as if calculating every word. "Her name is Emma. I haven't seen her since she was a couple of weeks old. And I'm afraid my mother is going to be so attached to her that I'll never get her back."

"You *want* her back?" Kendall's brow creased.

Lelani pressed her hands to her flushed cheeks. "I don't know *what* I want. Sometimes I think I do. I think I want her and that I want to be a mother. And then I ask myself, What can I give her? And then I don't know." Lelani shook her head as silent tears streaked down her cheeks. "I just don't know."

Now they all gathered around Lelani on the sectional, wrapping their arms around her. Most of them were crying too. Megan couldn't remember a stranger Christmas, and yet something about it was very sweet too. Bittersweet.

The group hug slowly evaporated, and they all sat around the sectional wiping their eyes and blowing their noses. Then Kendall got up and marched into the dining room as if on a mission. When she returned to the living room, she was holding the platter of untouched fruitcake that she had sliced and liberally doused with brandy.

"Be careful with that thing," warned Megan. "If you get it too close to the candle flames we'll probably all go up in smoke."

"Man, are we a mess or what?" Kendall sat down and passed her strange offering to the three of them. "But when all else fails, we can always get snookered on fruitcake!"

"Not you," warned Lelani as she took the platter from Kendall.

"That's right," agreed Anna as she took a dark slice and gingerly sniffed it.

"Yeah," said Megan, "we're cutting you off."

"Fine!" Kendall held up her hands dramatically. "Like I said, *let them eat fruitcake!*"

Thirty

Christmas Day

"We're going with you," announced Lelani as Megan was about to pull on her coat.

"What?" Megan peered curiously at Lelani. "To the mission?"

"That's right."

"What do you mean by *we?*"

"She means *us,*" said Anna as she came down the stairs, trailed by a sleepy-eyed Kendall.

"And my little dog, too." Kendall smiled as she held up Tinkerbell, outfitted in a red velvet jacket and matching hat.

"Seriously?" Megan was stunned. "You guys are going to come work at the mission with me?"

"That's the plan," said Anna.

"All for one and one for all," said Lelani.

"Will they have turkey?" asked Kendall hopefully.

"And dressing and potatoes and cranberries," said Megan, "all the trimmings."

As Kendall drove them into downtown Portland they even sang Christmas carols, making up the lyrics for the lines they couldn't remember. At the mission, a good-size crowd of homeless people had already lined up by the entrance.

"The doors open at eleven," said Megan as Kendall parked her car in back. "But dinner isn't served until noon. Before that there'll be gift giving and music and things."

Because they were shorthanded, the mission director was thrilled to have more volunteers, and the four of them were given red felt Santa hats to wear, along with assigned tasks. Megan and Lelani went straight to work in the kitchen. Kendall and Tinkerbell assisted Santa in giving out gifts, which were care packages donated by local churches. Anna joined the musical group, which consisted of a couple of guys and more instruments than performers. She surprised everyone when she played the guitar and sang beautifully.

Shortly before it was time to serve the meal, Gil showed up with Marcus and Edmond in tow. "We're the cleanup crew," announced Gil, much to everyone's surprise.

"But how did you know they needed help?" asked Megan.

Gil grinned at Lelani. "She called and suggested I pick up a couple of buddies to help out. These guys were willing."

"That's great." Megan smiled shyly at Marcus, adjusted her Santa hat, then started to pick up a large stainless-steel tray of sweet potatoes.

"Let me help with that," he offered.

"Thanks." She stepped out of the way and watched as he lifted it.

"Was that okay?" whispered Lelani.

Megan grinned at her. "Better than okay."

"Do you think Anna will be mad?"

Megan glanced at Anna, who was getting ready to sing another Christmas song. Her eyes were on Edmond, who was standing nearby, and a huge smile lit up her face. "Oh, I think she's okay with it."

They all worked together. The guys got stuck in the kitchen, and the girls helped to serve the food, joking and smiling at a crowd of mostly old guys.

"This is the prettiest group of servers I've ever seen here at the mission," commented a grizzled old man with a missing front tooth. He was grinning directly at Kendall now.

"Thanks, honey," said Kendall as she heaped a large spoonful of mashed potatoes on his plate.

"Merry Christmas," said Lelani as she added some dressing next to his turkey.

He nodded. "Merry Christmas to you, too, lovely lady."

Now Megan ladled gravy over his potatoes. "That enough for you?" she asked with a bright smile.

"More'n enough, sweetheart." He gave her a big grin. "Merry Christmas to you, too."

"Thanks," she told him. "This might just be one of my favorite Christmases." As she continued to ladle out gravy, greeting the appreciative guests (and even the ones who weren't), she knew this was a unique Christmas that she would always remember.

"Hey, Megan, this is kind of like that Jesus story you told us," said Kendall when there was a little break in the line. "You know, the big party where no one came and the servants went out to the streets to invite people."

Lelani laughed. "Yeah, our party last night wasn't too well attended, but there must be a couple hundred people here."

"Go figure," said Megan. But the comparison didn't escape her. This place was filled with all kinds of needy people, whether their needs were emotional, spiritual, physical, financial. They were here, aware of their neediness and being served. Last night, Megan and her four friends had been in great need as well. And when they had all admitted it, God had met them there. He brought them together and, despite their various problems and challenges, God had begun some kind of miracle in their midst, a miracle that Megan wanted to see him continue. Really, what kind of Christmas could be better than this?

... a little more ...

When a delightful concert comes to an end,

the orchestra might offer an encore.

When a fine meal comes to an end,

it's always nice to savor a bit of dessert.

When a great story comes to an end,

we think you may want to linger.

And so, we offer ...

AfterWords—just a little something more after you

have finished a David C. Cook novel.

We invite you to stay awhile in the story.

Thanks for reading!

Turn the page for ...

- **Discussion Questions**
- **A Conversation with Melody Carlson**
- **An Excerpt from *spring broke***

Discussion Questions

1. Why do you think Lelani struggles so much to forgive herself for her poor choices and for the disappointments she has caused others? If you were Lelani's friend, what would you say to her about this? What do you think God would want to say to Lelani about her failures?

2. Why does Anna so readily accept Jake's apology and resume a relationship with him? Is it possible for a person to forgive someone without exposing herself to more potential pain? Explain.

3. Compare Jake's treatment of Anna to Edmond's treatment of her. What makes Anna blind to Jake's flaws and Edmond's best qualities?

4. What do you think about Lelani's choice not to tell Anna about Jake's advances? Could she have done anything different to affect Anna's perception of that situation or to preserve their friendship?

5. Lelani finds relief from anxiety by learning how to trust God. What does *trusting God* mean to you? How do you practice letting go of your anxieties?

6. Compare the advice Gwen and Mrs. Abernathy give to Megan about dating a man who doesn't share similar faith values. Which perspective most closely represents your own? What would you have done in Megan's situation?

7. Do Kendall's housemates and friends make strong enough efforts to discourage her plans to pursue Matthew? What, if anything, should they have done differently? What is a person's ultimate responsibility in preventing a friend from making poor choices?

8. What will it take for Kendall to see how self-destructive her behaviors are? Do you think a crisis pregnancy will change her? Why or why not?

9. Why is being without family (or in conflict with family) during the holidays especially hard for the four women of Bloomberg Place? Which character most closely represents your own family situation? How would you cope with spending Christmas as she must?

10. What kind of neediness plays a role in each of the four women's central problems? Megan suggests that God is especially generous to those who admit their needs. How does her observation compare to your own experience of God?

A Conversation with Melody Carlson

The women of Bloomberg Place have pretty diverging opinions about God and religion. What kinds of challenges and opportunities does this dynamic give you as a storyteller?

It's a great way to imitate life by showing that we all evolve into our faith in various ways and from all sorts of places. In other words, there is no formula. And I believe that one of the most dynamic ways to "share" faith is simply to live out life, honestly and humbly and with the hope that God will shine through.

Do you think today's young adults have an easier or harder time than other generations did when it comes to talking about faith topics with people who don't see eye-to-eye?

I think it's always been "hard." But I also think we sometimes make it hard. We put too high of expectations on ourselves. Take Megan. In the book, she struggles with what to say, how much to say (which I think is typical), and yet it seems that her housemates are more impressed with who she is and her actions than when she attempts to "preach" at them. And isn't that how it is in real life too?

That Kendall really doesn't have a clue! Tell us: Is there hope for her?

I know Kendall is a piece of work, but she makes me laugh and I actually really like her. With all her flaws (which are many!) she has this kind of transparent honesty (even though she often tells lies) and I can't wait to see how she turns out by the last book. I absolutely have hope for her. Not only that, I'm sure that when Kendall finds God and turns her life around, she will impact everyone she meets. Okay, the impact might be painful, but it'll probably be memorable, too.

Have you ever had to spend Christmas without your closest family members? What was that like for you?

I spent my nineteenth Christmas in a foreign country and, being young and independent, I didn't think it was going to be a big deal until I heard "I'll Be Home for Christmas" playing on someone's tape deck. That was sad. But my housemates and I did our best to have a fun Christmas—and we attempted to be family.

What's your honest-to-goodness opinion of fruitcake?

Ha-ha! I actually like it! And during that Christmas away from home the first time, I tried to make one. My housemates were divided on it. Some thought it was good, some thought it should become a Yule log—even though we had no fireplace.

An Excerpt from *spring broke*

One

Megan Abernathy

"I'm starting to get seriously worried about Kendall," Lelani said as she stirred milk into her coffee. "She hasn't been herself lately."

"She's been pretty bummed," Megan admitted quietly. It was unlikely that Kendall would be awake this early, especially after discovering those "puppy potty pads" for Tinkerbell. Still, Megan didn't want to take any chances of being overheard by their landlady. "I think Valentine's Day was especially hard on her."

Lelani nodded. "Yes. Not only was she without a guy, but pregnant as well."

"And her favorite jeans are too small." Megan topped off her coffee. That detail seemed pretty minor to Megan, but to Kendall it had been a huge crisis.

"It doesn't help matters that Matthew is treating her like a stalker."

"You can't really blame him," Megan pointed out. "I mean she sort of was stalking him."

"I suppose." Lelani frowned. "Still, he could show a little more compassion. It's not as if she got pregnant on purpose."

Megan knew this was a tough issue for Lelani. She'd been through a similar situation herself and had a tendency to be extra hard on irresponsible dads. "But to be fair to Matthew, Kendall isn't a hundred percent certain that it's his baby yet." This was just another bone of contention as far as Megan was concerned. Kendall had finally admitted that she'd slept with more men than just Matthew last fall. Not only had she been stupid, she'd been careless.

Megan knew it was unkind to judge Kendall like that, and she never expressed these thoughts out loud, but it's how she felt. And it was just one of many reasons why Megan felt that sex outside of marriage was a mistake.

"What if it is Matthew's?" ventured Lelani.

Megan sighed and shrugged. "It seems like it shouldn't really make a difference. I mean, Matthew has no intention of leaving his wife for Kendall."

Lelani nodded and lowered her voice. "But Matthew's got money, and when Kendall gets in a snit, she starts talking paternity suits and how she'll take Mr. Hollywood to the cleaners if he doesn't agree to some huge settlement."

"A settlement that would probably come out of his wife's earnings as much as his." By now everyone seemed to accept that Heidi Hardwick's acting career was more successful than her husband's. It was also no secret that this Hollywood couple's relationship had been over a few bumps.

"Can you imagine what this news might do to their marriage?" Lelani shook her head sadly.

"I know that Kendall sometimes hopes her pregnancy will end it and that Matthew will come running to her."

"And they'll all live happily ever after." Lelani sighed, then took a sip of coffee.

"What a mess."

"It's no wonder that she's depressed. Being single and pregnant isn't easy. I guess we should be more supportive of her. Especially when she's as down as she's been these past few days. I keep thinking she'll bounce back."

"It seemed she had more resilience before." Megan rinsed her mug and placed it in the dishwasher. "Remember how upbeat she was when the pregnancy test was positive?"

"But that might just be hormonal. I remember having moments of unexplainable happiness during my pregnancy too. Then I'd get blue. It's kind of a roller-coaster ride."

"So we just hang on tight and hope that she stays on the track?"

Lelani smiled. "And try not to say the wrong things."

"Tell me about it." Megan lowered her voice again. "The other day Kendall was talking about terminating her pregnancy. I was just minding my own business. I mean, she knows how I feel about abortion. She knows how we all feel. So then she looks me in the eyes and asks me what I would do if I were her."

"Seriously?"

"Yes."

Lelani's brow creased. "What did you tell her?"

"That first of all, I wouldn't be in her shoes, since I'm committed to abstinence until I get married."

"You're making me a believer too."

"Then I told her that I'd have the baby, but that I'd probably adopt it to a loving family."

"And?"

"She fell apart."

"Oh no."

Megan looked at the kitchen clock. "Well, I better get to work. Cynthia's gone this week, and Vera has been stressing over absolutely everything. I wouldn't dare be one minute late lest she go into a rage."

"Despite the fact that she makes you work overtime?"

Megan made a half smile. "But, oh, I'm so lucky to have this job," she imitated Vera's voice now. "'Hundreds of young women would love to be in your shoes, Megan.'" Then Megan looked down at her Cole Haan loafers. "Of course, Vera would then make fun of my shoes and suggest I wear something a bit more stylish."

"You *lucky* girl!" teased Lelani.

Still, as Megan walked to work, she did feel lucky. Or maybe just blessed. But as the morning sun shone down, Megan felt hopeful for the day ahead. Oh, sure, Vera could be a witch. What else was new? But this was one of those rare February days with hints of spring in the air. The plum trees that lined Bloomberg Place had burst into pale-pink blooms, and the sunny faces of daffodils were making their cheerful appearances. Spring had always seemed a promising time of year to Megan. New life, freshness, the hope of things to come.

Of course, that's probably not how Kendall felt these days. Despite the new life that was growing within her, Kendall seemed more confused and worried and troubled than ever. And why shouldn't she be? A surge of empathy rushed through Megan. Poor Kendall!

As Megan turned onto Main Street, she felt a stab of guilt for not being kinder and more understanding toward her perplexing friend. Naturally, she couldn't help but disapprove of Kendall's lifestyle and choices. At the same time, she should be careful not to condemn her. And she did want to help Kendall. But how? Often it seemed that Megan's words only irritated her. And for that reason, Megan had been trying to keep her mouth shut. Really, other than praying for Kendall, there seemed little that Megan could do.

As Megan got closer to the design firm, she spied the homeless lady who often waited for her. By now Megan knew that her name was Margie. But she hadn't been around much during the past few weeks.

"Hello," called Margie, grinning widely to expose her missing tooth.

"I've missed you," said Megan as she fished inside of her bag. She usually kept a couple of dollars or McDonald's gift certificates handy, but since Margie had been gone, she'd gotten out of the habit.

"I've been sick."

"Really?" Megan extracted a five from her wallet and waited.

"I stayed at the shelter for a while. A lady there took me to the free clinic and they gave me some medicine."

"So you're okay now?"

"Oh, yes. And so glad to be out of that nasty shelter." She frowned. "So noisy and dirty in there. I can't stand it."

Megan had never asked Margie too much about herself. In fact, Margie had never spoken this many words. "So where do you stay now?"

Margie gave her a mysterious smile. "Oh, here and there."

Megan handed her the five.

"Oh, God bless you, dear!" cried Margie.

"God bless you, too."

Megan entered the design firm, a lavishly decorated place with expensive furnishings, authentic art, and pretty much useless accessories. Not for the first time, she noted the sharp contrast between this fancy place and poor old Margie's world. To be honest, Megan sometimes felt totally disgusted by the entire principle of decorating—so much money wasted on making someone's overly priced home into a showplace. But then it had never been Megan's career goal to land here. Hopefully she would land a teaching job by next fall. In the meantime, she was thankful to be gainfully employed. Certainly she wasn't getting rich. But she made enough to pay her bills.

As Megan hung up her coat, she noticed Margie still standing on the sidewalk out front, gazing up at the sky with an expression of wonder and delight. Megan wondered why it was that some people wound up homeless. To be fair, Margie seemed content with her lot in life. Compared to wealthy yet grumpy Vera Craig, Margie seemed downright happy. Go figure.

Megan went straight to work on a floor plan that Vera wanted finished by two o'clock so that she could show it to Helen Ferguson. So far her design was coming along just fine. But a little before noon, Megan's phone rang. To her surprise it was Kendall, and she sounded upset.

"I need help," cried Kendall.

"What's wrong?"

"I'm—I'm in trouble."

Okay, that went without saying, but what was Kendall really saying? "What kind of trouble do you mean?" Megan spoke slowly and clearly. "What is going on?"

"I need you to come home—" Kendall broke into fresh sobs. "Right now!"

Megan glanced at the clock. It wasn't quite time for her lunch break, but this sounded dire. "Okay. I'm on my way."

Megan grabbed her bag and her coat and headed out to the reception area.

"Early lunch?" Ellen, the receptionist, frowned at her.

"Kind of an emergency. But I'll make up the time."

"I'm sure that Vera would be pleased to hear that."

And hoping that Ellen wouldn't inform her, Megan hurried out and jogged the six blocks back to 86 Bloomberg Place. Halfway there she realized that she should've gotten more information from Kendall. Perhaps Kendall was having some kind of medical emergency—maybe something was wrong with the baby. In that case she should've called 9-1-1. Or maybe Megan would have to drive Kendall to the hospital. Fortunately Kendall had a car. Megan wondered why Kendall hadn't called Lelani instead. They seemed to be closer. But then Lelani was harder to reach at Nordstrom, and employees weren't supposed to take personal calls.

In a way, Megan felt honored that Kendall would call her in a time of crisis. She just had no idea what to expect. Megan prayed as she jogged. With a sharp pain in her side, Megan went into the house and found Kendall sitting in the living room. Still in her bathrobe, she had Tinkerbell in her lap and tears running down her cheeks.

"What's wrong?" Megan asked breathlessly as she sat down on the sectional next to Kendall. "Are you okay?"

"No. I'm not okay."

"What is it?" Megan placed a hand on Kendall's arm. "Is something wrong with the baby?"

"No—that's not it."

"What is it then?"

"I'm broke."

Megan's hand slipped off Kendall's arm, and she sat up straighter and just stared at Kendall. "Huh?"

"I'm broke and a creditor just showed up and—and it was horrible!"

"That's why you called me at work?" Okay, as kind and understanding as Megan had wanted to be, as sympathetic as she'd been feeling toward Kendall, as much as she'd prayed for her, Megan wanted to throttle her now! Kendall had sounded like she was facing a life-or-death emergency—because she was broke? Like that was news? When had Kendall not been broke? They all knew that her finances were a disaster. That's why she'd taken in renters to start with. Good grief!

"I—I thought you could help me," sobbed Kendall. "You're so—so sensible."

"What is it you *thought* I could possibly do?" Megan knew that her voice sounded harsh and angry. Okay, she *was* angry. This was ridiculous!

Besides, hadn't she already attempted to help Kendall to sort out this mess? Hadn't she helped her to start making the minimum payments and suggested ways to consolidate her bills? But Kendall hadn't listened. Instead she'd gone out and accumulated more debt. In her pathetic attempt to snag Matthew, she'd made more ridiculous purchases, maxed out more cards. And then she'd learned she was pregnant.

"I don't know." Kendall turned and looked at Megan with watery blue eyes. "I just thought you would know what to do."

Megan knew what she'd like to do—and say. But then she remembered that she was a Christian. So she took a long, deep breath and steadied herself. "Fine. At least you're willing to admit that you're broke, Kendall. They say the first step to recovery is acknowledging you have a problem."

"I have a problem," said Kendall in a tiny voice.

"You have a lot of problems."

Kendall nodded sadly. "I know."

Of course, Megan doubted she could help Kendall with all of her problems. In fact, Megan felt doubtful she could help her mixed-up housemate with much of anything. Really, only God could help someone like Kendall. But then Megan spied Kendall's latest shopping conquest. An Hermès bag that she'd "gotten on sale" after the holidays. It was now tossed down by the coatrack like an old piece of rubbish. "I have an idea," said Megan.

"What?" Kendall looked up hopefully.

"We'll do some early spring cleaning around here and have a garage sale."

"A garage sale?" Kendall frowned. "What could I possibly sell in a garage sale?"

Megan eyed the bag again. "Oh, I'm sure we could find a few things."

Other Books by Melody Carlson

These Boots Weren't Made for Walking
(WaterBrook)

On This Day
(WaterBrook)

Ready to Wed
(GuidepostsBooks)

Finding Alice
(WaterBrook)

Notes from a Spinning Planet series
(WaterBrook)

The Secret Life of Samantha McGregor series
(Multnomah)

Don't Miss the Rest of the 86 Bloomberg Place Series

Catch up with Kendall and the gang as their lives take unexpected twists and turns in the rest of this great series.

i heart bloomberg
now available

spring broke
available March 2009

three weddings and a bar mitzvah
coming fall 2009!